A DATE WITH THE HANGMAN

My right arm felt numb and my head began to go around in stately circles, humming like a distant motor.

"Relax, Dr. Branch," The voice came from the other end of a dark tunnel. "You'll go to sleep very shortly. Then I shall have the pleasure of hanging you."

The rope was looser now and I tried for the last time to get my knees under me. I couldn't raise my head. The black cloud had come back and rested on my head and it was as heavy as tons of coal. The idiot speck of consciousness I had left flickered and went out, and I turned on great black wheels in an infinity of humming wheels. . . .

D0556441

THE DARK TUNNEL

ROSS MACDONALD

Originally published under the name
KENNETH MILLAR

BANTAM BOOKS
Toronto • New York • London • Sydney

THE DARK TUNNEL
A Bantam Book / published by arrangement with the author

PRINTING HISTORY

*Dodd, Mead edition published 1944 under the name of
Kenneth Millar*

*Published in 1950 and 1955 under the title
I Die Slowly by Kenneth Millar*

Bantam edition / October 1972

2nd printing ... October 1972	*4th printing ..... April 1973*
3rd printing ... October 1972	*5th printing .... August 1974*
6th printing ... July 1983	

ISBN 0-553-23514-1

Published simultaneously in the United States and Canada

---

*Bantam Books are published by Bantam Books, Inc. Its trade-
mark, consisting of the words "Bantam Books" and the por-
trayal of a rooster, is Registered in U.S. Patent and Trademark
Office and in other countries. Marca Registrada. Bantam
Books, Inc., 666 Fifth Avenue, New York, New York 10103.*

PRINTED IN THE UNITED STATES OF AMERICA

H   15 14 13 12 11 10 9 8 7 6

Although it bears a certain physical resemblance to the University of Michigan at Ann Arbor, Midwestern University is, like all the characters in this story, a figment of the author's imagination.

To the memory of
John Lee

chapter i

DETROIT is usually hot and sticky in the summer, and in the winter the snow in the streets is like a dirty, worn-out blanket. Like most other big cities it is best in the fall, when there is still some summer mellowness in the air and the bleak winds have not yet started blowing down the long, wide streets. The heart of the city was clean and sunlit on the September afternoon that Alec Judd and I drove over from Arbana. The skyscrapers stood together against the powder-blue sky with a certain grotesque dignity, like a herd of frozen dinosaurs waiting for a thaw.

Alec drove his car into a parking-lot off Jefferson and we got out and headed for the Book Tower Building. His legs were not long for his height, a couple of inches less than my six feet, but his long, aggressive stride compensated for the length of his legs and I had to stretch mine to keep up with him. At thirty-nine he was so fit that years of deskwork had failed to bow his shoulders.

"Well, here we go," he said. "Wish me luck."

"Like hell I will. You know what I think of your going in the Navy. Anyway, I'm the one that needs the luck."

"You don't have to worry, they'll take you."

"Maybe," I said. "The Army turned me down last year."

"That was last year. They've given up using Superman as a standard."

"Perhaps the Army has. The Navy's still pretty

fussy, I hear. They want only men with hawk eyes who were born with a caul and can't drown."

"Where does that leave me?" Alec said. "You've got ten years on me."

"They'll snap you up in a hurry, and you know it. They've been casting yearning glances at you ever since Pearl Harbor."

Behind his optimistic square face and casual wise-cracking manner Alec had a brain that cut through administrative work like a buzz saw and stacked it in neat piles like lumber. He had been head of the War Board at Midwestern University since war broke out and had piloted the university through the transition from a peacetime to a wartime program.

His mind was as broad and humorous as his mouth, but when he got hold of an idea he held on like a bull-dog. Now he had the idea that he wasn't doing enough for the war effort and should join the Navy.

We walked the rest of the way to the Book Tower Building in silence and took the elevator to the Naval Procurement offices on the ninth floor.

The brown-faced officer behind the information desk stood up and put out his hand when Judd told him his name. "I've heard about you, Dr. Judd. I'm pleased to meet you, sir. My name's Curtis."

"How do you do, Lieutenant," Judd said as they shook hands.

"Didn't you help set up the V-12 program at Mid-western?" the officer asked.

"That's right. By the way, this is Dr. Branch."

Curtis and I shook hands. "I've heard your name, too, Dr. Branch," he said with an expression that couldn't remember where.

"I'm secretary of the War Board," I offered. "Not forever, I hope."

"What can I do for you gentlemen?" asked Curtis.

"Tell us how to get into the Navy," Judd said. "I've sent hundreds of boys over here in the last couple of years but I don't know what to do now that I'm here myself."

"It's easier to get in than to get out," Curtis said with a white enamel smile, "if you've got the qualifications. Let's see, I'd better take you one at a time."

He picked up a pen and took a slip of paper from a pile in the drawer of the desk. Then he turned to Alec and asked with a smile, "How many years of college?"

"Too many," Alec said. "About eight as a student, I guess, and fifteen as a teacher."

"That should be enough, eh? Dr. Branch?" He picked up another slip.

"Seven years as a student, and I've been teaching five."

"Well," Curtis said, "the first thing you men have to do is have your eyes tested. So many are rejected on account of eyes that we put that test first. Just take these slips down the hall and have a chair." He handed us our slips and pointed to the right. "And Dr. Branch, you'd better take your glasses off to rest your eyes while you're waiting for the doctor."

I took off my glasses. Curtis said, "Good luck," as we went out the door. I followed Alec down the hall to the bare ante-room of the eye-testing department, and we sat down on two folding chairs against the wall.

I returned to the subject that Alec and I had been arguing over for days: "I still don't get it, Alec. You're an irreplaceable man doing an essential job. What the hell do you want to join the Navy for?"

He said with the cheerfulness of an obstinate man who intends to go right on being obstinate: "I told you. I have an urge to know what the wild Waves are saying."

"I'm trying to be serious and all you do is make lousy puns. It's not that I care what you do. I'm wondering what's going to happen to the War Board after you leave."

"It'll muddle along the same as it has for the last two years. I'm not indispensable. Nobody's indispensable, except Harry Hopkins. And anyway, they haven't taken me yet."

"They will," I said. "They'll send you to Fort Schuyler for indoctrination and then give you a job somewhere doing exactly what you're doing now. Your character is your fate, and you're an executive. They'll keep you away from water as if you had hydrophobia, and put you aboard an office building."

"Not if I can help it." His jaw pushed out. "I'm tired of fighting this war with the seat of my pants."

"Johnny wants a gun," I said bitterly. "Where would we be if everybody felt like that? It takes a lot of guts sometimes to go on holding down a civilian job when you want to get into the fun and games."

Alec didn't like that. He flushed and snapped, "I suppose Guadal and Salerno were fireworks displays."

"Not to the men who were there. That's not what I mean and you know it. I mean simply that you're more useful where you are than you would be anywhere else."

"What about you?" Alec said. "Have you a hidden talent for naval warfare? What's the War Board going to do without a secretary?"

"You're confusing the issue. If the Navy doesn't get me, the Army will. They turned me down last year but they won't this year. And I just happen to prefer the Navy, if I can get in. I like water better than land."

"My position exactly."

"Like hell it is. You're too old for the draft, and you'll never see sea duty anyway, unless you go to sea in a filing cabinet."

"That's right," Alec said with a grin that did not change the stubbornness of the jaw. "Make mock of my grey hairs." He hadn't any: the close-cut nap of hair on his head was as black as mine.

The examining yeoman came in, a narrow-faced young man in a white tunic.

"Which of you men is first?" he said. He went into

the adjoining room and switched on the light over an eye-testing chart on the far wall.

"Go ahead, Alec." He got up and followed the yeoman, who shut the door behind him. In no more than a minute, he opened the door and came out smiling.

"Favorable verdict?" I asked.

"20/20. It sounds like something by H. G. Wells."

"Next," the examiner said through the doorway. I stepped in and closed the door.

"Stay where you are." He handed me a piece of cardboard with a round hole in it. "Now look through this hole with the right eye and walk forward until you can read the letters at the top."

I moved forward a couple of steps and read the jumbled alphabet aloud. Another two steps and I could read everything on the card.

"O.K.," the yeoman said. "Now go back and try it with the left eye. Read them backwards this time."

I had to trek nearly the whole length of the room before I could read the smallest letters at the bottom of the card.

"Not so good," the yeoman said. "How do you account for the comparative weakness of your left eye? Did anything ever happen to it?"

"Yes," I said. An old anger woke up and moved in my stomach. "A Nazi officer hit me across the face with his swagger stick in Munich six years ago. That eye's never been the same since."

"No wonder you want to get into this war," he said. "But I'm afraid the Navy won't take you. Maybe the Army will, I don't know."

"What's my score?"

"Not good enough, I'm sorry to say. Your right eye just about makes the grade but your left is way down. Too bad."

I said, "Thanks," and walked out to the front office. I didn't realize I could still be angry after six years, but my legs were stiff with rage. I put my slip on Curtis's desk and sat down to wait for Alec.

Curtis saw the figures on my slip and the look on my face and said, "That's too bad, Dr. Branch."

"Thanks. Where's Judd?"

He jerked his thumb towards an open door. "He's being interviewed. It takes half an hour or so." He went back to work on a pile of papers in front of him.

I remembered the glasses in my hand and put them on and looked out of the window. What I saw was a street in Munich on a night six years before: brown stone walls like carved cliffs in the lamplight and four men in black uniform coming out of a doorway like an arched cave, walking in step. I saw again like a repeated nightmare the stick raised above the white hostile face, and the girl getting up from the road with bloody knees. I felt the hot pain of the swishing stick across my face and the pleasure of bruising my knuckles on the white snarl and hearing the head strike the pavement.

A sharp pain in my right hand reminded me that the place was Detroit and the time was six years later. I looked at my hand and saw that I was clenching my fist so tightly that the nails were digging into the palm. I lit a cigarette and tried to relax.

I had been waiting for about half an hour when Alec came into the outer office. His back was straighter than ever, if possible.

He handed Curtis a sheaf of papers and said, "Can I take the physical now?"

"Not this afternoon," Curtis said. "Any morning, though. To-morrow morning if you can make it. We open at 8:30 and the earlier you come the shorter time you'll have to wait."

"I'll be here at 8:30 to-morrow," Alec said, and turned to me. "Sorry to keep you waiting."

"Finished?"

"As much as I can do to-day." His voice lowered sympathetically as we went out the door: "You didn't come in for your interview. Didn't you make it?"

"My left eye is not the eye of an American eagle,"

6

I said. "I'd still like to meet Carl von Esch, to talk over old times."

"Don't let it ride you." He squeezed my arm. "The Army's sure to take you when your number comes up again. They're reclassifying, you know."

"Don't worry, I won't brood," I said, and manufactured a grin. "It looks as if you'll make it, doesn't it?"

"If I can pass the physical. The officer who interviewed me was pretty encouraging."

"Congratulations."

We took the elevator down and went out into the street. The sky was still blue and bright but the memory of the night in Munich hung across it like a shadow. There was a first faint chill of winter in the air, and I felt older.

On the way back to the parking-lot neither of us said anything. We were good enough friends not to have to talk, and I had nothing to say. Alec seemed to be thinking about something. The lines that slanted down from his blunt nose were deep and harsh, and he didn't walk as fast as he had before.

Even after we reached the car and headed out of the city, the silence remained unbroken. He'd have unfinished business to worry about, I thought, and let him worry. He drove smoothly and automatically by instinct, and his brain went on working on something else.

When we were approaching Dearborn, I got tired of reading billboards to myself and said, "Are passengers allowed to talk to the driver of this bus?"

"Eh?" He smiled a little sheepishly.

"What's eating you? You tell me not to brood and immediately pull a Hamlet yourself."

"Sorry. Matter of fact, I want to talk to you about this. Let's go in there and have a beer." He nodded his head at a tavern that we were passing.

"I could do with a beer."

He turned down the next side-street and parked, and we got out and walked back to the tavern. It was a long, dim room lit by red neon, with a black bar running the length of it punctuated by red leather stools. The juke box at the back of the room looked like a small French chateau that had swallowed a rainbow. As we entered somebody put in a nickel and it began to cough rhythmically.

The place was nearly empty and we had one end of the bar to ourselves. We slid onto stools and Alec ordered two beers from a waitress who wore powder like a clay mask.

When we got our beer, I said, "What's on your mind?"

He wasn't ready to talk. "Look about you," he said. "The twentieth-century inferno, and we pay to sit in it. Red light like hell-fire. Ear-busting noise, and we pay the juke to lambaste our ears. Bitter beer."

"And horrible hags to serve it," I said. At the other end of the bar the two waitresses were giggling together over the exploits of their grandchildren.

"Walk down the streets of Detroit and what do you see," Alec went on. "Grey streets bounded by grey walls. Men caught in the machines. The carnivores creep between the walls on rubber tires. The parrots squawk from the radio in every home. The men run round in the buildings like apes in iron trees. A new kind of jungle." He drained his glass and ordered more.

"Baloney," I said. "Look at the other side of the medal. Hot lunches for children and advanced medical facilities. Cars for everybody—after the war. Education for everybody now. It's a fairly Utopian jungle to my mind."

"I won't argue. I'm a country bumpkin and Detroit always gets me." He was born in Detroit. "But education isn't everything. A car in every garage isn't everything, nor a helicopter on every roof."

"You sound like Thoreau," I said. "What good is a telegraph line from Maine to Texas, if Maine has nothing to say to Texas?"

"Exactly." He was talking now, and he let me have

8

it: "Education isn't everything. There's a certain doctor of philosophy, for example, that I suspect of doing a pretty barbarous thing."

"Dr. Göebbels?"

"This is serious. You can keep it under your hat."

I nodded.

"I'm telling you because I may need your help. I've got to clean this thing up before I go into the Navy."

"I'll help of course," I said. "But what do you want me to help do?"

He answered my question in his own way:

"I'm not in a position to go to the F.B.I. I'm not certain I'm right, and if I'm wrong I can't ruin a man's career for nothing. But there's been a leakage of information from the War Board to Nazi agents. You know we handle some pretty confidential stuff, and I've got to plug that leak. If I can uncover enough evidence to turn the case over to the Federal boys with a clear conscience—"

"Christ, do you suspect a member of the board?"

The five other members of the board flashed through my mind like actors in a disconnected movie short. Hunter, Leverett, Jackson, Vallon, Schneider. The president of the university, an *ex officio* member, attended some of the meetings, but he was above suspicion. Jackson was too: a former braintruster, head of the economics department, and a grassroots American liberal.

Hunter, a small brown man who looked like an efficiency expert and knew fifteen languages, hated the Nazis so much that when he was in Washington on a government assignment, the Dies Committee almost investigated him. Colonel Leverett commanded the troops on the campus and had taught at West Point. Vallon, of Romance Languages, was the descendant of a Rochellois Protestant who had come to America at the beginning of the eighteenth century. He was a slim, elegant man who wore a ruby on his left hand and looked like a prosperous actor. Vallon

9

was said to have a Puritan conscience but I had never met his conscience.

Schneider was a German, doctor of philosophy of Heidelberg and head of the Department of German at Midwestern since 1935. He had left his chair at the University of Munich in protest against Nazi philosophies of education soon after Hitler rose to power. His classic letter of resignation to the chancellor of the University of Munich had been published in translation in the United States, and made several hundred dollars in royalties for the International Red Cross.

"Do you suspect Schneider?" I asked.

"Yes."

"Why? On what grounds?" His judgments were impulsive at times and I wondered if this was a time.

"Who else?"

"That's what I was thinking. What about me, then? I need the money more than Schneider with his ten thousand a year."

"Sure. Do you suspect yourself? Do you love Germany?" His irony was as subtle as a blowtorch.

"Not passionately," I said.

"Schneider loves Germany."

"Maybe he does. But he hates the Nazis and Hitler. Remember what he said about Hitler in that open letter? 'When a hyena drapes a lion's skin over its narrow flanks and attempts to improvise a lion's bearing and a lion's voice, the imposture is immediately and pitifully apparent to all sensitive eyes and ears, and to all discriminating noses.' Something like that."

"There's such a thing as protesting too much," Alec said. "There have been wolves in liberal's clothing before."

"There's such a thing as suspecting too much."

"Perhaps. If Schneider really hates the Nazis so violently, why did he leave his son in Germany to be educated after he left himself?"

"That doesn't prove anything. I heard that the Nazis

wouldn't let the boy go. He stayed with his mother's family in Germany and then they conscripted him."

"They let him go two years ago," Alec said. "He's been in this country since 1941."

"Well, you seem to know more about it than I do. But you haven't shown me a case against Schneider."

"There's been a leakage of information from the War Board," he repeated in a whisper like a leakage of steam from a boiler. "Maybe Schneider isn't responsible. If he isn't, who is? Who else is there?"

"How much do you know about Vallon? Your secretary, Helen Madden, has access to everything we touch. I'm not accusing anybody, but how much do you know about her?"

"Enough," he said. He drained his glass and got off the stool, looking at me slantwise. The jaw muscles under his ears moved like a tangled bunch of worms. "Helen promised to marry me last week."

As I got off the stool, I saw my face in the mirror behind the bar. It was red and flustered-looking. I said, "Oh! Congratulations," and Alec said, "Thanks."

We went out the door and around the corner to the car and drove back to Arbana through the domains of King Henry the First, American model. Alec had relapsed into his deaf-mute phase, a new thing to me though we had been friends for years. I sat in the seat beside him and thought about Schneider. The only thing I knew against Herman Schneider was that he privately held the opinion that Shakespeare was a German on his mother's side. And that he was vain of his beard, which he treated like a pet mink.

We had driven into Detroit in the morning and lunched there, so it was barely four o'clock when we got back to Arbana. The little city was a relief after Detroit, which gave me the megalopolitan blues in spite of what I had said to Judd. Arbana is different. In the leafy season it looks almost like a forest from an airplane, there are so many trees. Now in September the trees were beginning to turn, but most of the leaves were still green. There was green grass on the campus, and when Alec stopped the car in front of McKinley Hall I could hear the power-mowers humming.

He said, "No hard feelings, Bob. You're perfectly right to keep an open mind, of course. I've got to go over to the board office to catch up on some work, but I'd like to talk to you to-night."

"Fine. About Helen, I think she's a fine woman. I was just using her as an example, but I picked one hell of an example. What time to-night?"

"Will you be free at ten? How about my office up in McKinley? There'll be nobody to disturb us."

"Right. See you at ten." I slammed the door and Alec drove away to the Graduate School. I could have gone to the library and done some work but I didn't feel like working. I decided to go up to the English Department office to see if there was any mail in my box, and started up the walk to McKinley Hall.

McKinley Hall is the British-Museum-classic building five stories high and a block long, which houses the college of arts and the administrative offices of Midwestern University. Arbana is the Athens of the West and McKinley Hall is its Parthenon and I am Pericles.

I started up the sweeping steps of the stupendous portico without even an alpenstock to lean on. There were students sitting on the steps, mostly girls in sweaters and young soldiers in their new winter uniforms. It was the end of the summer term, and they were holding post-mortems over the examinations they had been writing. A few pioneer couples were holding hands.

As I reached the top, Hunter the linguist, professor of comparative literature, came out through one of the swinging glass doors. He was a small, wiry man with little black eyes like licorice drops and a face as brown as his Harris tweeds.

"Hello, Hunt."

"Hello, Bob, how did it go?"

"It looks as if Alec will make it. They turned me down."

"They did? I thought you were in good shape."

"It's not my shape they objected to. My left eye is weak."

"That's tough. What's the matter with your eye?"

"I had an accident a few years ago in Munich—"

"Oh, yes, Alec said something about that. You weren't as lucky as I was. One time in Naples they put me in jail for brandishing a Leica in the harbor, but there was no rough stuff and they let me go next morning."

"My crime was worse. I objected to the murder of a Jew."

"What happened?" Curiosity shrank Hunter's small eyes to raisins.

"He was killed. But there's more to it than that, it's a long story. When we get together sometime, remind me to tell you about Ruth Esch—"

"Ruth Esch? Do you know Ruth Esch?"

"Do you know her, Hunt? We were engaged to be married—years ago. If she's alive, we still are, as far as I'm concerned."

"I didn't know. You shouldn't be so secretive. No, I don't know her, but she's coming here."

"Coming *here*?" My heart hit me under the chin. "When?"

"This week, I think. If it's the same Ruth Esch—"

"Is the woman who's coming here an actress? Tall? Red-haired?"

"I wouldn't know, but Schneider can tell you about her. She's been given a special instructorship in his department to teach German conversation."

"You don't know where Schneider is now, do you?"

"I was just talking to him in his office. If you hurry you should catch him."

"Thanks. I want to talk to him," I said, and opened the door.

Hunter called after me, "I hope it's the right girl." As I climbed the stairs to the second floor, my brain pounded out the words over and over like somebody practicing on a typewriter in my head.

Schneider was just about to leave when I reached the German Department office on which his private office opened. He was standing with his topcoat on and a grey Homburg in his hand, giving last-minute instructions to the departmental secretary.

Dr. Herman Schneider's appearance was as impressive as his reputation, which was awesome. Until 1934 he was the greatest Shakespearean scholar in Germany. It was generally acknowledged that he knew more about the First Folio than Heminge and Condell, and that some of his footnotes were as valuable as whole books by other men. As the president of the university said when Schneider came to Midwestern to become head of the Department of German: "With the advent of Dr. Schneider, we may say with some assurance that the cultural centre of gravity of the earth has shifted perceptibly towards the American Middle West." This was printed in the newspapers, and print never lies.

I stood behind him and waited for him to finish talking to the secretary, not realizing that our conversation was going to shift the cultural centre of the earth again. It's not that it wasn't an impressive conversation, to me at least. When he finally turned and gave me the full benefit of his beard, I was quite overpowered.

He was a huge man with large brown eyes, deepset under a bald dome for which his black beard compensated. He would have stood about five feet kneeling in prayer, if such a Jupiter of a man could ever feel the need of prayer. His belly, once the pride of the Hofbrauhaus, was a cenotaph to thousands of perished liters of beer.

"What can I do for you, Dr. Branch?" He spoke with the slightly exaggerated and aggressive courtesy of many Germans. His English was better than my German, but seemed to rumble in his belly and lollop around in his throat.

"I was just talking with Hunter, Dr. Schneider." Schneider called all college teachers doctor and expected the same in return: his beard demanded it.

"Oh, yes, he and I had a very pleasant conversation a few minutes ago."

"He mentioned a certain Ruth Esch, who is coming to teach in your department."

"Yes," Schneider said. "Yes, that is so. A very talented young woman. Why do you ask?" A hardness that may have been suspicion made the mellowness of his voice seem suddenly shallow.

"Is she an actress, a tall, red-haired girl?"

"Why, yes. I hadn't realized that her fame had penetrated to America. I must tell her."

"It hasn't so far as I know. I knew her in Munich."

"You did?" He seemed astonished and his eyebrows jumped like black mice. "She played a season with the Schauspielhaus in München. You saw her on the stage, perhaps?"

"Yes, I did. But I knew her personally as well. We were very good friends, in fact."

The black mice had convulsions and even the beard was perturbed. "Is that so? I didn't know you had ever visited Germany, Dr. Branch."

"I was there for a month in 1937, studying the influence of English romanticism on the Continental garden." On a travelling fellowship you have to study something that justifies travel. "I don't often talk of my visit to Germany. It ended unpleasantly."

"Unpleasantly?"

"Very. I was arrested and ordered to leave the country. I have an irrational prejudice against Jew-baiting."

"It is a commendable prejudice, Dr. Branch." He spoke as if he meant it. "And it was in 1937, then, that you met Ruth Esch?"

"Yes."

"You were close friends, you say? *Wunderbar!*" The enthusiasm seemed a little forced. "Fräulein Esch was a pupil of mine, you know. A charming and talented girl. I am greatly looking forward to seeing her again. Dr. Branch, you must make one of the party at our reunion."

"Thank you," I said. "I should like to very much. When will she arrive?"

"When? Will you excuse me for a moment? I must make a telephone call."

"Certainly."

He unlocked his office and closed the heavy oak door behind him. I sat on the edge of the secretary's desk and thought about Ruth. I remembered her every time Germany was bombed and many times between, but I had been afraid she was dead or in some way lost to me for good. Now coincidence had reached across an ocean and she was coming to Arbana. For the first time in six years, I felt the ambiguous bittersweet ache of being in love. Would she be the same? Would I seem the same to her? Six years of Hitler's Europe are like a century.

When Schneider opened the door five minutes later, he woke me from a day-dream thronging with bright, possible futures. He closed the door carefully behind him and said, "Dr. Branch, it is late to ask you, but will you have dinner with me to-night?"

His beard loomed benignantly and the amiability of his expression surprised me. To a full professor, especially a German one, an assistant professor is an *arriviste,* just up from the purgatory of an instructorship. Besides, I was in the Department of English, and the greatest Shakespearean scholar of Germany knew what American departments of English are. Hell, yes.

Schneider had never gone out of his way to be friendly to me before, but now he was smiling at me like a father and saying, "It would be so pleasant to talk with you about Fräulein Esch, and about old times in München. She was my favorite pupil, and to think that she is a common friend!"

Scratch a bronze statue of Jupiter made in Germany and you get a sentimental ooze, or so I thought. I resented his emotionalism, perhaps because enthusiasm over a woman resents competition. After all, he was a widower.

But I didn't refuse the invitation: I wanted to find out more about Ruth Esch, and he could tell me. I also wanted to find out more about Dr. Schneider.

"I'd be delighted," I said.

"Will seven suit you?"

"Perfectly. When is Ruth to arrive?"

"She will arrive on the nine o'clock train from Detroit tonight. Perhaps you will come with me to the station."

"I certainly will."

He ushered me into the corridor and locked the door of the German office. Before we separated, he patted my shoulder clumsily and said, "My boy, it will be a charming reunion. Charming."

As he strode off, I felt a little like a matador to whom a bull has been making advances: interested but dubious.

He turned and bellowed, "Seven, don't forget. Just a family party."

I hope I smiled urbanely as any matador. I felt like a character in Ernest Hemingway.

chapter ii

I REMEMBERED that I had come into McKinley Hall in the first place to see if there was any mail for me, and climbed the stairs to the English office on the third floor. The secretary was gone and the door was locked and I had left my keys in my apartment. I thought of using my knife on the lock as I had once or twice before, but decided it would be too much trouble. I went downstairs and out the front door, and crossed the street to the coffee-shop on the other side.

When I went in, I saw Hunter sitting by himself in a booth at the back. He raised his hand and I sat down opposite him and ordered coffee.

"Is it the right girl?" he asked.

"Yes. She's coming here to-night."

"You look excited."

"I am. She's a wonderful woman. You'll meet her."

"I hope so. She's an actress, you say?"

"She was when I knew her. Apparently she studied under Schneider before he left Germany. She never mentioned him to me so far as I can remember."

"You told me to remind you to tell me about her sometime. How about now?"

"All right." I told him about Ruth Esch and the month I spent in Munich in 1937 and how it ended.

I was twenty-three that year, and still a student. I was travelling on a fellowship and gathering material for my doctoral dissertation. After a couple of months in London, where I wore out the seat of a pair of pants in the reading room of the British Museum, I went to Munich at the beginning of November to do a month's work there. I didn't get as much work done as I expected to. I found better things than libraries in Munich, and worse things.

My second day in Munich I was looking for the American Express Company to change some traveller's marks into money, when I saw a huge crowd lined up on one of the main streets. I joined the crowd to see what was up, and heard people talking in tones of delighted awe about Der Führer. Great square banners of red silk marked with black swastikas hung high above the road on wires, and gasoline torches flared on square red pillars at every corner. Along the curbs like a human fence there were lines of black-helmeted elite guards standing at attention, each second guard facing the crowd.

It looked to me as if Adolf Hitler was going to come down that street shortly, and I stayed where I was. I filled and lit a briar pipe which I had bought in London, and waited for the circus to begin.

Sudden music blared from loudspeakers on the lampposts, and the crowd's hum died into staring silence. The music sounded like an obsolete popular song to me, but the crowd liked it and the Germans are a music-loving people. I went on puffing at my pipe.

Before six bars of music had been played, something happened to my pipe. It was whisked from my mouth and shattered on the pavement at my feet. A fat man beside me shook his jowls and growled at me in a low, intense German. I gathered that he objected to the aroma of tobacco. It seemed that a lot of other people did, too, because a little circle of my German neighbors were glaring at me as balefully as hell. I felt uncomfortable and started to move out of the circle.

The fat man gave me a petulant push and I pushed him and he sat down against a woman's legs. The woman stepped around him and I saw that her legs were beautifully made.

A man's voice said, *"Ruhe!"* in a rasping whisper, and I looked up and saw the nearest elite guard stalking me with his eyes. I wanted to get away but the crowd had closed around me and the fat man was getting up panting with rage. The woman he had fallen against stepped between us and said something to him about an *Auslander*. Red hair flared under her black lamb hat like gasoline fire, and even in German I liked the sound of her voice.

She turned to me and I liked her face: it was calm and beautiful, with no mob-hatred in it.

"Come with me," she said in English, and put a black-gloved hand in the crook of my arm. She said, *"Bitte,"* and the crowd made way for us. At the risk of breaking up the party, I went with her.

When we reached the edge of the crowd, she turned to me. "Don't you know the Horst Wessel song? You mustn't smoke in the presence of such sublime music."

She didn't smile. I looked for irony in her eyes, which were green and cool as the sea, and saw it flickering deep down near the sea-floor.

"I'm afraid I didn't realize the seriousness of my offense," I said, trying to match her irony. "Thank you for intervening."

"Not at all." She smiled, so that she suddenly looked like a young girl. "I'd be jolly sorry to see anybody torn limb from limb."

"Are you English?" I asked. She spoke English with a slight German accent, but her tone and idiom sounded English to me. English people who have lived abroad for years sometimes acquire a foreign accent.

"No. I'm German. I had an English governess. You're an American, aren't you?"

"Yes. But I don't even know how you knew I was an *Auslander*. I was so surprised when that fat fellow knocked my pipe out of my mouth I didn't even think of trying to explain."

"You look like an American, and you act like one."

"How does an American look and act?" I said, for the sake of continuing the conversation.

"Well, tall and healthy and quite—neither beautiful nor ugly." The color on her cheek-bones deepened faintly and she laughed with some embarrassment. "And you Americans have a certain blue-eyed look. It's not immaturity, exactly. A kind of naïveté, I suppose, as if the world weren't such a bad place after all—"

"Is it?"

She stopped smiling and looked at me. "How long have you been in Germany?"

"One day," I said, and changed the subject: "How does an American act?"

"As if the world weren't such a bad place after all," she retorted. "As if a single man could cope with any difficulty, and fists were effective weapons. If an Englishman were pushed and had his pipe broken, he'd appeal to the nearest bobbie."

"I shouldn't have pushed him," I said as I felt my ears turn red. "It was a childish thing to do."

"I'm glad you pushed him," she said, and her eyes danced like ripples in sunlight. "I felt like kicking him. He was very officious, a very kickable type."

The music had stopped and her laughter tinkled in the silence like a bell. We were standing clear of the crowd against a building, but several people turned and frowned at us. I wondered if laughter was *verboten* in the Third Reich.

"We mustn't talk," she whispered.

Noise flooded from the loudspeakers as if somewhere a dam of sound had burst, and broke in waves over the street.

"Wagner," the girl beside me whispered. "That means he's coming."

The waves of music swept the street bare of everything but sound and power, flattening the individual will like ocean combers rolling on the pavement.

When the sound receded, it left a throbbing vacuum for Der Führer to fill with his presence.

A little man in a brown raincoat came down the center of the street with his peaked nose thrust out like a brown rat walking in a dry riverbed. At his right a fat stoat, bloated with the blood of stolen chickens, waddled in step with the leader, and at his left a rabbit with a twisted foot limped along. Hitler and Göring and Göebbels, triumvirate of the new order that was to be in Europe.

The crowd was humming like viols and low drums, like bees around the queen. I felt vaguely embarrassed as if I was witnessing a sexual act, and looked at the girl beside me to see how she was taking it.

She was standing on tiptoe with her chin raised to see, her breasts high and pointed under her taut black coat. Her upper lip was twitching as if there was a nerve of hate there that she couldn't restrain, and I saw her take her lips between her teeth. Her face was pale and drawn tight over the delicate bones of her cheeks and jaw. There had been a gay and youthful beauty in her face, but now it was pinched by a bitter interior wind. Then and there I wanted to take her with me out of Germany.

After the strange triumvirate marched a little group of generals whom I did not recognize, and then a troop of S S guards like a mechanical black snake made of men. A brown caterpillar of storm troopers crawled behind them with breeches and leather leggings on its hundred legs. Then came a company of goose-stepping soldiers in army uniform, kicking out stiffly in unison as if they were all angry at the same thing and to the same degree. I had a grotesque vision of radio-controlled robots in field grey, marching across a battlefield towards smoking guns on pointed toes like ballet dancers and bleeding black oil when they fell down dead.

The girl beside me touched my arm and said in a low voice, "Let's get out of here."

I turned to her and she seemed smaller. Her mouth looked soft and defenseless, and was pale where she had bitten it. Her face was as white as a pearl and her black lashes shadowed her eyes. She looked very tired.

The circus was over and the crowd began to break up. We moved away with it, she leaning lightly on my arm.

"What's your name?" I asked. "Mine is Robert Branch."

"Ruth Esch."

"Will you have tea with me? You look as if you could do with some tea."

"I've never learned to like tea," she said, "even when I was in England."

"Have you been in England? I just came from there."

"Did you? I have been there often with my mother. She had friends in England."

"You speak English almost like an Englishwoman."

"Thank you," she said and smiled, more to herself than to me.

"If you won't have tea, will you have coffee with me?"

She hesitated. "Well, I really have an engagement with Thomas, you know. He'll be expecting me. On the other hand, he's not likely to go away."

"I'm sorry, I didn't know you had an engagement. Don't stand anybody up for me." I wondered who Thomas was and felt jealous of him already.

"Stand anybody up?" she said gravely like a child repeating a lesson, but there was laughter in her eyes.

"Break a date, call off an engagement," I said. "Americanese."

"Oh, Thomas wouldn't really care so much. Even when you stand him up, his arms still reach to the floor."

"What?"

She laughed at my surprise. "He lives in a cage at

23

the Zoological Gardens. He's a chimpanzee and I go to see him nearly every day."

"Are you interested in animals?"

"I like Thomas," she said. "He's so very human. The Nazis haven't thought it worthwhile to indoctrinate him."

"Are you an anti-Nazi?" I asked. "You look like one."

"*Danke schön.* We won't speak of it, if you please. By the way, are you a scholar?"

"A sort of one. Why?"

"Are you quite poor? Most scholars are."

"Not particularly," I said. "I've got a pretty good scholarship. In fact, I seem to be quite rich in German money."

"Then you may give me coffee over here." She pointed to the plate-glass front of a restaurant across the street.

I said, "Thank you very much," and meant it. She spoke and moved with the independence and dignity of a woman who could not be easily picked up. I felt that my one-guinea pipe had been broken in a good cause.

We crossed the street and entered the restaurant. The air inside had a hothouse warmth and was laden with the scent of expensive perfumes and expensive cigars. The men and women at the tables looked well fed and well dressed. Most of the women wore Paris dresses and had the slightly unreal, glazed look of the too perfectly groomed, the look of orchids and rich men's wives and daughters and top-flight politicians' mistresses. The rich men were there in clothes cut in Savile Row and Bond Street, and the officers in black S S uniforms and brown shirts were the top-flight politicians. At the far end of the room, a string orchestra in Hungarian peasant costume whined and throbbed and lamented. A faint sweet odor of dead and rotting Babylons came up through the cracks in the wainscotting, but the expensive cigar-smoke covered it over.

A waiter led us to a table and we had thick Turkish coffee in tiny cups.

"Oriental splendor," I said. "Are you by any chance a beautiful Armenian slave-girl?" Without her coat, Ruth Esch was more beautiful than before. She wore a high-necked, long-sleeved tunic of black wool above which her skin shone starkly. Her shoulders were wide for a woman but slender and delicately curved. Her bright hair burned steadily around her head like downward flames.

She said with a little laugh, "I'm not Armenian exactly. I'm a Troyan."

"Troyan? Do you mean Trojan?"

"Shakespeare says Troyan. I'm playing Cressida this week."

"Shakespeare's Cressida? Really? Are you an actress?"

"A sort of one." She was mimicking me. "The leading lady at the Repertory Theatre is under the weather this week, and they've given me her part. I was to play Cassandra."

"I can't see you as Cressida," I said, and recognized the blunder as soon as I said it.

"Oh. *Warum denn nicht?*" She was enjoying my confusion.

I blundered on: "She's a wanton, a light, giddy weathercock of a girl. You're not, that's all."

"Must an actress commit murder to play Lady Macbeth? Anyway I'm much giddier than you think."

"It was a silly thing to say. I take it back."

"It *was* silly," she said, "since a boy played Cressida in Shakespeare's day. You might at least reserve your comment until you see me act."

"Is there a performance to-night?"

"Yes."

"I'll come and see you to-night."

I had never seen *Troilus and Cressida* acted on any

stage. It is one the least popular of Shakespeare's plays because it handles love and honor with gloves off, and calls a spade a dung-fork. Achilles is a treacherous and perverted boar, Troilus a love-sick fool, Helen of Troy an international courtesan, Cressida a two-bit floozie. But Ruth played Cressida with an understanding that gave the play a quality I did not know it had. Her Cressida was a brainless, warm-blooded girl who could not resist the flattery of a handsome lover. She didn't try to gloss over Cressida's weakness with tragic effects, but gave her a certain pathos as a victim of environment and her own character. Moving about the stage in her tight bodice and flowing skirts, she was the image of feminine grace without dignity, and affection without consistency or restraint.

The image depressed me: with a girl who could act like that, you'd never know where you were at. But my depression didn't prevent me from going to her dressing-room after the final curtain to ask her to have supper with me. I wasn't the only one who went. The small bare room was full of people laughing and talking in German, and there were masses of flowers on both sides of the dressing-table where Ruth was wiping off her grease-paint.

I was a stranger and a foreigner and I felt like a fish out of water. But she greeted me gaily and familiarly as if I was an old friend, smiling at me in the mirror.

"Was I giddy enough, Mr. Branch?"

"You were wonderful," I said. "You still are."

"Even with grease on my face? Incredible."

"You're incredible, too. Will you have supper with me?"

"But I've just dined with you."

"Will you?"

"Please go away, everybody," she said in German. "I must change my clothes. Mr. Branch, you may wait for me in the hall if you wish."

I waited in the dim hall outside her door and in ten minutes she came out dressed for the street.

She looked happy and excited, with bright color in her cheeks and flashing eyes. Though the play as a whole had not been liked and the theatre had not been full, her performance had been well received. Especially by me.

"I think you did a marvellous job," I said.

"Thank you. But let's not talk of it now. I am finished with work for to-day."

"I'd like to go some place and celebrate. Where could we go to celebrate?"

"Celebrate what?"

"Meeting you. I thought German girls were dull and had thick ankles."

"We're a very giddy lot," she said. "Giddy, giddy, giddy. I thought American men had long grey beards like Uncle Sam."

"I shave mine off every morning but it grows again during the night. Like mushrooms."

She laughed, and we went out the stage-door into a side street.

"I know where we'll go," she said.

She took me to a cabaret where the wine was very good. We were served at a table in an open booth like the booths in American restaurants. In the centre of the long low room, a tall black-haired man stood against an upright piano, playing an accordion and singing a German song about Hamburg on the Elbe. He was very pale in the bright light, and his heavy black beard sprinkled his shaven jowls like black pepper on the white of a fried egg.

He had a rich baritone, though *Schnaps* had raised slivers on its surface.

"That singer should be able to sing blues," I said to Ruth.

"Buy him a glass of beer and ask him for *St. Louis Blues*," she suggested.

"Does he know *St. Louis Blues?*"

"Try him."

When he had finished chanting about Hamburg on the Elbe, I ordered him a glass of beer and asked for *St. Louis Blues.* He sat down at the piano and sang it in English. For three or four minutes I found what every American abroad is unconsciously looking for, the illusion that he's at home. I forgot that the great city around me and the girl on the other side of the table were mysterious and alien to me. I was an American college boy out on a date and the world was my oyster and there was an R in November.

A thin young man with a long nose and corrugated fair hair came past our booth before the singer had finished.

Ruth said, "Hallo, Franz," and the fair young man turned and smiled at her with teeth that were too good to be true.

"Why, Ruth," he said in German, "it's good to see you again."

"I'd like you to meet Mr. Branch," she said. "Mr. Branch, this is Franz."

I rose, and he gave me a hand like leather-covered wood and clicked his heels. He looked about my age but there was something faded about his eyes that made me wonder if he was older.

"How are you," I said. "Won't you join us?"

"Delighted," he said in English and sat down on the long seat beside me. "You're American, are you?"

"Yes. I'm sorry, I didn't catch your last name."

"Franz has repudiated his last name," Ruth said with a smile. "He's an Austrian baron but he refuses to admit it."

"I've enough personal crimes to answer for without assuming responsibility for the crimes of my ancestors," Franz said, smiling like a precocious boy. "My ancestors were in the aristocracy racket."

"And you've been in the United States," I said.

"Apparently I still talk United States adequately. Sure, I lived in California for several years. They deported me for being a Wobbly. That's one of my crimes."

"A Wobbly? You're older than you look."

"And younger than I feel. Thanks. How have you been lately, Ruth?"

"Very well, I—"

Two young men in black uniforms went by the open end of the booth. They looked in but neither spoke. Ruth turned pale and bit her lip.

Franz got up and said, "I must be going. I hope I have a chance to talk with you sometime, Mr. Branch. I haven't been in the States for ten years. *Auf Wiedersehen.*"

He was gone almost before Ruth could say, "Good night, Franz." As he went out, I saw the deep wrinkles on the back of his brown neck and the leather patches on the elbows of his shiny suit.

"He's a surprising sort of person," I said to Ruth. "How old is he?"

"Over forty," she said.

"Really? He looks about twenty years younger."

"Danger keeps some men young. It destroys some but it keeps some men young until they die."

"What kind of danger?"

"There are many kinds of danger," she said, "especially in the Third Reich. . . . I'm sorry but I think I must ask you to take me home."

"Of course," I said and got up. "I haven't offended you, have I?"

"No." She touched my arm. "No, you haven't offended me. It's just that I'm suddenly tired."

I helped her on with her coat and we went out to the street. We had to walk blocks before we found a taxi near the Bahnhof, and then it was a run-down affair standing high on its wheels like a horseless buggy.

When we got in, she leaned back against the worn leather seat and sighed before she gave the driver her address. The motor spluttered and the rickety cab moved away.

"We Germans are a poor people," she said as if in apology.

"There are things more important than automobiles, Fraülein Esch, and you Germans have many of them." My words sounded wooden in my ears.

"Please don't call me Fraülein. I hate that word. Will you call me Ruth?"

"I'd like to. If I may see you again."

"I want to see you again. There are so few people I can talk to anymore."

"You haven't talked much to me."

"I will," she said. "I'm fearfully—loquacious. Giddy and loquacious."

"To-morrow for lunch?"

"If you wish."

"Thank you."

"Thank *you*. I'm afraid I've spoilt your evening, and now you're inviting me to spoil your luncheon."

"That's the first giddy thing you've said. You've lit up my evening like a Christmas tree. Is there something the matter, Ruth?"

"No, I'm just tired."

"Who were the S S boys that passed our table? You looked as if you didn't like them."

"Did I? I must cultivate a dead—is it dead face?"

"Dead pan," I said. "Poker face. Your man Hitler has one most of the time."

"He's not my man Hitler," she said sharply. The driver cocked an ear. She changed her tone: "He's not my man. Der Führer belongs to all of us."

The driver stopped the cab and smiled at us benignantly as we got out. "Heil Hitler," he said.

"Heil Hitler," Ruth replied.

She turned and gave me her hand, which was slim and cold.

"Heil Ruth," I said under my breath. "When and where to-morrow?"

"Well, I'll be working here in the morning—"

"May I call for you here? At twelve, say?"

"That would be very nice," she said. She looked so soft and sweet in the lamplight I thought of kissing her, but she turned and ran up the steps with a wave of her hand and the massive panelled door closed behind her.

Before taking the cab back to my pension, I got out my new map of Munich and marked the location of her apartment in two colors, with the street and number in large block capitals.

Next morning after breakfast, I set out for the Englischer Garten to kill two birds with one stone. I was supposed to be studying English romantic influence on the continental garden, and it happened that Ruth's apartment house overlooked the Englischer Garten. I walked around the great park all morning and thought more about Ruth than I did about English romanticism.

At five minutes to twelve I was in her street scanning a tall row of blank-eyed stone houses with faintly Asiatic tilted eaves. Her number signalled in brass from above an arched doorway, and I knocked on the locked door. It opened immediately.

"Mr. Branch! I'm so very glad you've come." She looked glad. *"Kommen sie nur'rein."*

She motioned me in and I passed her in the doorway. Her morning freshness made me think of lilies of the valley.

"Lilies without, roses within," I said to myself.

"I beg your pardon?"

"I was just quoting a little verse. It comes over me all of a sudden and I have to quote verse. You're looking very well."

"So are you," she said as she led me down the hall.

"I feel well. I've been walking in the Englischer Garten all morning."

"Have you? Did you see the water-birds—the water-fowl?"

"Yep. And the pagoda, and the Greek shrine on a hill. Is it by any chance a shrine of Venus?"

31

"What a funny question. Why do you ask?" She opened a door and stood aside to let me enter.

"Because I said a brief prayer to Venus there, invoking her aid."

Her eyes passed over me like a cool wave as I entered the room. "That's rather a compliment, I suppose. A very courtly one. I didn't know Americans—"

"Were capable of courtliness? You should see me with the powdered wig and ruffles that I wear around the house when I'm at home."

She laughed for no good reason and said, "Won't you sit down?"

I sat in an armchair by the window and she sat down facing me on a straight chair beside a desk. There was a typewriter with paper in it on the desk. Beside us two tall windows with the shutters thrown back opened on the air. Venetian blinds hid the room from the street.

"I saw you in the street," she said.

"I wondered how you got to the door so fast."

She blushed and I said, "I like this room."

It was lovely and strange like the green-eyed woman. Chartreuse walls with Chinese bird-prints, pale green curtains the color of new leaves on a willow-tree, dark green leather chairs. Noon light seeped through the curtains and filled the room like quiet water. I felt like a fish at the bottom of a pool, a little strange but I liked it. Her hair shone steadily in the underwater light like an inextinguishable aureole.

"Do you live here by yourself?"

"Yes, I am a bachelor girl."

"I have no family, either."

"Oh, I have a family. My mother is dead, but my father lives on his estate near Köln."

"And you left him for a career?"

"No, not exactly. I am not eager for a career. I do what I can. My father is a deputy in the Reichstag and I have not seen him since 1934."

32

"Because he supports Hitler? Hell, I sound like a questionnaire. Ask me some questions."

"I don't mind your questions," she said. "I think I can trust you. You'd be much more subtle if I couldn't."

"You can trust me all right, but that's no reason why you should answer my questions."

"I like to. There are so few people I can trust. My father would not be a member of the rump Reichstag if he wasn't a Nazi. He was a member of von Papen's *Herrenklub,* and he has supported Hitler since 1933, like many other rich men in Germany. He has been afraid of the people since the Revolution of 1918, afraid that the Communists would gain control of the country and seize his estates. Now he still has his estates but he has nothing else. Nothing at all."

"Not even you," I said.

"He has my brother Carl."

"What does he do?"

"He was a student."

"Was?"

"He is not anymore." There was a look of complete loneliness on her face as if she was an alien in a strange country. Two days in Germany had given me the same feeling but it was superficial compared with hers. Germany was not the only country I had.

She didn't want to talk about her brother and got up to offer me wine. We had Chianti out of a bulbous bottle with a long neck.

Then we went downtown on a streetcar and had lunch together, and after that we went to the basement of the Hofbrauhaus for beer. I drank a couple of liters out of huge crockery mugs. I was feeling jolly and she was as light-hearted again as a young girl. I felt very jolly and forgot about Hitler and loved all the jolly, sweating Germans who were drinking beer and eating pale sausages in the basement of the Hofbrauhaus.

I said to Ruth, "Munich is a wonderful city."

33

Something about my enthusiasm brought the ice age back to her eyes. "You're fortunate to be able to think so. You don't have to live in Germany. There is insane anger in this city, and all over Germany. Last summer I saw a group of teen-age boys kill another boy by beating his head on the sidewalk, because his father happened to be a Jew. When I tried to stop them, they drove me off with stones, and there was nothing I could do."

"Why don't you leave Germany? You could get a job in America, or anywhere."

"Because I am a German and I can't escape being a German. I am going to stay here."

The jolly faces seemed suddenly to glisten satanically along the tables and the pale sausages to wriggle like worms. We got up and left the rathskeller. As we came into the street, a regiment of boys went by at the double, looking to neither left nor right. Above the stone buildings, a single bomber circled, learning to understand cities from the air.

For a month Ruth and I were together almost every day. We walked in the Englischer Garten and went to the opera. We took a bus to Garmisch-Partenkirchen and skied in the mountains. We went riding along the Isar on rented horses, and I learned how female centaurs carry themselves. I was in love and young enough to forget, or almost forget, about Hitler and the certainty of war, but I don't think she ever forgot. There was always a secret strain in her face as if she was carrying a weight hidden under her clothes.

By the second week I was urging her to marry me and come to America. She wouldn't leave Germany. By the fourth week I was desperate. She hated the Nazis, yet she wouldn't leave Germany and to me there was no sense in it.

On the last day of the last week we were sitting together in her apartment, and I said for the twentieth time, "Marry me and come to America."

"Marry me and stay in Germany," she mocked me.

34

"It isn't the same. I have a living to make. My life is in America."

"My life is in Germany. The people are angry and wild, they've let the nightmares out of the inside of their minds. I must stay here because I am not insane. Is that egotistical of me, Bob?"

"It's the truth," I said, "but sane people aren't going to be happy in Germany. You're not happy now."

"What regard Americans have for happiness. I have no wish to be happy. Nobody is happy. I wish to stay where I'm needed."

"What can you do for Germany?" The question sounded cruder than I intended.

Her throat and mouth were still as marble. I thought if the Winged Victory of Samothrace had a head it would be her head, serenely proud and brave. "I can remain myself," she said.

With the abstract part of my mind I wouldn't argue against her, but the rest of me was twenty-three and wanted to carry her out of the country on a white charger. I stood up and put out my hands for hers and pulled her up to me. When I kissed her, she kissed me back but the firm body against me did not yield. There was an integrity of will in her that could not give in, and even in passion she seemed remote, though her lips were soft and opened under my kiss and her hand was cool on the nape of my neck.

I could think of no more arguments and said. "I suppose it's time we were going to Frau Wanger's."

A friend of Ruth's who lived in a flat near hers had invited her to tea and asked her to bring her American, me. I was flattered by Frau Wanger's invitation because she lived by herself with a dachshund and her small daughter and had very little to do with men. She was a political widow. Like some other decent German women she had left her husband when he turned Nazi, and had lived since by tutoring foreigners in German.

35

By the time Ruth and I reached her flat the little drawing-room was crowded. When I was introduced, there was a good deal of heel-clicking and bowing from the waist, but there was no satanic flicker in the eyes, and neither insane anger nor South German sentimentality in the cool tones of the conversation. Franz was there and gave me a dazzling smile. Several of the other men were like him, younger-looking than their eyes and quick-moving when they moved. The women looked intellectual and tough as if they had laid aside their sex. Several of the names were Jewish. Frau Wanger's friends were not Nazis.

On the contrary. While we were drinking our tea, there was a series of scrabbling taps on the door of the apartment. The dachshund squealed and jumped into Frau Wanger's lap, and Ruth got up and opened the door. A heavy, grey-haired man staggered in, one side of his face glistening with blood from a gash over the eye.

"Dr. Wiener, you are hurt!" Ruth exclaimed.

There was complete silence in the room and we could hear the old man's quick breathing. He opened his mouth to speak but his jaw shook and he could not. Some drops of blood fell from his stained beard onto his shabby black vest. Ruth helped him down the hall to the bathroom to tend his wound. Franz cursed once between his teeth and the room filled with low sounds of excitement and indignation.

"This is terrible, terrible," Frau Wanger said to me in English. "What will you tell Americans of our country when you return home?"

"I'll tell them about you and Ruth and Franz," I said. (I'm telling them now.) "What happened to the old gentleman, do you know?"

"Dr. Wiener is a Jew," she said.

In a few minutes Ruth came back into the room holding Dr. Wiener's arm. His head was bandaged and his face was washed as pale as the bandage. He shook in his chair and could not hold his cup of tea. Ruth held it for him.

There was only one thing to talk about but nobody would talk about it in front of the injured Jew. The party broke up and the guests went home. Several of the women apologized to me for Germany when they said good-bye. The men held their tongues but there was a look of firm humility on their faces, more impressive than pride or anger. Only Franz sat on in a corner by himself, composed and self-contained.

Dr. Wiener went on trembling in his chair, trembling with rage and humiliation, trembling with terror. S S men had attacked him at the head of the street, he said, and flung him down in the gutter. They had kicked him like a dead dog in the gutter, him! a respected physician before they took away his practice, a scientist and a family man and a veteran of the last war. He spluttered with rage.

He went on trembling with terror. He must not venture forth on the streets of this accursed city, this doomed Sodom, in the light of God's day. He must move in darkness, skulk in back streets, live underground like a rat in a tunnel, because he was the unchosen of the chosen of Moloch. He wept with humiliation and trembled with terror. He was afraid to go home.

"I will take you home, Dr. Wiener," Ruth said and put her hand on his arm.

"I'll come, too, if I may," I said.

"I'm afraid I can't," Franz said from his corner, smiling as if at a personal joke. "I think those S S men are looking for me."

"Stay with me as long as you wish," Frau Wanger said. "Both of you."

"*Vielen Dank*," Franz said. "Until dark." He stayed in his corner, relaxed but ready like a boxer between rounds.

Dr. Wiener said, "You are very good. But I must

go home to my wife. She must not be left alone." As night fell in the German cities, Jews were safer in the streets and less safe in their houses.

He got up and walked slowly to the door on knees that were bent with age and weakness. Frau Wanger said *Auf Wiedersehen* with anxiety in her voice, and Ruth and I went down the long stairs with Dr. Wiener between us, each of us holding an arm.

He walked slowly and heavily but bore most of his own weight. We went out into the street and along the deserted sidewalk. The brown stone buildings looked ancient and obtuse. The lighted windows seemed to burn with a mad, inner fire consuming a doomed city.

I said to Ruth, "Why are they after Franz?"

"He's a worker for the Austrian *Sozialdemokraten.* He came to Germany to fight *Anschluss.* He should not have come."

"You must not stay," I said. "Will you marry me and come to America?"

She spoke across Dr. Wiener, who was moving like a sleep-walker, lost in the old melancholy dreams of the Jew. "I love you. When all this is over, I will go with you if you want me to. Now there is work to do in Germany. It will take years. It may take all my life."

"You're going to stay, then?"

Before she could answer, four men in black uniform came out of an arched doorway at the head of the block and approached us walking in step, their polished belts shining dully in the lamplight. Their black metallic bodies were like the products of a foundry and lent no humanity to the street. We stood still and watched them come. Ruth took two steps towards them and stood still again. We moved up behind her. The four S S men passed under a street-light and their shadows lengthened towards us on the pavement.

Their heels clicked on the concrete like four metronomes synchronized, and they came to a halt facing us, as if somebody had pressed a button. The smallest of the four, a slim, elegant job with a baby face whose works alone must have cost a fortune in marks, spoke to Ruth in German:

"An Aryan lady promenading with a Jew. How charming."

In the face of what he feared, Dr. Wiener had stopped shaking. I felt his arm stiffen under my hand.

"A von Esch promenading with Nazi cut throats," Ruth said. "Equally charming."

"You treacherous whore," said the beautiful young man. "Get out of my way and go home."

She struck him across the face and he seized her arm and twisted it and flung her into the road. She fell on her hands and knees.

I stepped in front of the old man and hit out at the officer. He stepped back and raised his stick in the air. Out of the corner of my eye I saw Ruth get up from the road with blood on her torn stockings and run towards us. The stick came down across the side of my face and my left eye seemed to burst in my head. I struck wildly at the white sneering face and jarred my arm on flesh with bone and teeth under it. I heard a live skull thud on the pavement.

Something hit me over the head and I saw black swastikas swarming in a red sky.

The first thing I saw when I came to was a framed and enlarged photograph of Der Führer accepting a bouquet of flowers from a little girl in a white dress. It moved me deeply.

I raised my head and the shifting weight on top of it and looked around me. I was lying on a bench against the wall where the photograph hung, in a long, dimly lit room. Most of Dr. Wiener was lying on the next bench, but parts of his head and face were missing. I went over to him but he did not say anything because he was dead. I felt his cold hand.

Ruth was not there but several officers of the law were. I had attacked a Nazi officer, Captain von Esch, and they suspected me of worse crimes. They questioned me all night. They would not answer my questions about Ruth Esch. I would not answer their questions about Ruth or Franz or anyone else.

In 1937, the Nazis were still leery of mistreating American citizens, although they had killed one or two and imprisoned and deported several newspaper correspondents. In the morning, two Gestapo men in plain clothes collected my luggage, took me to the Bahnhof and put me on a train for Switzerland. I didn't see Ruth after that.

chapter iii

WHEN I finished Hunter said, "And that's the end of the story, eh?"

"I hope not," I said. "It's beginning to look as if it isn't. But I haven't heard anything of Ruth for six years."

"I suppose you tried to get in touch with her——"

"I did what I could. They wouldn't let me back into Germany but I wrote letters to everyone I could think of. The Repertory Theatre, Frau Wanger, the manager of her apartment building. I even called her father in Köln by long distance but I couldn't get in touch with him. All I ever found out was that she wasn't in her apartment anymore, and she wasn't at the Repertory Theatre."

"Maybe they concentrated her," Hunter said.

"That's what I was afraid of. I even thought they might have killed her. It was the uncertainty that got me more than anything. It still gives me nightmares. You're walking across a bridge with a girl and she falls through a trap-door into dark water and disappears. You're dancing with a girl in a bright ballroom and the lights go out and when they come on she's dead in your arms with her scalp peeled off and hanging into your face."

"Christ you've got a grisly imagination. Skip the horrible details, eh?"

"That night in Munich wasn't imagination," I said. "Nor the six years of wondering what happened to her."

"But it's over now. What did Schneider say?"

"I didn't have much of a chance to talk to him. I'm going out to Schneider's for dinner to-night and then we're going to meet her at the station. She's coming on the nine o'clock train from Detroit."

"So it's a romance with a happy ending."

"I hope so. Six years is a long time but I know how I feel about her."

"Good luck to you. We need an Héloise and Abelard love-story around here. The faculty gets more and more bourgeois every year, more and more like a flock of insurance company employees. You'll be Prometheus the Firebringer if you can show us a little *grande passion*. Why, this town hasn't had a spot of the pure flame since the assistant dean of women went to Australia and had a baby on sabbatical leave."

"I can't promise anything like that. My intentions are strictly honorable. In fact, I can't promise anything and I prefer not to talk about it."

"No doubt that's why you've been talking about it for an hour," Hunter said with a lopsided smile. He looked at his watch and got up to go. "It's nearly six. I'll be looking forward to meeting Ruth Esch."

"You'll meet her," I said. "Thanks for lending an appreciative ear. And don't use it against me if she's already married."

Hunter flicked his hand at me and left the shop. I finished drinking my final cup of coffee and got up to follow him out. When I was paying my check, an elegant grey suit mounted on whalebone and plush came through the door on elegant painted legs. Helen Madden's figure was the kind that makes other women look vulpine when they pass it in the street. Her face was not so stunning but it was pleasant enough: a wide, amiable mouth, a straight nose, intelligent brown eyes, and hair that must have cost her seven percent of her salary.

"Hello, Bob," she said. "I'm glad you happen to be here. There's something I'd like to ask you."

"I'm sorry I can't stay. I've got a dinner engagement. But let me be the first to congratulate you."

She blushed and looked happy. "Did Alec tell you?"

"Yes. It's the second-best news I've heard this year."

"What's the best?"

"I'll tell you to-morrow when I'm sure. There's many a slip between cup and lip, especially when the cup runneth over."

"Don't be so mysterious. You're just like Alec."

"Has he, too, been whispering cryptic nothings into your ear?"

"It's past a joke." Her voice had a faint hysteric screech which I had never heard in it before. "Come and sit down for a minute."

She sat down in a booth and I sat opposite her.

"What's bothering you, Helen?" This was the first time I had ever spoken to her like an uncle, but our relations were always shifting. Friendship between the sexes is invariably complicated, even when it is not impossible. Helen and I had gone around together a bit but it came to nothing by mutual agreement. We hated each other a very little, because we couldn't forget that we might have loved each other.

"I suppose it's nothing really," she said. "But Alec has seemed strange lately. He hardly noticed me when he came into the office this afternoon."

"I can't understand why."

"Bob, is something on his mind? I know he's anxious to get into the Navy, but that hardly accounts for the way he's been looking. He's been terribly grim the last few days. And he never used to be that way at all."

"He's over-working," I said. "There's a lot of business to clean up before he leaves. And he's got his ups and downs like anybody else."

"Not Alec. I've been working with him every day for nearly two years. Alec is the original vitamin-fed personality, and when he acts grim he has a reason."

I couldn't tell her what I knew just then so I introduced a diversion. "There's been no trouble between you, has there?"

"None at all. And there won't be." Her voice was warm and firm again, the voice of a woman sure of her man.

"Why should you worry, then? He has a tough job. Forget you're engaged to him in the office. Outside of the office, forget that you're his secretary."

"And end up with schizophrenia," she said with a smile. "You don't know of any special trouble he's having then?"

"Of course not," I lied. "And if I did know of anything I wouldnt' tell you. Alec can handle any trouble he'll ever get into. Watch him when he gets into the Navy. He'll be the terror of the seas."

"Run along to your dinner engagement, Bob. You've made me feel better. Alec's secretive about his feelings, you know, and I guess it's been getting me down. Heavens, I've been acting like a calf."

"Not a bit. I'm sorry I can't stay."

"I told you to run along. Good-bye."

I looked at my watch on the way out, and made a bee-line for my apartment. It was nearly six-fifteen and my engagement with Schneider was for seven. But if I was going to meet Ruth at the station, I had to shave and change my clothes.

My livingroom-bedroom-kitchenette was ten minutes from McKinley Hall, but I made it in less. By the time the tower clock rang the half-hour, I had finished shaving. Two minutes later I was tying my tie when the phone rang.

I picked it up and said, "Branch speaking."

"Hello, Dr. Branch, this is Dr. Schneider. I tried to get you before but you were out."

"I just got in a few minutes ago."

"I merely wished to suggest that I pick you up in my car. Save gas, you know. I have to run into town anyway."

44

"Thanks," I said, "but it's a fine fall evening and I think I'll walk. I'll see you shortly."

"Oh, of course, if you're going to walk— We can drive down to the station together. Good-bye." He hung up.

I looked at the clock on the mantel. I had twenty-five minutes to walk out to Schneider's place, a distance of about a mile and a half, and I put on my coat and started immediately. Germans like trains and guests to run on time.

He had bought the house on Bingham Heights when he first came to Midwestern. I had never seen it from the inside, because Schneider was not usually hospitable to his academic inferiors, but I had seen it from the road. What made it interesting was the university grapevine report that it had cost Schneider most of the small fortune he had brought with him out of Germany.

He couldn't have bought real estate in a better place. Bingham Heights is an escarpment overlooking Arbana from the north. Cut off from the city proper by a hundred-foot cliff with a stream running along its base like a moat, it constitutes a sort of upper town for the aristocracy, the deans and department heads and retired automobile millionaires. But any ordinary man can reach this plutocratic eyrie by a scenic road which winds up to the heights.

It was just on seven when I reached the top of the cliff, but I stood for a minute to catch my breath. The road ran near the cliff at the top of the rise, and beyond the wire cable and white posts of the guardfence, fifty feet of scraggly bushes sloped down to the bare lip of the edge. From the road I could look down over the city.

The still trees and the quiet buildings seemed to lie under amber in the evening light. Fifty miles away Detroit vibrated steadily like an engine that could not stop, and planes and tanks in an endless stream roared and rattled away to war. But in the fall of 1943,

Arbana seemed as peaceful as ever. I could have stood and watched it for an hour, but Schneider was waiting and like a little man I went to meet my dinner.

The road curved away from the cliff and ran along the top of the escarpment two or three hundred yards from the edge. There were houses standing in spacious grounds on both sides of the road, but the houses to my left, between the road and the cliff, were bigger and looked as if they cost more. The third house on the left, a long, low white brick building with modernistic shoebox lines, was Schneider's. It stood in several acres of landscaped grounds, terraced down to the cliff edge and surrounded by trees which had been left standing when the house was built. A concret runaround driveway masked by elms led in from the road. The porch was at the back for the sake of the view, and the front door opened directly onto the driveway.

When I came down the driveway, Schneider was standing in the doorway waiting for me.

"Dr. Branch," he said, "I was beginning to despair of you."

"I'm sorry if I'm late. I didn't hurry particularly because you said you were going to drive into town and I thought you might pass me on the road."

"Oh, I decided not to go. I can do my errand tonight quite as well. Shall we go in?"

He spoke very amiably but there was awkwardness and strain in his gesture when he moved aside to make way for me. I noticed his eyes when I passed him and they were dull and opaque like brown wood.

He followed me in and took me down the central hall to the living room at the back. The floors were blue varnished concrete, slippery and smooth like semi-precious stones. There was a big Persian rug in the living room with the same deep blue in it, relieved by old, decadent rose. The lights were fluorescent and invisible and came on like dawn when Jupiter pressed the switch. The fireplace was big enough to roast a two-hundred-and-fifty-pound pig.

I wondered where Schneider's money came from. The Nazi chiefs had always objected to money going out of Germany, except for what they invested abroad themselves. Was Schneider a Nazi investment as Alec thought? It was strange that he had left his son in Germany for seven years after he left himself. But perhaps he couldn't help himself. I thought of Ruth.

"Won't you sit down," Schneider said, nodding toward a chair by the window. "Martini?"

"Thanks, I will."

He poured and handed me my cocktail and sat down with his own on the curved leather seat in the bay window which overlooked the garden.

I sipped my drink and said, "May I ask how you happened to get in touch with Ruth Esch?"

"Of course, my dear boy." I have several grey hairs among my raven locks, and I dislike being anybody's dear boy. "It's really very simple, though it seems strange now that I tell of it."

"It's a strange world," I said. "Melodrama is the norm in 1943."

"Exactly. Ruth's story is a case in point. She has had six grim and terrible years, experiences which must have been most arduous to a woman of her culture and sensibility. She was imprisoned by the Nazis for alleged treason activity."

"When?"

"In 1937, I believe."

"So that's what happened. You've been in touch with her, then?"

"Yes, of course, during the last few weeks. Ruth has been in Canada for several weeks. There has been some difficulty about her entering this country, but it's cleared up now. I have been able to prevail upon the Department of Justice to relax, in her case, their somewhat stringent attitude towards so-called enemy aliens."

47

He stroked his beard as if it were a trophy he had won, but I didn't resent his vanity. If he really had helped Ruth to get into the country I'd get up early every morning and currycomb his beard with loving care.

"How on earth did she get out of Germany?"

"She escaped. She has said that she would tell me more when she arrived, but she would not trust the details to the mails. All I know is that she escaped into Vichy France, and from there to Algeria. The Vichy-controlled administration in French North Africa put her in prison in Algiers. This summer I heard of her through the War Department, and was able to procure her release. She was taken to England and from there secured passage to Canada. And now she is to teach here at Midwestern. With her thorough knowledge of the German language and society, she will be a most valuable instructor in the A S T Program."

"There's no doubt of that," I said. "But it seems to me that she owes you a very great deal."

"Do you think so?" he said. There was a deep and tragic irony in his smile. He got up and turned his back on me to look out into the twilight that was rising from the ground like thin smoke into the pale sky. I stood up and looked out of the bay window over his shoulder. A few ragged clouds were scudding north and out of sight above the house. The curved window in which we stood was like the glassed-in prow of a boat, headed nowhere across a darkening sea.

Something moved in the garden and broke the illusion. I looked down towards the far end and saw a man get up out of a deck-chair on the last terrace by the cliff-edge. He stood for a moment with his back to the house, looking up into the moving sky. His body was slim and straight against the horizon and he stood with his legs apart like a young man, but in the evening greyness his hair looked snow white.

Dr. Schneider rapped on the window and the man in

the garden turned around and saw us and started up the flagstone path to the house. He moved quickly and easily like a cat, his Angora hair blowing in the wind. When he came closer, I could see that he was a young man, hardly older than some of my students. His face and hair were very blonde, almost albino, and his eyes were as pale and empty as the sky.

Schneider turned to me and said, "My son Peter. I don't believe you know him."

"I haven't had the pleasure."

"I seldom see him myself. He's a consulting engineer, you know, and his job takes him all over the country. He just got back from Canada and is taking a short holiday."

"Really? Did he meet Ruth Esch?"

"No, I don't believe so."

"Of course not," Peter Schneider said from the doorway. I turned and looked at him. If his eyes had not been incapable of expression, he would have been glaring at his father. "Canada is a large country, you know."

His accent was surprisingly good, less evident than the old man's, although Peter had only been in the country two years.

Dr. Schneider moved around me and said, "Of course, you were in Toronto, weren't you? Peter, I'd like you to meet Dr. Branch. Dr. Branch, my son Peter." There was no warmth and no fatherly condescension in his voice. The two spoke to each other as equals and their relation puzzled me.

"How-do-you-do," Peter said and put out his hand. I answered him and stepped forward to shake it. It was soft and strong like his face, which was as rosy and smooth as a baby's.

The strength of his face was in the bones. Under the light drift of hair the brow was wide, with bulbous ridges above the eyes. The nose was blunt and straight and the sharp, triangular chin looked determined, but the lower lip was thick and soft, like a woman's or a sulky boy's. His face, strong and petulant at once, was handsome enough, but two things made it strange. His eyelashes and eyebrows were so light that he seemed to have none, and his steady eyes were almost colorless and held no meaning. If the eyes are the windows of the soul, Peter Schneider's soul had long ago pulled down the blinds and gone into another room.

"I know Toronto a bit," I said.

"Really?"

I turned to Dr. Schneider. "Where was Ruth in Canada?"

He looked at his son and said nothing. Finally he spoke: "I don't know."

An elderly woman with drooping eyes and mouth and breasts came into the room and stood twisting her apron until Schneider said, "*Ja?*"

"Dinner is ready," she said in German and stumped away on flat slippered feet.

I looked at Schneider and he said, "My housekeeper. I brought her with me from Germany and she has refused to learn English. Mrs. Shantz is an ignorant peasant, but she is a good cook."

When the dinner had reached the coffee and cigarettes stage, I was ready to agree with him. Frau Shantz spoke only German but her cooking had a pleasant French accent. Good food and two Martinis had made me very comfortable from the neck down, and even Peter, though his invisible eyebrows kept their complacent scowl, had broken down and begun to talk.

Partly in the hope of finding out more than they had told me and partly for the sake of talking about her, I told them some of the things I knew about Ruth. I watched their faces when I described her attempt to protect the old Jewish doctor.

Dr. Schneider surprised me by looking entirely sympathetic and saying, "She was very brave, very brave. If more Germans had such moral courage, certain—ah—conditions would be impossible."

50

"She's a virtuous woman," I said, "with the courage to follow it through."

"Courageous, certainly," Peter Schneider said. "Nobody can deny it. But why do you call her virtuous, Dr. Branch? Is virtue merely physical courage, the early Roman *virtus*?"

"Moral courage as well," I said, looking into his eyes to see what he was getting at. His eyes said nothing: it was like looking into the depths of a wash-basin. I went on: "Her feelings were decent and right and she acted in accord with them."

"Naturally, we sympathize with her feelings because they agree with our prejudices, against anti-Semitism for example. But is virtue merely a matter of the feelings of the individual? What if the feelings are wrong? Say I have an uncontrollable urge to maim small children, is such an act sanctioned and made virtuous by my mere possession of such an impulse? I distrust the feelings of men in general. I subscribe to the doctrine of original sin."

"I hadn't thought of you as a religious man, Mr. Schneider," I said in the hope of insulting him. "You'd base your ethics in dogma or revelation then, would you?"

"Of course not, I was speaking figuratively. I base morality in the common good. If you act for the common good, you are doing the right thing."

"Whose common good?"

"The good of the community. The political group or state, whatever the group happens to be."

"Is there no morality above the state?"

"Obviously not. Morality varies from place to place. In Russia it is not considered moral to deprive colored people of civil rights. In America and India it is considered moral."

"That merely proves that the state or community can be wrong."

"Who is to decide that the state is wrong? The individual following some inner light?" There was a sneer in his tone but his face was blank of anything but the permanent scowl which grew more complacent by the minute. I looked towards Dr. Schneider at the head of the table. His eyes were hooded and his face was shut up.

"Call it inner light if you wish, or conscience or the super-ego. Whatever you call it, it knows that some things are wrong."

"You are an unconscious anarchist, Dr. Branch. You would set up the feeling or impulses of the individual against the laws, against the good of the state."

"If the laws are evil, they are not for the good of the state. Denying the validity of the individual conscience leaves no check on the state. Whatever it does is right."

"If it is successful, yes," Peter Schneider said, as if that clinched the argument. "If unsuccessful, no."

"Successful in doing what?"

"In furthering the interests of its people, or as many of them as possible."

"You're arguing in a circle," I said, "but let that pass. Can the good of the majority of the people sanction, or perhaps even include, the persecution or misery of a minority?"

"Obviously," Peter said, and leaned forward across the table. "I cite the Negroes in the United States."

"And the Jews in Germany?"

"You're trying to drive me into an anti-Semitic position, Dr. Branch."

"Not at all. I'm trying to drive you out of an anti-Semitic position."

"Nonsense. I merely said that the individual could not be sure of being right when he takes the law into his own hands. Especially a woman, a young girl."

"You seem to share Hitler's prejudice against women," I said, "as well as his prejudice against Jews."

"I have no concern with Hitler," Peter said.

Dr. Schneider spoke for the first time in minutes, "It is not entirely courteous to argue so strenuously with a guest. You must accept our apologies, Dr. Branch." His voice was a light monotone which contrasted with his usual rich blatancy. It sounded as if he was afraid to speak but couldn't help himself.

I said, "The conversation is both interesting and instructive. I believe that Mr. Schneider was about to expound an old Turkish doctrine regarding the inferiority of women."

"Ach, women," Peter said. "You Americans are hagridden by your women. They ride on your shoulders and strangle you with their legs. Their legs are pretty, of course. But why should they be treated as equals? Would you give equal civil rights to a race-horse?"

"If it had equal intelligence and other human qualities."

"Are women equal in intelligence to men?"

"Not if they're not educated. The Middle Ages proved that."

"Why attempt to educate them? Women can perform their natural functions without education. Most of them are hardly more complicated than a child's puzzle. Press three buttons in the proper sequence and the gates open. The gates of Aulis and the gates of hell. Abandon hope all ye who enter here."

Suddenly I could contain my anger no longer and it boiled over. "I abandon the argument. Your political and social ideas have the fascination of the horrible as far as I'm concerned. And the horrible loses its fascination very quickly."

What Peter said had convinced me that if he wasn't a Nazi intellectual he had missed his calling. I stood up with a vague notion of walking out of the house, but the thought of Ruth held me. She was coming there tonight and evidently didn't know what kind of family she was walking into.

Peter stood up and said, "Come now, Dr. Branch, you must learn to be a better loser. We must have no hard feelings over a small argument of purely academic interest."

I bit back my anger and said, "I suppose I did fly off the handle. I must be getting the professional habit of resenting contradiction."

Dr. Schneider produced an artifical laugh which bounced twice against the roof of his mouth and fell flat.

"Not contradiction, sir. Merely disagreement," Peter said. "We are probably using different words to mean the same thing."

I let even that pass.

Dr. Schneider got out of his chair and said, "It's some time before we're due at the station, Dr. Branch. Would you care to look over my house?"

I said I would and Peter excused himself. A moment later I heard his light feet go up the stairs two or three at a time. His father showed me the library with its shelf of first editions, the copper-screened back porch overlooking the lights of Arbana, the small, warm conservatory opening off the porch, and even the utility room where the furnace sat drinking oil and glowing contentedly. Dr. Schneider became quite amiable again after Peter left us, and he waxed lyrical over his radiant heating system which kept the floors warm enough to sleep on all winter. He seemed to love his house better than he loved his son.

I listened enough to answer when I had to, but material possessions bore me, especially when they belong to other people. I pricked up my ears, though, when he offered to show me the *salle d'armes*. A special room for fencing seemed incongruous in the house of a man of Dr. Schneider's age and weight.

"I'm rather interested in fencing," I said. "Do you fence?"

"When I was a student, I indulged in some sabre-play." He touched his left cheek, which was seamed with scars. "But I have not fenced for thirty years. Peter is a considerable fencer, I believe."

"Really? I did some intercollegiate fencing when I went to college, but I've never competed with the sabre. We used foils and épée, with masks, of course. I've got no scars to show for it."

"Our sabre-fencing at Heidelberg was a crude and bloody business," Dr. Schneider said with an emotion that surprised me. We moved out of the utility room under the staircase into the central hall, and I noticed Peter coming down the stairs. "Since my Heidelberg experiences I must confess I have detested fencing, and especially the sabre. It is a butcher's implement."

Peter was at the foot of the stairs now, and he stood there listening.

"If that's the way you feel," I said, "it's surprising that you have a fencing *salle* in your house."

"It was part of the house when I bought it, and I left it as it was. Peter sometimes uses it when he is here, and, of course, it lends a certain touch to the house."

"The manorial touch," I said. "Your establishment is on a feudal scale, Dr. Schneider. I'd like to see your fencing room."

As we went down the hall, Peter joined us and said, "My father has been maligning the sabre, Dr. Branch. It is the most beautiful of weapons, and the most difficult."

"The Italian sabre has its points, certainly. I've played around with it but I never really learned it."

We went on discussing the sabre as we entered the *salle d'armes*, but after Dr. Schneider switched on the light my mind wasn't on what I was saying. It was wondering where Peter Schneider had picked up the smudge of lipstick on his cheek. I hadn't seen it there before he went upstairs, and Frau Shantz, the middle-aged housekeeper, didn't look as if she used lipstick or as if Peter Schneider could conceivably kiss her.

Dr. Schneider pointed at a row of long, narrow cases on a table at the end of the room and said, "There are the foils, Dr. Branch, if you are interested."

When I went to look at them, Dr. Schneider spoke in an angry whisper which I couldn't catch. When I turned around, the lipstick had disappeared from Peter's cheek and he was casually tucking a handkerchief into his breast pocket.

"I'm afraid it's the least interesting room in the house," Dr. Schneider said.

"On the contrary. It brings back very pleasant memories, probably because I won a round-robin once and this recalls the scene of my former triumph. It was the only thing I ever got a letter for in school."

To anyone but a fencer the room would have been less interesting than an average hotel room with nobody living in it. It was a large, square, empty room on a rear corner of the house, with tall windows on two sides. There were crossed sabres over the door, and a few wire masks and pads hung on the white plaster walls. A corrugated rubber mat ran across the exact center of the room.

But the black rubber mat and the faint memory of old sweat along the walls excited me for a minute. I took a foil out of its case and moved it in the air.

Peter stood beside his father watching me. I looked at him and his mouth moved into a smile like soft rubber, but under the rosy flesh the strong and passionate bones of his skull were fixed in a durable, clenched grin. His blonde hair looked senescent in the white light.

"Would you care to play with the foils a little, Dr. Branch, since you do not affect the sabre?"

"I'd like to," I said, "if you'll be forebearing. I'm years out of practice."

Peter clicked his heels and bowed and started to take off his coat. I started to take off mine.

"I'm sorry to interfere with your sport," Dr. Schneider said, "but there's hardly time, I'm afraid."

I looked at my watch. "It's not eight-thirty," I said.

Peter spoke to his father in low, intense German. He must have thought that I didn't know enough colloquial German to understand him, because what he said was, "Hold thy noise, thou doddering fool."

Dr. Schneider said nothing, but he turned green like old bronze. He turned and walked stiffly out of the room.

"We'd better skip it," I said. "Your father seems to object."

"Of course not. There is plenty of time. My father is a wet blanket. Do you care to select a foil and a mask?"

"If you wish."

We put on masks, faced each other on the rubber mat, and saluted with our foils. The blunt, harmless blades crossed and disengaged. He lunged and I parried and lunged. He moved away very quickly and parried and lunged.

If you have once learned to swim, your muscles never forget what to do in the water. Though I had not fenced for years, my muscles remembered the parries and *ripostes* that had been trained into them. My footwork was slow but the foil lightly held in my fingers followed their direction like an extension of my hand. I touched Peter three times while he touched me twice.

He laid down his foil and took off his mask and I took off mine.

"You are quite an expert fencer, Dr. Branch." He spoke with what used to be called old-world courtesy before the old world lost its manners. But his fair skin was strained tight over the bones of his face.

"Hardly," I said. "I've probably spent more time with the foils than you have."

"No doubt you have. The sabre is my weapon. The foil is a pretty toy but the sabre is an instrument of war."

He moved quickly to the doorway and took down the two sabres from over the door. He thrust the hilt of one towards me and said, "Just feel it, Dr. Branch, the weight and balance and versatility."

While he stood opposite me on the mat and made his sabre whistle in the air, I looked at the one he had given me. It was not an Italian fencing-sabre with truncated point and blunted cutting-edge. It was a cavalry sabre, heavy and long, pointed like a pen and sharp enough to cut bread or throats. It was an instrument of war, all right.

Peter said, "On guard," and I looked up to see him giving me the fencer's salute with the other sabre. His blade whirled in the air and levelled out towards my bare head. Fear came down on me like a cold shower but there was exhilaration in it, too. My blade sprang up almost without my willing it to keep my skull from being split, and I parried the cut.

The sabres crossed and arced in the air. He struck at my head again and I riposted and tried to kill him by sinking my blade in his neck. He parried very easily and smiled at me. He struck at my head and I parried. A drop of sweat ran down my forehead and tickled the end of my nose. I was sweating with exertion and with the terror of death. The movements of my raised arm began to feel laborious and remote.

Two well-matched men can carry on unbroken play with sabres for minutes at a time, but we were not well matched. After the first few strokes, I could hardly meet his descending sword. My weapon became a burden too heavy to hold and the flashing metal dazzled my eyes.

He forced me back steadily towards the wall, his sabre falling like steady hammer-blows. The sweat ran into my eyes and clouded my glasses. Through them I saw the skull-grin shining in his face like a sign of death. My left heel struck hard against the wainscotting and ended my retreat. He struck at my head and I parried and he changed his tactics and thrust at my throat.

My nerve broke down and I forgot about everything but saving my neck. I dropped my sabre and moved sideways along the wall and his point crunched into the plaster. I started running across the bare room and his sabre came between my legs and tripped me. I went down hard on the concrete floor and my glasses fell off and smashed in front of my face. The back of my neck tingled for the final blow.

No blow came, and Peter's footsteps went past me towards the doorway in the second that I lay breathless. I raised my head and looked towards the door. My eyes were dimmed and stinging with salt sweat, but between his moving legs I thought I saw a woman in the dark hall outside the open door. She was shaking her head from side to side, so violently that her loose hair fell across her face.

Before Peter closed the door behind him, I saw enough to make me think that Ruth Esch was standing there waiting for him. Then I thought that there were shadows in the hall, that Ruth had been in my mind for hours, that my imagination was wild with fear and anger, and I half-doubted what I had seen.

I was suddenly conscious of my position, crouched on my hands and knees like a beaten dog, and I stood up. I picked up the broken pieces of my glasses and wrapped them in a handkerchief and put them in my pocket. The knob of the door turned quietly and I picked up the sabre I had dropped and stood facing the door as it opened.

Dr. Schneider was standing in the doorway wearing a topcoat and holding his Homburg in his hand. He showed his false teeth in a smile under his moustache and said, "I hope you enjoyed your exercise, Dr. Branch. I can see that you are a true swordsman. You hate to relinquish a sabre even for a lady's sake. But I'm afraid we must go now if we are to meet the train with any time to spare."

"Isn't Ruth here now?" I blurted.

"Why, no, it's only twenty to nine. I thought you understood that we were to go together and meet her."

"Of course," I said, and laid the sabre on the table. The last fifteen minutes seemed unreal to me already. I was not sure what was real and what was imaginary.

The only thing I knew for certain was that I had felt panic and had made a fool of myself.

I said, "Let's go."

There was nobody in the hall and I said, "Where's Peter?"

"He asked me to excuse him to you. He suffers from migraine and the unaccustomed exercise brought on an attack. He has gone to his room."

"I'm sorry to hear it. Will you give him a message?"

"Of course," he said as he let us out the front door. "What message do you wish me to give him?"

"Tell him that the épée is an instrument of war as well as the sabre, and that I know the use of the épée. Tell him that I'd be very glad to instruct him in its use."

"You are very kind, Dr. Branch. I'll be sure to tell Peter." He smiled with the deep irony I had seen in his smile before and left me at the door to get his car out of the built-in garage at the side of the house.

It was dark night now, and the stars were brilliant among the tall trees. The black Packard rolled up to the door like a gliding house, and Dr. Schneider got out and opened the right-hand door for me. I got in and he shut it behind me. He moved around the front of the car like a clumsy black bear in the headlights, and slid behind the wheel.

He shifted gears and we moved down the driveway in a cavern of elms.

I hadn't heard the door on his side close, and I said, "Your door's open."

He said, "Oh, thank you," and banged the door, but when the car turned right into the road his door swung open a little and I saw that he was holding it with his hand. The beginning of a new, bewildered panic squirmed in my chest but I said nothing for fear of making a fool of myself again.

The car picked up speed as we approached the curve where the road dipped down the side of the escarpment. I saw the headlights glare on the white posts of the guard fence and the scrubby bushes on the other side. The headlights swept dark space beyond the head of the cliff, as black and empty as the space between burnt-out stars.

My hand found the inside handle of the door on my side and I tried to pull it up. Then I put my weight on it to push it down. It wouldn't move. I looked at Schneider and he was staring straight ahead. The car was doing about forty and was heading for the guard fence.

His hand on the wheel jerked down and the car swerved to the right. I yelled, "Brakes!" but it was too late. The car crashed through the fence and plunged into the bushes towards the edge of the cliff.

Schneider cried, "Jump!" and tumbled sideways off the seat. His door swung open under his weight but I hadn't time to reach it. The big car was tearing through the bushes like a half-track.

I knew I couldn't find the brake with my feet in time to stop it, so I wrestled the wheel with my left hand and reached for the brake with my right. The car veered and bucked and came to a halt at an angle.

I got out on the driver's side and looked at it. One wheel was over the edge and the car seemed to tremble there like a balance on a knife-blade. Its headlights stared blindly out into the empty darkness like a stupid animal. I was angry and elated at the same time, and I put my shoulder against the front fender and heaved.

The Packard rolled over the edge of the cliff and I listened to hear it strike. For three seconds it was as if the two tons of metal had dissolved in air, and then I heard the rending crash of its fall into the shallow creek at the foot of the cliff. For two more seconds I listened to the water it had splashed up falling like heavy rain into the stream.

I felt better now. Schneider had tried to kill me and though I probably couldn't prove it, I had given him an accident that he'd have to report to the police. And they weren't making Packards for civilians anymore. After five years of sedentary life broken only by hunting and hand-ball and an unsatisfactory duel with sabres, it felt good to push a valuable automobile over a cliff with a clear conscience.

I heard scramblings in the low bushes behind me and I turned quickly with my fists clenched. I could see Dr. Schneider's shadowy bulk coming towards me in the darkness.

"I'm sorry that I was unable to save your car, Dr. Schneider—"

"But thank God you are safe, my dear boy—"

"And don't come any nearer," I said, "or I'll be tempted to throw you down after it."

"What is that? What do you mean?" But he stood still.

A light went on in the front windows of the house across the road and a moment later the porch-light went on. A man came out the front door in a dressing-gown and trotted across the lawn towards us.

I said to Schneider, "Figure it out for yourself," and walked around him to the road.

The man in the dressing-gown came running up to me and said, "What happened?"

I said, "We've had an accident. That gentleman's car went off the road and over the cliff."

"Good Lord! Did anybody go over in it?"

"No," I said. "May I use your phone?"

"Of course, certainly. In the front hall. The door's open."

He turned to question Schneider, who had limped diffidently up to the road, and I ran across the lawn to the house and called a taxi.

I went down the road and met the taxi at the foot of the hill. When I got into the front seat beside the driver, the clock on the dash said five to nine. The train from Detroit was just pulling in when we reached the station. Ruth Esch did not come on that train and nobody I knew was at the station to meet her.

chapter iv

I STOOD on the station platform, feeling frustrated and empty, until the late commuters scattered to their families and the train pulled out. When the lights and noises faded down the track into darkness and silence, I had a momentary childish wish to be on the train, headed for Chicago and points west. Then anger came back and took hold of me again, and I started towards McKinley Hall to meet Alec Judd.

He knew more about the Schneiders than I did. Perhaps he would know why they had lied to me about Ruth and tried to kill me. Even if they knew that Alec was suspicious of them, they had no way of knowing that he had told me about it unless they could read minds. So far as they knew, and so far as I knew myself, I was perfectly harmless. But I began to feel less harmless as the night wore on.

Walking through the dark streets to the university, I thought of a way of checking on Dr. Schneider's story about Ruth. The clock on the university tower rang the quarter-hour as I crossed the campus. If I was lucky I could find out right away.

I let myself into McKinley Hall with my faculty passkey. The basement corridor was as quiet and black as the inside of a sealed pyramid. I climbed the stairs to the second floor in the dark and went down the corridor to the office of the German Department. There was no light behind the pebbled glass door and the door was locked.

I took the automatic elevator to the fourth floor.

Bailey, head of the English Department and air-raid warden of the building, kept a flashlight in a desk in the English office. I found it in an unlocked drawer and flashed it around the room. There were several letters in my mailbox. I had no time to look at them now, and stuffed them in the breast pocket of my coat. When I got back to the second floor, the corridor was as quiet and dark as before.

I switched on the flashlight and looked at the lock, which seemed to be the same as the one on the English office, a spring lock of the Yale type. I took out my jackknife and set the lighted flash on the floor and went to work on the lock. After a few minutes of grunting and swearing, I managed to get the doorjamb thoroughly scratched and the door open. I picked up the flashlight and stepped into the office and closed the door behind me.

Most of the departments in the College of Arts did their business in the same way and kept similar files. The filing cabinets along the wall behind the secretary's desk were tall and dark green like the ones in the English office, and I was pretty sure they would contain the same kind of material: old examinations which could be shuffled and used over again, mimeographed material for courses, reports on graduate students and former students, information on teaching appointments in the department.

The cabinet drawers were unlocked and I soon found the appointment records. I riffled through the folders with one hand, holding the flashlight in the other. Damman, Eisberg, Erskine, Esch. Ruth's name was here then.

I jerked the folder from the drawer and sat down at the desk to examine it. The first sheet in it was a copy of a university contract on thin blue paper:

To Miss Ruth Gerda Esch,
Care of Professor Herman Schneider,
15 Bingham Heights Road,
Arbana, Michigan.

You are hereby notified of your appointment as instructor in the Department of German Language and
Literature, College of Literature and the Arts, for the
university year 1943-1944, with compensation at the
rate of $2400 for the year.

This was followed by the usual printed conditions.
The contract was dated September 15, 1943, one week
ago.

The rest of the contents of the folder removed any
doubts I had had that Ruth had been appointed to
teach at the university. There was a copy of the personal record which is kept for every member of the
faculty. The place-names and dates were pleasant to
look at, because Ruth had lived in those places and
done things at those times. Born in Cologne, Germany,
August 8, 1915. Ph.D. candidate at the University of
Munich, 1933-1936. Assistant Lektor for English at
Weltwirtschaftliches Institut, Kiel, Germany, 1936.
Member of company of Munich Repertory Theatre,
1937. There was nothing below that but white paper.
Six blank years.

I sat with my eyes on the dimly lit paper and tried
to imagine the blank years. Things I had read and
heard about German concentration camps and North
African prisons crawled across my bright, sweet memory of Ruth Esch. My imagination was like a wavering
flashlight beam in a terrible shifting darkness that
covered half the earth. Terror and hunger and long
silence broken by the sound of whips. Where had
Ruth been and what had they done to her and where
was she now?

The floor of the corridor creaked outside the office
and I doused my light and stood up facing the door. I
heard it open slowly and a hand fumble for the light

switch along the wall. Dr. Schneider? The step in the corridor must have been heavy to make the floor creak. I turned on the flashlight and threw its beam on the door. Alec stood there blinking like a groundhog in winter.

I could see his face but he couldn't see mine. He said, "Who is that?" He found the switch and turned on the lights. "Bob!"

"Turn off the lights. This is extra-curricular."

He turned them off and I replaced Ruth Esch's folder in the files by the light of the flash, and closed the drawer.

"What the hell are you doing here?" Alec said.

"Let's get out of here first and then I'll tell you. What the hell are you doing here?"

"I was on the way up to my office and I saw a light. How did you get in?"

I showed him the scratches on the door-jamb. "My pig-sticker."

"I wish you hadn't done that," Alec said as we stepped into the hall. "Those scratches are sure to be noticed."

"So what? There was something I wanted to find out and I found it out. Nobody's going to suspect me of being a Raffles, unless you turn stool-pigeon and sing to the cops."

"You're getting your jargon mixed," Alec said, and I could tell from his voice that he was smiling in the dark. "That's not the point. You can fry for all I care. The point is that Schneider is going to find out about those scratches and he's going to be very careful."

"It's about time he turned over a new leaf. He's been getting frightfully careless lately. In fact, his little attempt to kill me to-night was grotesquely inefficient."

"His what?"

"I thought that would hold you," I said. "Let's go up to your office. This is no place to talk."

We went up to Alec's office on the fifth floor. I

shared my office with two other teachers, but Alec was a full professor and had a room to himself. On two sides, books hid the wall from floor to ceiling. He had been a great scholar before war had made him an administrator. At forty, he was co-editor of the *Middle English Dictionary* which the university had been working on for years.

His desk stood in a corner against the wall between one set of bookshelves and the tall window which faced the door, so that the light came from the left when he worked there in the daytime. He hadn't used this office to work in for months, but the desk was still the desk of a scholar, littered with books and papers and philological journals. A cradle phone stood clear of the debris on a shelf which projected from the wall beside the window. A lamp with a green glass shade for night work hung on the wall above the telephone.

Alec pulled the chain which turned on the wall lamp and switched off the ceiling light.

"Sit down," he said and I took the old leather armchair at the end of the desk. He sat down in the swivelchair facing me across the corner of the desk, and opened a drawer. "Would you like a drink?"

"I think I would."

He produced a pint of Bourbon and uncorked it and handed it to me. I took a stiff drink and wiped the neck of the bottle and set it on the desk.

"What would the Dean say?" I wondered.

"He'd say give me some." Alec recorked the bottle and put it back in the drawer without drinking any.

"What's the matter?" I said. "Have you gone into training for the Navy?"

"No, but I've got a job to do. I'm going to search Schneider's office to-night. If there's anything there, I've got to find it before he sees those scratches on the door to-morrow. I wish you'd told me you wanted to get into that office."

"Why? Because you can walk through locked doors?"

"Yes," he said. "I'm a superior burglar. I borrowed Bailey's master key. They gave it to him so he could turn out the lights anywhere in the building for a blackout."

"I'm sorry if I interfered with your plans. But I've started to have plans of my own. Can I help with the search?"

"If you want to. It may be a big job. And it may lead to nothing. Now what's this about Schneider's attempting to kill you?"

"It's a fairly long story." I told it to him from the beginning, without adjectives but leaving nothing out. Not even the lipstick on Peter's face and the shadow of a woman I thought I had seen in Schneider's hallway. I told him what I had found in the German office.

When I finished, he said, "Is it possible that they used Ruth Esch's name to get you out there so they could kill you?"

I thought a minute. "I don't think so. Hunter told me about her first, and I went to Schneider and brought up the subject myself. Anyway, he couldn't very well fake the records in the German office."

"He could if he wanted to. But you say you don't know any reason why they should try to kill you."

"No doubt I'm an irritating type. I was indiscreet enough to blaspheme the organic totalitarian state at dinner. Then I beat Peter at foils. It's barely possible that he was just trying to frighten me with the sabre to get back at me for that. It's barely possible, too, that the automobile accident was an automobile accident."

"But you don't think so."

"No."

"Are you going to lay charges?"

"I've been thinking about it. But there's not much evidence beyond my personal impressions and a pair of broken glasses. Before I do anything I want to know where Ruth comes into this. And we'll see what we can find in Schneider's office. When I get the Schneiders, I want to get them for keeps."

"So do I," Alec said, and his mouth shut on the stem of his pipe like a mantrap on a leg.

"Do you know anything against Schneider that you haven't told me?"

"Very little, unfortunately, and what evidence I have is what you'd call circumstantial, I suppose."

"What is it? You can hang a man on the right kind of circumstantial evidence."

"There are two things, really. One of them points in the general direction of Schneider, and the other points straight at him but doesn't really prove anything. The first thing is this. When the Buchanan-Dineen bunch was rounded up in Detroit, a good deal of information was found in the hands of Nazi agents, information that was known only to certain men in the armed services and to members of our War Board."

"What kind of information?"

"Largely material on Army and Navy training programs at the university, enrollment figures, length of courses, curriculum of the various programs. They had a detailed analysis of all the courses, A S T P, V-12, and the rest—meteorology, aeronautics, naval architecture, Asiatic and European languages, army engineering—the whole business."

"It sounds like a leak," I said, "but not such a bad one."

"That's where you're wrong." The intensity of his seriousness seemed to draw his eyes back into his head. "Information like that can tell a highly trained spy more about the long-range plans of the United Nations than a whole mailcar full of short-term official orders. The Nazis have men who can put two and two together and get twenty-two, men who do research in the history of the future. And stuff like that is perfect raw material for them.

"I'll give you an obvious example. Last spring the

Army speeded up the A S T P course in Italian local government, and a couple of months later all the advanced students in that course were ordered away. Any spy who knew that and who knew his business could figure out where they were going, and why, and approximately when. The idea that enemy spies are interested chiefly in airplane plans and secret formulae is hardly more than a literary convention."

"I know. It's just that it's sometimes hard to recognize something important when it turns up in your own back yard."

"It's important all right. A smart German who knew all about our A S T P courses and could correlate the knowledge with information from other sources could figure out a hell of a lot. He could predict with a reasonable degree of accuracy a lot of the things that we'll be doing five years from now in Europe."

"In 1948? The war will be over long before then."

"No doubt it will, but the Nazis won't be finished if they can help it. Himmler's boys are laying plans now for carrying on underground even after Germany loses the war. But they're not going to get any more information from us."

"You said there was something else, something that pointed directly at Schneider."

"Right. There's a young man named Rudolf Fisher who lives in Detroit, a naturalized American of German birth. When the F.B.I. arrested Buchanan-Dineen and her little helpers, they picked up Rudolph for questioning. Evidently they had something which connected him with the Nazis, but they didn't have enough to make it stick. Anyway, they released him after a day or two."

"What's the connection with Schneider?"

"Well, it may be a connection or it may not. I think it is. For the last two winters Schneider's been giving an extension course in German language in Detroit, and Rudolf Fisher's been enrolled in the course both times and had perfect attendance."

"How do you know?"

"I've been doing a research job on Schneider. But it's in the files in the extension office for anybody that wants to look for it. Fisher's enrollment in Schneider's course would have given them a very neat respectable excuse for meeting once a week."

"That's supposing quite a lot. Fisher may simply have aspirations to culture."

"Then he chose a curious way to satisfy them. He was born in Germany and lived there until he was fifteen. What would a German want with a course in German conversation?"

There was no answer to that. Alec went on: "So far this sounds pretty flimsy, too flimsy to turn over to the F.B.I. That's why I want to search Schneider's office. We may turn up something concrete."

"The F.B.I. could do a better job of searching."

"But I can't set them on Schneider until I'm sure. You know what could happen to him if I raised a hue and cry, whether he's guilty or innocent. Public opinion would force him out of his job. There's been criticism of the university already for retaining a German on the staff. As I see it, there's perhaps one chance in ten that he's an innocent man, and I will not take the responsibility for wrecking a man's life until I'm sure of my grounds."

"I see that," I said. "But make it one chance in twenty that he's innocent. And one chance in a thousand that he'd leave incriminating evidence in his office."

"I'm not sure that it's so unlikely. So far as he knows, he's above suspicion. And he's going to hold his first extension class in Detroit to-morrow night."

"Is Rudolf Fisher enrolled?"

"I don't know. Registration isn't complete. But I gave Schneider the plans for the new A S T Program the day before yesterday, marked private and confidential, not to be copied and not to go out of his hands. He sent them back yesterday. If he copied them, the chances are the copy is in in his office now, and if we can find it we'll have the evidence we need."

"Let's go," I said.

"Wait a minute. There's something else we've got to find out, and we can attend to that first." He looked at his watch. "It's ten-twenty. We can't enter Schneider's office yet."

"One must observe the formalities, no doubt."

"There may be janitors in the building. In any case, we'd better wait."

"And while we're waiting, we can try and find out if Ruth Esch has arrived."

"We've been thinking about the same thing," Alec said.

"What else should I be thinking about? I've been thinking about her ever since I met the train and nobody got off."

He turned in his chair and lifted the cradle phone from the shelf behind his head. He dialed a number and waited while the phone rang twice.

Peter's voice answered: "Professor Schneider's residence."

"May I speak to Miss Ruth Esch?" Alec asked.

"Miss Ruth Esch?"

The line was silent for five seconds. Then Alec repeated, "Miss Ruth Esch."

"One moment, please," Peter said.

Alec put down the receiver and replaced the phone on the shelf. "Come on. My car's out front."

In six or seven minutes we reached the base of the road that climbed Bingham Heights. Alec drove up a side road a few yards and parked the car in a shallow ditch.

"We'll sneak up on the bastards," he said as we got out, "and see what we can see."

He went up the road to the heights like a locomotive on a grade, steady but puffing. I had less weight to carry but I felt the pace he set, and my heart had two reasons for pounding.

He stopped at the cliffhead to look at the smashed fence. The cables were still down and two of the white posts were jagged like broken teeth. The front windows were lighted in the house across the road, but there was nobody in sight.

"It looks as if he wanted to get through that fence quite badly," Alec said.

"He did get through."

"I suppose he figured he could jump out into the bushes and let you go over with the car. You said the door on your side wouldn't open?"

"It wouldn't open. I think he jammed it when he shut it for me."

"We should have a look at that car to-morrow. I want to look at the door. And I want to look at the steering-gear, just to make sure that it wasn't an accident."

"We'll have to wade a creek to look at it, unless the wreckers can get it out."

"I can wade a creek. That sabre business sounds fantastic, and this accident on top of it sounds more fantastic."

"The Schneiders have fantastic personalities," I said. "Shall we join them?"

We walked beside the road under elms and maples. The drying grass rustled faintly under our feet, and the wind whispered in the trees with the autumnal voice of an old woman.

"What in hell made you want to fence with young Schneider?" Alec said. "You're not Sir Lancelot."

"Wait till you meet Peter. He makes your adrenal glands play like fountains. Incidentally, you're not Edgar B. Hoover but I understand you're hot on the spoor of some spies."

"Shut up," Alec retorted pleasantly.

We turned into the Schneider driveway, walking on the grass in the shadow of the arching trees. We avoided the open triangle of concrete in front of the house and walked quietly under the trees to the side.

We stayed out of the fluorescent light that fell from the uncurtained windows and glared on the grass-blades of the lawn like white alkali dust.

There was a light on the screened porch at the back and I crept forward a few feet and craned my neck to look into the porch. Dr. Schneider was sitting there in a deck-chair reading a newspaper.

I moved back into the deep shadow where Alec was standing. Suddenly he put his hand on my arm and said, "What's that?" in a hissing whisper.

From the house came a ringing clash, repeated once and twice and three times in a regular time, like the sound of harsh cymbals. I knew the sound—foils have a duller ring—and ran across the lawn on tiptoe towards the lighted window of the *salle d'armes*. Before I reached it, the clashing sabres ceased.

I put my hands on the sill and stood on tiptoe to look into the room. The window was open but there was no sound.

Then the harsh cymbals rang again, once and twice and three times and four in steady beat. I could see the sabres moving above the sill, so quickly that their flashing seemed to hang in the air like solid wheels of thin silver.

I chinned myself on the sill to see the swordsmen and felt Alec's heavy shoulder moved against the back of my thighs to take part of my weight. One of the swordsmen was Peter Schneider. His back was to me but I saw his blonde hair and the way he stood.

The other swordsman was bareheaded, too, and faced me full in the light, a woman with green eyes and red hair that moved lightly on her head when she moved to parry and strike. Her breasts were sharp and steady beneath her raised arm and a blue flared skirt whirled round her knees in time with the whirling sabres. The woman looked dear to me and yet remote in the white air, like a lost thing found under water.

The sabres must have clashed thirty times in unbroken sequence but the play went on. They stood bareheaded under the flashing blows as if they trusted each other utterly. The woman's face looked dazzled and serene and Peter's body moved like a dancer's in love.

The woman stepped back and lowered her sabre and Peter laid his weapon on the floor and stepped towards her. She came into his arms and I saw his face go down to hers. She dropped her sabre and her hand came around to the nape of his neck. Her knee pressed forward between his legs and they stood there swaying in passion.

Alec took away his shoulder and my heels came down on the ground. I felt disembowelled and stuffed with kapok. A goblin monotone in the howling wilderness of my brain began to recite brisk little rhymes about what a four-letter day it was for me, and repeated them like a cracked record. Phut shut blut slut rut gut mut.

Alec had pulled himself up to the window and I chinned myself beside him on the wide sill. The kiss was still going on, far beyond the Hays office maximum. A charming scene. A charming couple, Peter Schneider and Ruth Esch. I couldn't see too much of them.

Dr. Schneider made a sudden appearance in the doorway at the far end of the room. He seemed interested in the scene, too. He stood glaring.

Then his mouth opened so that his false teeth glittered in his beard. He said in German in a loud voice: "Stop that!"

The young lovers sprang apart like the two halves of an apple separated by a knife. I couldn't see Peter's face, but Ruth's face looked pale and angry as she turned to face him.

Dr. Schneider walked towards them ponderously and quickly, his black beard shaking on his chest. With a grunt he stooped and picked up the woman's sabre and brought the flat of it down across her shoulders. I heard it swish in the air and he raised it for a second blow.

Peter, in a voice like the yap of a dog, said a German word which implied that his father's sexual practices improved on nature's simple plan. Without waiting for a further development of the theory, I dropped to the grass and sprinted around the back of the house and onto the porch. I heard Alec pound up the steps behind me as I ran in the open back door.

When I reached the door of the fencing room, Dr. Schneider was lying on the floor on his back. Peter was kneeling on his father's outstretched arms and briskly slapping his face. Just a family party.

"This will teach you to mind your business," Peter said in German. The old man's curses were muffled and he gasped for breath.

The woman was standing above the two men, looking down at them. She glanced up and saw us and I stepped into the room with Alec at my shoulder. She fell back a pace and her hand flew to her mouth, but she said quite calmly then:

"Peter, you have guests."

Peter came to his feet facing us in a single fluid motion. His face was scarlet with fury and for a moment he crouched slightly with his shoulder muscles bunched under his sweater as if he would leap at us. I wish he had.

The woman touched his arm and said, "Please."

Peter drew a hand across his rage-puffed lips. Then he said, "Dr. Branch."

I heard the woman take a short, hard breath. She looked at me with wide green eyes in which bewilderment moved like water under wind. Had I changed so much?

Before I could speak, Peter said, "Forgive me for being found in such an undignified position. My father is in his manic phase again. Happily it never lasts long, but I sometimes have to act decisively in order to avoid a Dostoevsky climax. Prince Myshkin, you know."

Dr. Schneider was getting to his feet, his face contorted with effort and indignation. "It is you who are insane!" he exploded in German. "You are insane and corrupt."

"Hold thy noise, pig-dog," Peter said in German. "Or thou wilt be made to regret it."

"I regret begetting you. You are twisted and insane. And as for this thing—" The old man pointed at the woman with a stubby finger that vibrated in the air —"you will take this thing out of my house."

"Your house?"

"Out of my house. To-night. I cannot stand it."

Dr. Schneider stamped to the door with his shoulders hunched as if in despair. I wondered what he despaired of. The woman stood straight and watched him go past us out of the room. Her eyes flared with hate like the green flame of copper foil.

Peter turned to me and said, "My father is temporarily insane, as I said. But pardon me, I believe you know my fiancée, Dr. Branch? Miss Ruth Esch."

She said, "Do you remember me, Bob? I've changed, I know. Though I said I would remain myself." Her voice was harsher than it had been.

"You haven't changed at all," I said. "I knew you right away."

But she had changed. Anyone changes in six years, and she had been in prison. Her hair was as bright as ever but her green eyes were not so clear. The bones of her face were more prominent and there were faint hollows in her cheeks and along the line of her jaw. Her skin was ravaged by time and the hardships she had undergone, and she looked older than she was.

Yet the strong and delicate shape of her head was the same and her body was as I remembered it. Slim and straight as a boy's, with small, high breasts and narrow hips and firm legs like a dancer's. I stood and looked at her and wondered if I had dreamed I saw her kiss Peter Schneider. But he said she was his fiancée and she had not denied it. I couldn't think of anything to say.

Alec had not spoken till now. He said, "I'm afraid I don't know Miss Esch, and Mr. Schneider."

"Mr. Judd," I said to them.

Ruth bowed stiffly and Peter clicked his heels. Alec's frown deepened at that.

My story was ready. "I came to inquire if Miss Esch had arrived safely. Mr. Judd was good enough to drive me out. We were just going to knock on the front door when we heard the sound of fighting. We came in without knocking."

Peter coolly looked me up and down. "Unwisely, perhaps? Do you frequently intervene in family crises with which you have nothing to do?"

"I dislike patricide," I said. "I dislike homicide of any kind."

Peter turned red again. He was turning red as regularly as a traffic light. But he spoke very calmly and precisely. "Good evening, Dr. Branch. And Mr. Judd. You have seen that Miss Esch has arrived safely and now, I believe, there is nothing to detain you."

I looked at Ruth and she turned away. There was a red weal across the back of her neck where the sabre had struck her. I said, "Ruth," but she didn't look at me.

Suddenly, I felt like a romantic boy. Six years is a long time. The six years from 1937 to 1943 were a very long time in Europe. Much water had flowed under the bridge, and much blood, and then the bridge was blown up. I had known her for one month and she had made no promises.

I turned and walked out of the room and Alec followed me to the front door. It was locked but I turned the key in the lock and we stepped out onto the driveway. We had nothing to say to each other as we went down the road to the car. At least I had nothing to say, and Alec held his peace.

We found the car and drove back into Arbana. My head was buzzing, not with ideas. Ruth Esch had changed all right. She had changed from my girl into Peter Schneider's.

Yet she had probably saved my life. It was pretty clear that she had been in Schneider's house all evening: I remembered Dr. Schneider's phone-call when I first mentioned Ruth to him in the German office, the lipstick on Peter's face, the woman in the doorway who had shaken her head at Beau Sabreur. A queer thought dragged through my head and left a narrow slime of doubt: had she objected to my decapitation because an automobile accident is a less dangerous way to commit murder?

"Drop me at my apartment, will you, Alec? I'm going to have a drink and go to bed."

"No more housebreaking to-night?"

"Not for me. I'll see you in the morning."

"Right." He stopped the car at my corner and I got out.

Before I slammed the door, I said, "Good luck."

He needed it.

chapter v

THE steam heat was on and the apartment was stuffy. I took off my suitcoat and threw it on the chesterfield and went out to the kitchen. With boiling water and lemon juice and rum I made myself a large toddy to take the rasp out of the buzzing in my head. As I drank the toddy, the buzzing sank to a murmur like water lapping with low sounds by the shore. But my brain was not yet the complete blank I wanted it to be.

I ran the water in the tub and took off my clothes and had a hot bath. Half-floating in the hot green water, I contemplated my navel like a yogi trying to forget the world. Pale navel I loved beside the Shalimar. For a few minutes I almost dozed. The telephone put an end to that.

I wrapped a towel around me and left a trail of water across my living room carpet and caught the telephone on the fourth ring. "Hello."

The answer was very low but I recognized Alec's voice. "Listen, Bob. I think I've found what I was looking for in Schneider's office. Now get this—"

"Where are you?"

"M E Dic office. Don't ask questions. I think there's somebody in the building. Get this." He spelt it. "T A I L L O U R. Write it down."

I put down the receiver, took a pencil and an envelope out of the breast pocket of the coat on the chesterfield, and wrote it down. Taillour. When I went back to the phone, the free signal was buzzing. I hung up and the buzzing went on in my head.

I called the university number and asked for the Middle English Dictionary office.

The operator said, "There will be nobody there at this time of night, but I'll ring it if you wish."

She rang four times and nobody answered.

I gave myself a few swipes with the towel and put on my clothes again. On the way out I passed the telephone stand by the living room door and saw the envelope on which I had written Alec's word. I picked it up and looked at it. Taillour. There were two clicks in my brain like a billiard carom. 'Taillour' was a Middle English spelling of tailor. The German word for tailor is *Schneider*.

So what? It was a roundabout way of telling me what I already knew, that Alec had something on Schneider.

Two smudged words on the envelope caught my eye. It was postmarked Kirkland Lake, Ontario. What the hell? I had had no letters from Kirkland Lake. Then I noticed that the envelope had not been opened: it must have been one of the letters I had picked up in the English office when I went there to get the flashlight.

I looked at the address:

> Dr. Robert Branch,
> English Department . . .

The black script shimmied under my eyes like highly trained fleas. It was Ruth Esch's handwriting. I looked at the postmark again. September 20. To-day was September 22. Or was it the twenty-third? I looked at the clock on the mantel. No, not midnight yet.

I ripped open the envelope and saw the signature "Ruth" and started to read. It was a long letter but I read it standing up. I forgot to sit down.

The letter said:

Dear Robert Branch:

I know you must be the Bob Branch I knew because you are a professor of English as you said you were going to be, and took your first degree in 1934.

Please don't expect a coherent letter. My nerves have been shaken, and I'm so excited. For a long time I felt like an old woman and now I'm feeling young again. I am in Canada, and I'm coming to the United States. I have been appointed to teach in your university. Isn't that a remarkable coincidence? It will be so good to see an old friend again.

Dr. Herman Schneider, the head of your German Department, but of course you must know him—and oh, Bob, he has been so kind to me!—sent me a university catalogue. Just to-day I was looking through it, and I found your name in it. And you are a professor already! You are advancing very rapidly.

This is frightfully confused, isn't it? I haven't done any writing for so long. For months I hadn't even any paper to write on. I made up things in my head and forgot them again. You know, I almost forgot my English when I was in prison. But during the last few weeks in England and Canada, it's been coming back again.

What a mooncalf you must think me! Here I'm chattering away and I haven't told you anything. But I sat down to write to you as soon as I came upon your name. I should have waited a little.

I wrote the above nonsense in the morning just after I found your name in the catalogue. It's terribly silly but I'm going to let it stand. At least it shows I still have some spontaneity of feeling—for a long time I thought I had no feeling left. Does it seem strange to you that anyone should be proud of possessing human feelings? It is not strange in Germany. But I'm talking cryptically like a heroine in melodrama.

I'm feeling more composed now, and I wish to tell you what has happened, so that you will know what to expect when we meet again. To think that I shall see you and Dr. Schneider in a few days!

Perhaps it will revive painful memories in you, but I must tell you these things. I wrote you letters from Köln, but they could never have reached you. I know my father intercepted some of them, for he tore them up before my eyes. But I'm wandering again. I must begin at the beginning.

You have not forgotten that terrible night in München when you and Dr. Wiener were attacked on the street. One of the four S S men who attacked you was my brother Carl. I can make no excuses for Carl. He was—I hope he is no longer—a fool and a knave. But perhaps I can explain him partly. My father is no better. Sometimes I have thought that all Germany was populated by fools and knaves. It is not true, but there is much truth in it.

Once my brother was a fine student and a liberal, a leader in the Youth Movement. But Hitler took over the Youth Movement and Carl went with it. He never had a strong character and the Nazis caught him young and made him an officer and corrupted him. He became a Nazi and a Jew-baiter long before I met you, and I refused to see him anymore.

Carl was stationed in München when you were there in 1937. My father set him spying on me because I was a disgrace to the family. I had dropped the "von" from my name. I had been a pupil of Dr. Schneider, who had been forced to leave his chair at München on account of his liberal opinions. I had been removed from my lectureship at the Institut. It was even said that I consorted with Jews and democrats and revolutionaries. My father was afraid that the Nazis might make him suffer if I got into trouble, that the sins of the children would be visited upon the fathers. But he dared not speak to the Gestapo directly. Accordingly, he sent Carl after me.

You know part of what happened then. The three S S hoodlums knocked you senseless. Carl told me later that you were forced to leave the country but, I never learned what happened to Dr. Wiener. They kidnapped me, and Carl took me by automobile to my father in Köln.

My father locked me up in one of his houses in Köln with a servant to guard me. He said I must stay there until I came to my senses. I remained locked up in the house for four years, but I did not come to my senses. I tried to escape many times. Only when I tried to escape I was mistreated. I had books to read, and writing-materials, but I could not send the letters I wrote and I could not leave the house except to walk in the courtyard under guard.

It sounds like a story of the Middle Ages, doesn't it? The cruel father and the girl shut up in the tower. But there are worse things than that in the Dark Ages of my country. My lot was really an easy one. I fared better than some of my friends. Do you remember Franz? Years after it happened, I heard that he was concentrated and gradually cut into little pieces over a period of weeks until he died. He died but he did not speak of his friends. Many of them are still active in Austria and Bayern. Their time is coming soon, when the Gestapo will be the underground and the honest men that are left will walk in the open air and speak their thoughts.

I told you I would never leave Germany until the Nazi insanity was over. I never would have left it if I could have done anything at all. But as the years went by, I came to feel as powerless as a mummy or a ghost. I could see the Rhine far off through the barred windows of my room and the barge-trains moving up and down on the river, but not once in four years could I get so far as to dip my hands in the water. I was shut up in a dim old house in Köln, while Austria and Czechoslovakia were swallowed up and Poland and France fell and Germany invaded Russia and decency was blotted out in Europe.

My chance came at last when the R.A.F. bombed Köln. The house was partly destroyed and my guard was killed. I got away while the bombs were still falling and took refuge with friends in the underground. They helped me across the border into Occupied France—I can't tell you how—and eventually I got into Vichy France. For months I worked with the French underground, helping refugees from occupied Europe get from France into Spain and Portugal. After four years of uselessness, I was finally doing something to fight the Nazis. It was the best time in my life, but it didn't last long.

The Vichy police got on my trail and I went to Marseilles and escaped to French Africa on a cargo-boat. But they caught me in Algiers and put me in prison. I don't like to think of that prison. Have you read Koestler's *Dialogue with Death?* I have just been reading it these last few days—it is so good to be able to read again, whenever and whatever I wish. Anyway, the prison in Algiers was something like Koestler's Spanish prison. Someday I will tell you about it.

When the British and American forces invaded North Africa, I foolishly expected to be released from prison immediately. So did the other political prisoners, at least all that I knew—we were not allowed to talk but we had means of communicating with each other. But it was months before any of us were released. When democracy compromises with fascism, the result is a hybrid which looks more like fascism than democracy.

Finally, through an American officer who inspected the prison, I got in touch with Dr. Schneider, who I knew was at Midwestern University. I believe that it was through his efforts that I was released, though he had said very little about it in his letters. I can never repay him—he has even secured me a position at the university. I didn't tell you I have a contract all sealed and signed. And just this week I received permission from the Department of Justice to live and work in the United States.

I am anticipating myself again. You must have patience with my narrative style.

I was released in June of this year and taken to England by airplane. I spent weeks there trying to obtain permission to come to the United States. Then I was advised to come to Canada and try to make arrangements from there. After more weeks of waiting, I secured passage from England to Canada. Several weeks ago I reached Toronto and got in touch with Dr. Schneider again. Through his good offices I have now at last been given permission to come to the United States. I expect to leave here for Arbana very soon.

You must wonder what I am doing in a gold-mining town in northern Ontario. Perhaps my reason is rather foolish but if there is any risk it is my own. Dr. Schneider's son, Peter, who is here with me—a charming and intelligent young man—thinks that my reason is sensible. I will tell you when I see you rather than in a letter, because my letter may be opened by the censor.

Auf Wiedersehen, Bob Branch. I am looking forward to seeing you. And please do not be embarrassed if you have a beautiful wife and three pretty children. I am not a romantic any longer—I am nearing thirty and sometimes I feel much older—and I would love your wife and children.

Indeed, I *will* love them; because, of course, you are married. I want so much just to live for a while in a peaceful place with good people who are my friends.

Ruth Esch.

When I finished the letter I stood and thought for a minute without moving, if the kind of circles my mind was moving in can be called thinking. Peter Schneider had been with Ruth in Canada, perhaps for a couple of weeks. Even then he was a fast worker. I had not been overwhelmed by his charm, but then he was my rival. If I was a competitor at all, and I didn't feel like one. She must have been very willing, to be corrupted so quickly. I remembered what Dr. Schneider had called her, and had a sudden vision of two white German bodies grappling in darkness. I felt sick with a moral sickness I had felt once before: when I was four or five I walked into a little wood and found a small snake trying to swallow a large toad.

My mind veered away from this and went on travelling in circles. A day or two before, Kirkland Lake had been in the news. Twenty or so German prisoners had escaped from a Canadian prison camp near there. Most of them had been caught again, a few had been killed resisting capture. What was the errand which Ruth had been afraid to mention in her letter and of which Peter had approved? Had the two of them gone to northern Ontario to help German prisoners to get away?

But even in a state of emotional bewilderment I

saw that this logic was a bit hysterical. The sincerity and pathos of her letter flooded back into my mind and confused me more. I couldn't believe that letter was an exercise in literary deceit. Perhaps she knew even less than I did about Peter Schneider, perhaps he had fooled her completely. Then I remembered that she was an actress. Perhaps she had fooled me. My feelings ran hot and cold, and the snake and the toad grappled amorously in the underbrush, eating each other behind the bedroom door.

The toll of the tower bell made me start and look at the clock on the mantel. It was midnight, and I had been on my way to McKinley Hall to find Alec. I cursed myself for a dawdler and went out the door, stuffing the letter in my pocket.

I lived on the north side of the campus, ten minutes from McKinley Hall, which is on the south side. I covered the distance in five minutes by trotting and cutting across the dark campus, and approached the building from the rear.

There was one light on in its block-long length. It seemed to be on the fourth floor. Of course, the Middle English Dictionary office. Alec must be up there again. I looked for a light on the fifth floor immediately above the Dictionary office, but the fifth-floor windows were all dark. No light in Alec's office second from the end.

The walk that ran along behind the building was unusually dark. The flood-light on the corner must have burned out, I thought, and I looked up as I passed it.

As I raised my eyes, a light flashed on in the second window from the end on the fifth floor, Alec's office, and a man leaped at me from the lighted window. He howled like a dog and stretched out his arms as he leaped outward and I cowered against the wall in terror, quivering like a beaten animal. No human being could make that leap to the bare pavement.

The howling man dived headfirst to the sidewalk in front of me and I heard his skull break with a sound like an egg dropped on the floor. One leg thrashed in a convulsion and the body crumpled and lay still. Blood spattered and glistened darkly on the dim pavement, and I moved sideways along the wall to avoid it.

Then I remembered the flashlight still in my pocket. I turned it on the upturned face. There was no face. Dark blood was flowing from the head like oil in steady, wormlike streams. I felt the pulse. No pulse. I straightened the twisted body and the ruined head moved limply sideways like a pumpkin on a string.

I knew by the hair and the clothes that it was Alec. I said to myself, I'm going to kill Schneider, and I heard the words said aloud by someone. I must have said them because there was nobody else there.

My mind began to function again after the shock, and a sudden thought jerked me upright and accelerated my heartbeat ready for action: whoever had pushed Alec out of the window must still be in the building. Before I could move I heard the faint sound of a woman's shout from somewhere high up in the building, and then something that sounded like a door being shaken violently in its frame.

I looked up at the lighted window from which Alec had fallen and saw that it was half-open. Again the woman's shout came keen and distressed out of the dark building, and then there was the crash and tinkle of broken glass. Somebody was breaking into Alec's office. My heart pumped faster but I stood where I was and watched the window.

I heard the woman's shout again, louder and more anguished now. She was calling, "Alec!"

The woman's head appeared at the window dark against the light. I couldn't be sure but it looked like Helen Madden. She leaned far out and looked down at me and the dead man with the flashlight beam on his face. She screamed. Her scream ended in a tearing sigh like the last vomit of despair, and her head and shoulders fell out of the light and left the window empty.

I let myself into the building and ran up the west

stairs, turning on the lights at the ends of the corridors as I went. So far as I could see the corridors were empty. I waited too long, I thought, I've given the Schneiders time to get away.

When I reached the fifth floor, I could see from the head of the stairs that Alec's door was open, throwing a cone of light across the hall. When I reached the door, I saw that one corner of the ground-glass pane in it was broken. I stood in the doorway breathing heavily, and looked into the room.

The green-hooded lamp above the desk was on, and it cast a greenish light over the woman who was sprawled on the floor beneath the window. I went to her and saw that it was Helen. Her eyes were closed and her breathing was quick and light. It looked as if she had simply fainted. I straightened her out on her back, pulled her skirt down over the bare gooseflesh of her thighs, and let her lie. As long as she stayed unconscious I didn't have to tell her.

When I stood up, I noticed that the receiver of the telephone dangled on its cord from the shelf below the lamp, hanging almost to the floor. It was swinging slightly, making little clicks against the corner of the desk. Just as I reached for it, I remembered fingerprints and got down on my knees to put my ear against it where it hung. I could hear nothing, not even the dial tone. Then I heard voices, very faint as if from a long way off, like voices on a record-player when the tube has blown out. I could not understand what they were saying. The rustling voices ceased and I stood up again.

The only sign of a possible struggle besides the dangling receiver was the broken glass in the door. But I had heard the crash. Helen must have broken it to get into the office after Alec fell. Perhaps she heard him fall, perhaps she had even seen the Schneiders running away. Or was it Peter Schneider alone?

I stepped around the woman on the floor to look at the window. The lower half was open, a single steel-framed pane about four-feet square that opened at the bottom and swung outward from the top. The top corners of the pane slid down oiled grooves in the upright sashes at the sides when the bottom was pushed out, so that when the window was wide open, it formed a horizontal plane midway in the four-foot square, supported by steel arms. The window was only partly open now. The outswung pane formed an angle of about thirty degrees with the vertical sashes where it met them at the top, leaving room for Alec to have crawled out at the side and jumped from the concrete sill.

But the window was not wide open, as it would have had to be if Alec had been pushed. He had not been dead or unconscious when he fell: he had yelled and thrown up his arms. Had the Schneiders partly closed the window after pushing him out? I had seen nor heard nothing. And why had they turned on the light?

I remembered the light in the window on the fourth floor beneath Alec's office, and a sudden doubt took hold of me. Had Alec been pushed from the Dictionary office? I had been taken by surprise in the dark, and with my glasses broken, I could be mistaken about the window.

I ran down the stairs to the fourth floor. The door of the Dictionary office was open and the light was on. All the windows were closed and fastened. The door to the inner room where the files were kept was open and I glanced in. It was dark and there was no sound. I turned out the light in the outer room and went back to Helen.

Her breast was rising and falling more slowly and regularly. I put my ear to it and heard her heart beating strongly. I wet my handkerchief at the drinking-fountain in the hall and wiped her face with it. Her eyelids fluttered and she began to stir.

Then, for the first time, I thought of the police. To avoid touching Alec's phone, I went down the hall to my own office to call them. The lieutenant at the desk said he'd come right over himself, and I told him to bring a doctor for Helen.

I went downstairs to let the police into the building. When I opened one of the glass doors at the front, the police car was drawing up to the curb. Two men in dark uniforms got out and came up the walk and mounted the steps. They walked quickly but laboriously, as if every building were a tomb.

"My name is Branch," I said as they came up between the pillars. "I just called you."

"I'm Lieutenant Cross," said the wider of the two policemen. Their backs were to the light from the street and I couldn't see their faces. "This is Officer Sale."

"Did you call a doctor for the girl?"

"Yeah, this is probably him now." Cross jerked his head at a car that had just turned the corner. "Go and get him, will you, Sale?"

Sale went to the car that had stopped at the curb and came back with a middle-aged man in a camel's-hair coat and a dither.

"Dr. Rasmussen," Cross said to me. "I guess you better look at the body first, doctor, just to make sure."

"Very well, lieutenant. Where is it?"

I took them through the building and out one of the back doors.

"You said the dead man's name is Judd," Cross said. "Is that the Judd on the War Board?"

"Yes."

I could see the body on the sidewalk, lying as still as if it had always been lying there.

"There he is," I said.

The policemen turned their flashlights on the dead man.

"Jesus," Cross said, "he certainly is mashed up."

The doctor squatted down by the body, drawing his light coat up around his hips so its hem wouldn't draggle in the blood on the sidewalk. He stood up shaking his head:

"He was dead the minute he hit the sidewalk. Did he jump from the roof?"

"Fifth floor," I said. "But he didn't jump."

"From that window there?" Cross said, pointing at the lighted window of Alec's office.

"Yes. That's where the girl is."

"Oh, yes, the girl," Rasmussen said. "I'd better get up there. Nothing I can do here."

I unlocked the door, which had relocked itself, and the doctor followed me in.

"Second from the end on the fifth floor," I said. "The light's on and you can't miss it. I think she just fainted, and she may be conscious now."

"Right," he said, and started up the stairs. I went out to the sidewalk where Cross and Sale were still standing.

"What happened to the light on the corner of the building?" Sale asked. In the light of the lieutenant's torch I could see that he was a tall man of thirty or so with a sallow skin and a broken nose.

"What light?" said Cross.

"This is the way I go home and there's always a light here. On the corner." Sale turned his flashlight on the corner of the building. The light was there all right, and the bulb was in place.

"We'll look at that later," Cross said. "Maybe it just blew out."

He turned to me. "You got any idea how this happened, Mr. Branch? You said he didn't jump."

"I saw him fall from that window. I think he was pushed. I know he didn't commit suicide."

"How do you know?"

"I knew him. He wasn't the kind of a man who would kill himself, and he had no reason."

"That you knew of?"

"He had no reason. I talked to him on the telephone half an hour before this happened."

"Oh, you did? You say you saw him fall. Where were you when he fell?"

"Walking on this sidewalk. About where you're standing."

"You say you think he was pushed. Did you see somebody push him?"

"No. I didn't see anybody. I simply know that Judd was not capable of committing suicide."

"The damnedest people do," Cross said. "What did he say on the telephone?"

"He wanted me to come over here."

"Did he say why?"

"No." I wanted a more receptive audience before I brought the Schneiders in, and I had to have a talk with the president of the university.

"Where does the girl come in?"

"I don't know, you'll have to ask her. She was Alec's fiancée. She must have been in the building and heard him cry out when he fell. She broke into his office and looked out of the window and saw him down here on the sidewalk and fainted."

"Jesus," Sale said. "Tough on her."

"You're not accusing *her* of pushing him?" Cross said.

"Of course not," I snapped. "They were going to be married. This thing is going to ruin her life."

"Looks like suicide to me, lieutenant," said the man with the broken nose.

"I don't know," Cross said. "I'm going to call the detective-sergeant. Can I phone around here, Mr. Branch?"

"There's a phone in my office on the fifth floor."

"Same floor as the room he jumped from, eh? I want to look at that room."

We entered the building and climbed the stairs to the fifth floor.

Dr. Rasmussen met us at the head of the stairs. "Miss Madden has regained consciousness," he said. "I put her on the settee in the Ladies' Room down the hall."

"I want to ask her some questions," Cross said.

"Not just now, lieutenant. She's had a shock and you'd better let her rest for a while. You can question her later, perhaps."

"Yeah, how much later?"

"I'd say give her an hour anyway. If she wasn't a good strong girl, I'd send her to the hospital for the night. But she's got a stiff upper lip."

"Did you tell her, Doctor?" I said.

"She knew. I confirmed what she knew." After a pause Rasmussen said, "Well, I can trust you gentlemen to see that she gets home safely. I might as well toddle home for a snooze. I think I'll have a delivery before morning."

"O.K., doctor, good night," Cross said. Rasmussen picked up his bag and waved his hand and went downstairs.

"Is that Judd's office?" Cross asked as we passed the open door.

"Yes."

"Hey, lieutenant," said Sale. "the glass in the door is broken."

"I think Miss Madden broke it. I heard the crash after Judd fell."

"I get it," Cross said. "You might as well stay here and look around, Sale. I'll be right back."

I took Cross to my office and he called the detective-sergeant. When he had finished, I picked up the receiver.

"Going to make a call?" Cross looked as if he felt he should be suspicious of me but couldn't quite make the grade. His broad, weather-reddened face was set in unimpressive creases of earnestness and his blue eyes were puzzled.

"I'm going to call President Galloway," I said. "He's got to know about this."

"I guess that's right," Cross agreed. "Stick around,

though, will you? The detective'll probably want to ask you some more questions."

"I'll stay in the building."

Cross went out the door and I dialed President Galloway's number. He lived in the presidential mansion, which was a university building on the opposite side of the campus from McKinley Hall.

While the phone rang, I looked at my watch. It was just after 12:30. How long ago had Alec died? It was midnight when I left my apartment. It must have taken me about five minutes to get here. Perhaps six. Alec had been dead about twenty-five minutes. In another twenty-five minutes, I hoped to have his murderer. But first I had to talk to Galloway.

On the fourth ring, a maid answered the phone. "President Galloway's residence."

'This is Robert Branch, professor of English. May I speak to the president?"

"It's very late. Could I have him call you in the morning, or take a message?"

"Tell him it's important university business. If he's in bed, you'll have to wake him up."

"One moment, please."

I waited a number of moments. Then I heard the president's voice say, "Galloway speaking," with the exaggerated briskness of a man still half-asleep.

"Robert Branch speaking. Alec Judd has been killed."

"Judd killed! Good heavens. How did it happen?"

"He jumped, or was pushed, from the window of his office in McKinley Hall. I think he was pushed and I think I know who pushed him."

"You do?"

I decided to hold it till he came over. "I'd prefer not to tell you over the phone. Can you come here now, sir?"

"Of course, Robert, of course. Where are you?"

"In my office in McKinley Hall. I can't leave here because the police want to question me. Fifth floor."

"You've called the police?"

"I called them as soon as it happened. I saw Alec fall."

"It must have been a terrible shock. You were close friends, weren't you? You called the local police, of course?"

"That's right."

"I'll be right over," Galloway said, and hung up.

I replaced the receiver and leaned back in my swivel-chair and looked at the telephone. I thought of the receiver dangling from the shelf beside Alec's window. Had he been phoning when he was attacked? If so, whom had he been phoning?

My mind jumped like a shot deer. He was phoning me! The line was cut off while I was writing 'taillour' on the envelope. I stiffened up and the chair tilted me forward.

Then I relaxed again and blew air out of my lungs. The deer had been missed by a mile after all. It couldn't have been much after 11:30 when he phoned me. Besides, he said that he was phoning from the Dictionary office on the fourth floor. What was he doing in the Dictionary office?

A sharp-nosed man in plain clothes with a beady eye and a clipped black moustache put his head in at the door. "I'm Haggerty," he said, "Detective-Sergeant Haggerty. Are you Professor Branch?"

"Yes. I believe you want to ask me some questions."

"Can you wait a few minutes? I want to examine this office down the line first."

"O.K., sergeant," I said, and he took his nose away with him.

I went on sitting in my chair. There was no sign of Galloway yet. The dangling receiver still bothered me. Suddenly it occurred to me that I could do something.

I dialed 'O' and the night operator answered, "University operator speaking."

"This is Professor Branch of the English Department. I'm investigating a certain matter for the president and I wonder if you can give me some information."

"What about? It depends on what it is," she said in the cagey way switchboard operators have.

"Is the line to Professor Judd's office still open?"

"Yes, it is. I turned my key a few minutes ago and there was nobody on the line. I asked if the line was being used and a policeman came to the phone and told me to leave it open."

"How long had the line been open? I mean, when was the call put in?"

"The original call from Professor Judd's office? I don't know, maybe an hour ago. I don't remember exactly."

"Did you hear anything that was said over the line?"

"Say, who is that talking? Are you really Professor Branch?" The false culture flaked off the surface of her voice like old fingernail polish. There is nothing like fear for a job to remove culture from a voice.

"Do you want me to quote some poetry to prove it?"

"No kidding, you're not trying to put me on the spot, are you?"

"Of course not. I'm Branch and I don't know or care who you are. Did you hear anything?"

"I'm not allowed to listen to conversation," she said more calmly. "But when a line has been open for quite a while we're allowed to switch in and make sure it's busy, that's all."

"Was Judd's line busy?"

"Well, it was open for about twenty minutes or so, so I turned the key and somebody was talking all right and I switched out again."

"About when was this?"

"I switched in about midnight, I think. No, it was just after midnight. The tower clock had just struck."

"How long after midnight?"

"Two or three minutes, maybe. I don't know."

"You didn't hear anything that was said?"

"We're not supposed to listen and I couldn't tell you anyway, Dr. Branch. It wasn't anything, anyway. It sounded like a gag."

"It was no gag. Can't you tell me anything?"

She said: "Sorry I have to go now. The policeman in the office wants to talk to me."

She clicked off.

chapter vi

I HEARD quick, heavy steps in the hall and got out of
my chair. President Galloway came through the door
with his head down as if he were butting his way in.
He had on trousers and a shirt and a grey suede wind-
breaker. The shirt was open at the neck and I could
see the matted grey hair on his chest. He had obviously come in a hurry and I wondered why he had
taken so long.

"A terrible business, Branch." His lined face was
pale and needed shaving. I had never seen Galloway
look perturbed or disheveled before. He was a former
head of the Department of Psychology, a good judge
of men and a smooth and subtle politician. Maybe
statesman is a better word: he presided with considerable dignity and some wisdom over a university community as large and complex as an ancient city-state.
But he was upset now.

"I'm glad I was able to get in touch with you, sir,"
I said, "and that you could come over."

"We've got to do what we can. Branch, do you
think Judd's death had anything to do with the War
Board?"

"I'm sure it had."

"I've been worried about the War Board," Galloway
said. "I heard indirectly at the time of the Detroit
indictments that evidence was turned up which led
in our direction."

"Alec said something of the sort this afternoon."

"It was evidently a blind alley," Galloway went on,

"but I called up one of the Federal men with the Detroit office who happens to be a friend of mine. Former student, in fact. I wanted to keep it unofficial. He came down here last week and we talked it over—off the record, of course."

"It might be a good idea to make contact with him now. This is likely to be a Federal matter."

"I called him before I left the house." A tired smile twitched the sagging muscles of Galloway's face. "As it happened he was at the Bomber Plant to-night and it took me some time to get in touch with him. But he should be here before long."

Thank God for that, I thought. I had no great faith in the sly-faced sergeant.

I said: "The Bomber Plant? What's the matter there?"

Galloway answered, "I don't know," and closed his face up like a fist. After a pause, as if to console me for the snub, he said: "A great boy, Chet Gordon. I had him in psychology seminar eight or nine years ago."

I remembered the name from my undergraduate days. "Was he an intercollegiate swimmer?"

"That's the man." After another pause he said, "You had something to tell me, Branch."

I gave it to him without trimmings: "Alec was murdered by Herman Schneider or his son, or both of them."

"Jesus Christ, Branch! Do you know what you're saying? Did you see them do it?"

"No."

"What grounds have you for this—accusation?"

"The Schneiders tried to murder me to-night. Shortly before Alec was killed, he called me on the phone and told me he had found proof that Herman Schneider had copied confidential War Board information. There are other things."

"Jehosophat." Galloway was regaining control of his proper names. "What other things?"

I told him what I knew, leaving out my suspicions of

100

Ruth Esch. If she was an innocent friend of the Schneiders, there was no point in ruining her university career before it began.

When I finished, Galloway said, "This is a big thing, Robert. I'm glad you called me before speaking to the police. A big thing. A scandal involving a man of Schneider's standing in the university could do us a great deal of harm. We must move with circumspection."

Circumspection was his favorite word: he had to consider the board of regents and the state legislature and the national reputation of the university. I wanted to see Schneider in handcuffs. I said:

"You can't hush up murder and you can't hush up espionage."

"Of course not, Robert, of course not," Galloway said in the soothing accents he used when he was most unalterable. "But we cannot be impetuous. Murder has not been proved. Stronger men than Alec Judd have committed suicide."

"I was with Alec an hour before it happened. He was in fine fettle."

"Of course, of course," which meant that he would move when he was ready. "Have you found this evidence against Schneider which you say he said he had?"

I didn't like the 'you say' construction but wasted no more breath. "No."

"Has a search been made for it?"

"I told the police nothing about it."

"Good. We can handle this in our own way. We must have a talk with Schneider. At least we can find out if he could possibly have killed Alec."

"Why not let the police handle it?" I said sharply. He had the temporizing brain without which few university presidents can last a year, and trying to co-operate with him was like shaking hands with an octopus while walking in quicksand.

"Chester Gordon will be here soon. He is a man of

wider experience, and greater discretion, than I should judge the local police to be. Meanwhile, I should like to discuss this matter with one or two members of the War Board."

"Don't call Schneider, sir."

"I shall call Herman Schneider," Galloway said softly, "and ask him to come over. I think you may trust me to be discreet." He looked at me out of blank, cold eyes over which the lids drooped slantwise.

I remembered that I was an assistant professor and said nothing. Galloway said, "May I use your phone?"

"Certainly. I'll go down to Alec's office and see if the police have found anything. The detective said he wants to question me."

"Go ahead." He sat down to phone.

When I opened the door, Haggerty was going through the drawers of Alec's desk. He looked up at me with a nasty look in his small eye like a rat cornering another rat:

"I hear you were having a little conversation with the university operator a few minutes ago. A very highbrow little confab, I bet you. I'm not an intellectual myself, but I hear it was a very highbrow little confab."

"That's what you said," I said with eighteenth-century courtesy. "I'm not a detective myself, but I thought I might learn something from her. It turned out I couldn't."

"Yeah, I know. But don't you think it might be a wise plan, professor, to leave investigation to the proper authorities? We're stupid, we're slow, we're dumb, but we're trained to find out things. Isn't that right, professor?"

"That's right, sergeant. I don't want to butt in." In the United States a college degree is a mystic symbol. There are a lot of men who have never been to college and can't get over it. It pays to humor them.

"O.K., now we know where we stand. You leave

investigation to me, I leave Shakespeare to you." His thin lips smiled narrowly: he had taken the curse off one college degree. I hid my Phi Beta Kappa key in my watch pocket.

Sale, the officer with the sallow face, was watching us as if he were enjoying himself. "Where's Cross?" I asked.

"He took the body to the morgue," Haggerty said. "I told him to send over the fingerprint man. He'll probably want your fingerprints, so he'll know which are yours and which are somebody else's, if there was somebody else."

"Don't forget Miss Madden's fingerprints. The lieutenant told you about her, didn't he?"

"I'm not planning to forget anything, professor. I went down there a few minutes ago and she said she was ready to talk to me when I get through with you."

"How is she?"

"She's O.K. Now I want to know what you saw. Everything you can remember." He sat down in the swivel-chair at the desk and I sat facing him in the chair I had sat in talking to Alec earlier in the evening.

Sale was standing behind us looking unnecessary but interested, and the sergeant said, "You better go down and guard the front entrance."

"O.K., Sarge." Sale went out closing the door behind him.

"Now you were walking on the sidewalk down below this window," Haggerty said. "What time?" He had taken out a black-bound notebook and waited with pencil poised.

"Five after twelve as close as I can figure it."

"What did you see? Tell me in the order you saw it."

"The first unusual thing I noticed was that the light on the corner of the building was out."

"Sale checked on that. The bulb was partly unscrewed. But that doesn't prove anything, it could've been kids."

"And perhaps Alec thought he could fly and just jumped down to greet me." The official assumption that Alec's death was suicide, unless it could be proved otherwise, was getting under my skin.

"Aw, c'mon, professor, don't be like that. I'm just trying to figure a case. We got to co-operate."

"Somebody turned that light out, and I think it was for a reason. And somebody turned on the light in this office."

"When was that?"

"I saw the light go on at the moment that Alec fell."

"Could he have turned it on just before he jumped?"

"He could have, I think, if he stood on the sill and pulled the chain through the window-opening as he jumped. But why would he do that?"

"Make it look like an accident," Haggerty said.

"You think it was suicide," I said, "but he had no motive for suicide. Alec Judd was a successful man, in general a happy man. He just got engaged to be married to Miss Madden, and yesterday he went to Detroit to apply for a commission in the Navy."

"What do you mean, 'in general'? Was something bothering him?"

"He was a little worried recently, but it wasn't the sort of thing he'd kill himself over."

"He was worried, eh? What about?"

"About the War Board. Certain things were bothering him."

"Such as?"

"He didn't tell me." Galloway wanted me to keep mum for the present, and I kept mum against my will.

"Now look, professor, this looks like suicide to me. I know you don't like to think so; he was your friend. But I've seen quite a few suicides. I've seen a couple right in this university."

"It was not suicide," I said.

"What makes you so sure? Did he look dead when he fell?"

"He was alive when he fell. I heard him yell, and it scared me to death."

"Did you see him jump?"

"I saw him the moment after he jumped. I could see him against the light from the window, flinging his arms up. He was feet-first but he turned in the air on the way down and landed on his head."

"Did it look like a jump?"

"It looked like a jump. But I know he was pushed."

"Look here, professor." He stood up and put his hand on the windowsill. "Is this the way the window was when you came up here after he fell?"

I got up and looked at the window. It was still open at a thirty-degree angle. Between the bottom sash of the outward-swinging pane and the outer edge of the narrow concrete sill, there was hardly more than a foot of clear space.

"This is the way it was," I said.

"Miss Madden didn't close the window, did she?"

"Not that I saw. She looked out, screamed, and fainted. No, she didn't close it."

"Right. Now how in hell could anybody push or throw a man as big as Judd through that little space, even if he was lying sideways? And you said he came feet-first and standing up. I don't see how anybody could push him out in that position even with the window wide open. Look."

He opened the pane wide, so that it made a right angle with the vertical sash. The metal supports at the side creaked as if it was seldom opened that far. As the bottom of the pane swung outward, the top came down, moving in grooves in the sash on each side, so that even when the four-foot square of window was wide open there were only two feet of clear space between the horizontal pane and the sill. Above the pane there was another two-foot space, bounded at the top by the bottom sash of the upper pane.

The upper pane was closed and had been since I could remember. I tested it with a push but it was firmly rusted in place.

"They could have opened the window wide and flung him out and closed it after him."

"Who are *they?* You didn't see anybody close the window after. You didn't see or hear any struggle before. Don't forget Judd was conscious, and he wouldn't co-operate with anybody chucking him out a window."

He paused and went on: "I'm sorry, professor, I think he jumped, and I'll think so until I see the evidence pointing the other way. I think he opened the window wide and climbed up and stepped out on the outer sill—"

"He couldn't have been knocked unconscious and stretched out on the sill so that he'd fall off when he moved?"

"Maybe if he was Tarzan of the Apes," Haggerty said. "That sill isn't eight inches wide. Anway, that's not the way you saw him fall. He didn't roll off, did he?"

"No."

"Well," Haggerty said, "he climbed out on the sill and stood out of the way of the window and partly closed it. He reached in and turned on the light—see, it's got a pull chain and he could even hold the end of it outside the window."

"Why would he turn out the light in the first place?"

"So nobody would see him climb out the window. Same reason he turned out the light down below on the corner."

"So now you think Alec did that."

"I just thought of it," Haggerty said, as if his own cunning surprised him. "He didn't want anybody to see him jump. A lot of suicides try to make it look like an accident. He probably called you up to convince you that it was going to be an accident."

"He convinced me that it was murder," I said. "Not an accident, and not suicide." This ratty detective can ratiocinate till doomsday, I thought, and I'll stick by what I know about Alec Judd.

"Tell the coroner," Haggerty said. "You'll be the main witness at the inquest."

I was still standing at the window trying to figure out how Alec had been murdered, and I noticed a tiny strip of white cloth on the upper righthand corner of the sash. When I looked more closely, it turned out to be a small piece of adhesive tape, one end of which was stuck to the sash.

"What do you make of this?" I said to Haggerty.

He squinted up his little black eyes and looked at the piece of tape without touching it.

"Adhesive tape, eh?" he said. "Damned if I know what to make of it." Damned if either of us knew.

There was a quick double knock on the door and President Galloway came in wearing a tie and suitcoat. His face, newly shaved and gleaming rosily, looked ten years younger. I looked at him in surprise, and he saw my look.

"I've an electric razor down in my office," he said, "and some clothes. I heard you men talking in here and rather than interrupt I went down and shaved. The external man is the father of the internal, you know."

And an administrative job is the mother of vanity, I thought. What I said was:

"This is Detective-Sergeant Haggerty, sir."

Galloway turned to Haggerty. "Was anything found on the body?—anything of importance, I mean."

"Nothing but personal stuff, sir. Pens and pencils and opened letters, pipe and tobacco pouch, things like that."

"Was his wallet in his pocket?"

"Yes, sir. Nothing missing that I could tell. They took the stuff down to the station."

A young man in uniform, carrying a large black case, came in the open door and Haggerty suggested that he take my fingerprints. He decorated my fingers with indelible black ink and then went to work on the telephone.

"Shall we go down, Branch?" Galloway said. "I asked them to come to the seminar room on the fourth floor. Quite a sensational subject for a seminar discussion."

"Quite," I said, not relishing his academic quaintness. "Did you call Schneider?"

"Why not? He is here." He turned to Haggerty. "I've called together several university officials to discuss this case, sergeant. Will you hold yourself in readiness in case we want information from you?"

"Yes, sir, I'll be in the Ladies' Room for a while."

"I beg your pardon?"

"Miss Madden's in the Ladies' Room," Haggerty spluttered. "I want to ask her some questions."

"Oh, of course," Galloway said and went out the door. In the hall he said to me, "What is Miss Madden doing here?"

"She was in the building when Alec fell, and saw him on the pavement afterwards. She fainted. They were engaged to be married."

"Miss Madden and Alec? It must have been a dreadful shock to her."

We passed the Ladies' Room and I jerked my thumb at the closed door. "She's been lying down in there for an hour or more. The doctor said she took it like a soldier, but I thought it best not to disturb her."

"Quite right," said Galloway. "Shocks like that have driven women insane."

We went down the stairs to the fourth floor. The door of the seminar room was open and the lights were on. From the hall I could see Jackson, executive assistant to the president and head of the Economics

Department, sitting at one end of the table, his broad bald scalp glistening in the light.

I said to Galloway, "I'll be in, in a minute," and went down the hall to the drinking-fountain. My heart had begun to accelerate again and my throat was dry.

When I got back to the seminar room, Galloway was standing at the end of the table beside Jackson. He was talking about Alec's death. I could see Hunter sitting on the far side of the table, his black stare fixed on the president, but I couldn't see Herman Schneider.

I was about to enter when a soft bass voice purred at my shoulder, "Can you tell me where Professor Branch's office is, please? I was told at the president's house that he is there."

"I'm Branch," I said. "Galloway's in here."

"My name's Gordon, Chester Gordon. How-do-you-do?" The bass voice was diffident, and the long dark face from which it issued had an inward-looking, almost sullen look. Gordon had sleepy black eyes set deep in a burnished outdoor face. His face was like an Indian's who distrusted all palefaces.

"How-do-you-do," I said and looked him up and down, having never seen an F.B.I. man to my knowledge. He had a short-distance swimmer's broad shoulders and thin flanks; they were neatly clothed in a grey business suit.

"You're the secretary of the War Board, aren't you?" Gordon said.

"Right. Shall we go in?"

"Thank you."

Galloway turned to greet Gordon. "I'm glad you could come, Chet. I shan't waste time with introductions, gentlemen. Mr. Gordon is an agent of the Federal Government."

I took a vacant chair beside Hunter, and Gordon sat down beside me.

Hunter murmured, "This is a damnable thing about Alec, Bob."

"Yes."

I looked up and saw Dr. Schneider watching me across the table. His face was set so hard that his beard looked false and tacked on, and his brown eyes were like marbles. He had begun to realize the significance of the meeting, if he hadn't all along.

Galloway closed the door and returned to the head of the table. When he spoke, his voice was impersonal:

"Professor Branch has a story to tell and, I understand, an accusation to make."

All eyes but two turned to me. Chester Gordon sat with his chin down, looking into the intricacies of his own brain.

I stood up and spoke:

"I'll come to the point immediately. You know what happened to Alec. Yesterday afternoon he told me that he was worried about the War Board, that he suspected a leakage of information from us to the spies who were recently arrested in Detroit. President Galloway and Mr. Gordon can confirm that suspicion, or at least the fact of its existence."

Gordon nodded and Galloway said, "That's so." Schneider did not move in body or face.

I went on: "Alec told me that he had some reason to suspect a member of the War Board of espionage, and he told me just this evening that he intended to search the office of the suspected person for incriminating evidence.

"He did so, and called me about 11:30, half an hour before he was killed, to tell me that he had found incriminating evidence in the office of Dr. Herman Schneider."

There were only five other people in the room, but their excitement was almost an audible hum. In the midst of it Dr. Schneider got slowly to his feet. I noticed that Gordon's right hand rested near the left lapel of his suitcoat.

"Gentlemen," Schneider said with heavy dignity,

"this is an outrageous slander. I am aware that Dr. Branch was a close friend—"

I cut him short. "I haven't finished."

"You have the floor, Dr. Branch," Galloway said.

"In addition to espionage, I wish to accuse Dr. Schneider of attempted murder and of consummated murder. To-night his son Peter tried to kill me. When his son failed, Dr. Schneider himself attempted to do the job by crashing his car on Bingham Heights. I don't know what reason they had for trying to kill me, but I do know why they killed Alec Judd. I accuse Dr. Schneider of being either the murderer or the murderer's accomplice."

"May I speak, President Galloway?" Schneider said in a rising voice which he tried to control.

"You may speak."

"Gentlemen, this accusation—these accusations come as a tragic surprise to me. You know my reputation and my past, though I do not choose to rest on them alone. I am not guilty of any of the actions which this misguided young man has seen fit to attribute to me.

"My son fenced a little with Dr. Branch to-night, and appears to have frightened him. Later, when I was driving Dr. Branch home, my car got out of control and plunged over the cliff near my home. I can understand that Dr. Branch may have been unsettled by the experience—I was shaken myself and barely escaped with my life—but it is certainly irrational to accuse me of trying to kill us both.

"Above all, I know nothing of espionage or of the death of Professor Judd. His death has come as a deep personal blow to me. Perhaps it has affected Dr. Branch even more deeply. But you must not condemn me, untried, on the word of one young man, a young man whose judgment has perhaps been unsettled by a series of harrowing experiences."

Schneider sat down wearily in his chair.

"Have you any evidence, Branch?" Jackson said

curtly. He was leaning forward across the table, the lines in his face drawn deep by earnestness.

"I have what happened to me, what Alec told me, and what happened to Alec. And a word he told me to write down when he called me from the Dictionary office before midnight. 'Taillour,' Middle English for 'tailor.'"

"And Old French," Hunter said.

"Schneider means 'tailor' in German," I said, realizing how feeble it sounded.

"Did he explain it that way?" Hunter said.

"He was cut off before he could say anything more. I believe he may have been attacked then."

Hunter said, "I know how you feel about Alec and all that. But tell me: if Alec had given you the word 'chasseur'—'hunter'—would you be suspicious of me?"

"There's more to it than that. You're not a German, for one thing."

"You don't like Germans, I know," Hunter said. "But your logic seems pretty tenuous, and I can't follow it."

Schneider was looking less strained by the minute, and I felt that things were slipping out from under me.

"Did you make a copy of the War Board report which Alec gave you, Dr. Schneider?" I asked.

"Yes, I did," he said coolly.

"May I ask why."

"Though you have no legal right to question me, there is no reason why I should not answer. I made a copy for further study, a copy which I intended to destroy when I had mastered its contents. Surely, it is not criminal to take serious interest in one's duties."

"Judd specifically instructed you not to make a copy."

"Your tone is not wholly tolerable, Dr. Branch. I do not recall that any such instructions were given me. If they had been, my making a copy would have been, at worst, an indiscretion."

"Have you anything more to say, Dr. Branch?" Galloway said. His voice was like dry ice, and the faces in the room were becoming hostile to me. I felt a surging desire to jolt them out of their stupid preconception that a respected scholar could do no wrong.

"I should like to ask Dr. Schneider another question."

"Ask your question," Galloway said, looking at me without great interest.

"Dr. Schneider, can you account for the movements of your son and yourself at the time that Alec Judd was killed?"

He meshed his hands over his belly and began to twiddle his thumbs. After a pause he said, "Of course I can, Dr. Branch. May I ask if you can account for yours? You must have some reason for this unusual attack on me, and I should like to find out what it is."

"Where were you at midnight?"

"I was at home. My son Peter was with me."

"Have you any way of proving it? Was Miss Esch present?"

"No, she has taken quarters in a hotel. But a policeman was there. He had come, rather tardily, to inquire after the details of our accident." Red lights flickered in his brown eyes like small triumphal torches.

"What was the policeman's name?"

"Moran, I believe. He is a motorcycle policeman."

There was a buzz of voices in the room. The meeting was on the point of spontaneous disintegration, and once that happened things would be where they had been.

I turned to Galloway. "I should like to check on Dr. Schneider's story. May I step over to my office and phone the police?"

"I'm willing to accept Dr. Schneider's word," Galloway said. Jackson said, "And I."

They're liberals and sportsmen of the old school, I thought, the kind of liberals and sportsmen that the Nazis have hornswoggled in every nation in Europe:

113

I'd rather be a son of a bitch and have a chance in the rough-and-tumble.

I said, "I'm going to phone." Galloway raised his eyebrows and looked with interest at the bare wall.

I went out the door leaving a silence like a vacuum which tugged at my coattails, and went upstairs to my office. I dialed police headquarters and Cross's voice answered the phone.

"Branch speaking. Is there a motorcycle officer named Moran there? I'd like to speak to him."

"Just a minute," Cross said, and in a minute Moran came to the phone and said, "Yes?"

"Did you interview Dr. Herman Schneider tonight?"

"Yessir. I got there late because there was a bad hit-run case on the other side of town."

"What time did you get there?"

"About twenty to twelve. Just a minute. I'll look at my book. Yeah, twenty to twelve. I called him up about an hour before and told him I couldn't make it till then and he said he'd wait up for me."

"Was Dr. Schneider there at twenty to twelve?"

"Yessir."

"Was his son Peter there? A blonde young man."

"Not when I got there. He came in a few minutes later."

"Did he get there before twelve or after?"

"Before twelve. I left right after twelve—I heard the tower clock. He was there for a while before I left."

"Was anybody else there?"

"Nope. The old man said he'd give me a cup of coffee, only his housekeeper was in bed. So no coffee."

"Thanks very much, officer." Thanks for a feeling of frustration.

"Nodatall, professor. Good night."

"Good night." I slammed down the receiver and went out into the hall.

As I passed the Ladies' Room, the door opened and

114

Haggerty came out grinning like a laboratory rat who had mastered the maze.

"Hello, professor," he said. "Are they still down there?"

"Yes."

"Have you solved the mystery?"

"No."

"Maybe there is no mystery. They'd better hear what Miss Madden has to tell them."

He moved aside and Helen Madden came up to the lighted doorway. She was so pale her skin seemed translucent, but her mouth was set and her eyes were dry.

"How are you, Helen?"

"I'm all right, Bob. I'll feel worse to-morrow and the day after."

"Are you willing to tell Galloway and the others what you saw? Sergeant Haggerty seems to think it's important."

"What others?"

"Jackson and Hunter and an F.B.I. man. And Herman Schneider."

"Where are they?"

"In the seminar room on the fourth floor."

"Yes," she said. "I'll tell them what I saw."

We went down to the seminar room with Haggerty trailing behind. Her legs moved stiffly like a sleepwalker's, and I took her arm on the stairs Her muscles were tense under the sleeve.

When we entered the room, the men there looked at her as if she herself had been dead, and got to their feet. I said, "Sergeant Haggerty wants Miss Madden to tell you what she saw."

Galloway came and took her arm and led her to a chair.

Jackson said, "Sit down, Haggerty," and turned to me. "Did you speak to Moran?"

"Dr. Schneider's statement is correct," I said.

"Is that all you have to say?" Galloway asked.

"That's all I have to say." I sat down.

Galloway said, "Miss Madden, you are very kind to come here at all. Please confine yourself to the relevant circumstances of Professor Judd's death as you know them."

She said: "Alec committed suicide. I can't understand it but—he killed himself." She let out her breath with the last three words.

I looked at Schneider and Haggerty across the table from me. They were practically smiling.

"I know this must be painful to you, Miss Madden," Galloway said. "Indeed, I am deeply conscious of its painfulness, and of your fortitude. But can you tell us how you—that is, what your grounds of judgment are?"

"Yes," she said. "I'd better tell you the whole thing. After Alec and I finished work to-night, he said he had an appointment and went off to it. I went to a movie and got out about 11:30 or so. On the way home I saw Alec's car in front of McKinley Hall, so I—I climbed in to wait for him. I thought he probably wouldn't be long and that he could drive me home. Anyway, I wanted to see him. He had been worried recently about the War Board and I was concerned about him.

"I sat in the car smoking until nearly midnight and it began to get quite chilly. Finally, when he didn't come, I thought I'd go up to his office and get him—I thought he shouldn't go on working after midnight anyway. I let myself in the side door and took the elevator up."

"What time was this, Miss Madden?" Galloway said.

"Midnight. I heard the tower clock strike before I entered the building. Alec's office was dark when I got there but for some reason I stood and listened at the door. I had a feeling that he was there in the dark office. I knocked on the door and called his name but he didn't answer me, and I began to feel terribly frightened.

"I tried the door but the self-lock was on and it

wouldn't open. Then I put my ear against the glass part of the door and I could hear a sort of whispering noise. It sounded very faint and queer, like—something on a radio program."

"Did you recognize his voice?"

"No, not then. But he spoke once before—before he jumped. I heard him speak quite loudly and clearly. His voice sounded strange and troubled but I knew that it was Alec speaking."

"What did he say?"

"He said: *'I don't feel like it, but I will if I have to.'* Then I heard the window creak and his terrible cry as he fell. Just before he fell the light went on. I was quite frantic and I tried to break down the door. Then I took off my shoe and broke the pane with the heel and let myself in. There was nobody in the room."

Her breathing was quick again and her forehead was wet. She put her hand to her forehead and then took a handkerchief out of her sleeve and wiped it.

"Thank you profoundly, Miss Madden," Galloway said. "Certainly there is only one inference to be drawn. Did it sound as if he was talking to himself when he said—what he said?"

"Yes. It sounded rather horrible and queer, not like Alec at all, though I know it was his voice—as if he was temporarily unhinged. He sounded—sick. Why did he kill himself?" she cried on a keen rising note. "If he was sick, I wanted to take care of him."

"Of course you did, my dear," Galloway said. "As you say, the poor man must have been temporarily unbalanced."

"*He was not,*" I said "I'd back his brain against the brains of all of you put together."

"Dr. Jackson," Galloway said as if I had not spoken, "would you be good enough to take Miss Madden home?"

Jackson said, "Certainly," and they got up and left the room.

Haggerty said, "I guess that settles the case, doesn't it?"

"Indubitably," Galloway replied, and the meeting broke up. Schneider was the first to leave and Gordon left soon afterwards. Galloway was careful not to look in my direction until he left, too, with Haggerty at his heels.

Hunter came up to me and put a hand on my shoulder. "Better drop it, Bob, at least for to-night. Go home and get some sleep, man."

I said, "Go to hell," and left him standing by himself in the room.

I went up to my office and locked the door behind me and sat down at my desk to wear out the telephone some more.

chapter vii

I PICKED up the telephone directory but I thought of a man whose name wasn't in the book because he had been dead for a long time. Heraclitus was the man. He said that everything in the world flows and changes constantly like a river, so that you can't fasten yourself permanently to anything. He was wrong.

You can fasten yourself to a man. The integrity of a man is the rock in the changing river. Suicide is a betrayal of friends, and Alec Judd was not capable of any kind of disloyalty. Therefore he had been killed. Because I was very angry, the thing seemed crystal clear to me: I could not believe that Alec killed himself without betraying him. Everybody else was wrong.

The Schneiders had an alibi for the time of Alec's death, but if they didn't kill him somebody else did. Perhaps Ruth Esch killed him. I was beginning to suspect her. A man will trust another man further than he'll trust a woman,—women are a different kind of animal. I wanted to find out if she had an alibi, too.

Schneider said she had moved into a hotel, and Moran had not seen her with the Schneiders. There were two good hotels in town, the Rogers House and the Palace.

I called the Rogers and was told that no Ruth Esch was registered there. I called the Palace and she was there.

"I'd like to speak to her," I told the operator. "Will you ring her room?"

"Certainly, sir." She rang several times and there was no answer.

"There is no answer, sir," the operator said melodiously as if she was singing a song. "May I take a message?"

"No, thanks. Can you tell me what time she registered at the hotel?"

"I'm sorry, sir, I cannot give you that information." Same old song, the telephone operators' *Internationale.*

"May I speak to the manager?"

"He is not here, sir," she lilted "But we do not give information about guests."

Before hanging up I said, "Thanks for the musical selections," because frustration was beginning to get me down. She switched off.

I felt a drawing tension in the roof of my mouth and a pressure on the nerves behind my eyes. I remembered it from childhood, the feeling of wanting to cry. I sat stupidly with the dead receiver to my ear, wondering if adult infantilism was getting hold of me and looking at the reproduction of the Laughing Cavalier on the wall above my desk. The Cavalier laughed and laughed, as roguishly as hell. But it wasn't the sound of laughter I heard.

From the dead receiver, as if from a long way off, came the sound of faint, indistinguishable voices. It was the sound I had heard when I listened at the dangling receiver in Alec's office after he fell. I pushed down the bar and got the dial tone and called the number of a taxi company. When they answered I said, "Sorry, wrong number," and they hung up.

Then I listened and heard the voices again. It must be switchboard leakage, I thought, the sound of the calls and the operator's voice at the university switchboard. I called another taxi company and got the same result. Apparently, you heard it whenever you put in a call on the university telephone system and the other party hung up.

Introducing the first and only complete hardcover collection of Agatha Christie's mysteries

Now you can enjoy the
greatest mysteries ever written
in a magnificent
Home Library Edition.

Discover Agatha Christie's world of mystery, adventure and intrigue

Agatha Christie's timeless tales of mystery and suspense offer something for every reader—mystery fan or not—young and old alike. And now, you can build a complete hardcover library of her world-famous mysteries by subscribing to <u>The Agatha Christie Mystery Collection.</u>

This exciting Collection is your passport to a world where mystery reigns supreme. Volume after volume, you and your family will enjoy mystery reading at its very best.

You'll meet Agatha Christie's world-famous detectives like Hercule Poirot, Jane Marple, and the likeable Tommy and Tuppence Beresford.

In your readings, you'll visit Egypt, Paris, England and other exciting destinations where murder is always on the itinerary. And wherever you travel, you'll become deeply involved in some of the most ingenious and diabolical plots ever invented ... "cliff-hangers" that only Dame Agatha could create!

It all adds up to mystery reading that's so good ... it's almost criminal. And it's yours every month with <u>The Agatha Christie Mystery Collection.</u>

Solve the greatest mysteries of all time. The Collection contains all of Agatha Christie's classic works including *Murder on the Orient Express, Death on the Nile, And Then There Were None, The ABC Murders* and her ever-popular whodunit, *The Murder of Roger Ackroyd.*

Each handsome hardcover volume is Smythe sewn and printed on high quality acid-free paper so it can withstand even the most murderous treatment. Bound in Sussex-blue simulated leather with gold titling, <u>The Agatha Christie Mystery Collection</u> will make a tasteful addition to your living room, or den.

Ride the Orient Express for 10 days without obligation.
To introduce you to the Collection, we're inviting you to examine the classic mystery, *Murder on the Orient Express*, without risk or obligation. If you're not completely satisfied, just return it within 10 days and owe nothing.

However, if you're like the millions of other readers who love Agatha Christie's thrilling tales of mystery and suspense, keep *Murder on the Orient Express* and pay just $9.95 plus postage and handling.

You will then automatically receive future volumes once a month as they are published on a fully returnable, 10-day free-examination basis. No minimum purchase is required, and you may cancel your subscription at any time.

This unique collection is not sold in stores. It's available only through this special offer. So don't miss out, begin your subscription now. Just mail this card today.

BUSINESS REPLY CARD

FIRST CLASS   PERMIT NO. 2154   HICKSVILLE, N.Y.

Postage will be paid by addressee:

The Agatha Christie
Mystery Collection
Bantam Books
P.O. Box 956
Hicksville, N.Y. 11802

So Alec had been telephoning and the other party had hung up and left the line open at Alec's end. But who was the other party?

As I pushed the telephone to the back of the desk, I noticed the ink-stains on my fingers. Fingerprint ink. Perhaps the fingerprint man was still in the building.

I went down the hall to Alec's office and looked in through the broken pane in the door. The fingerprint man was packing away his equipment in the black wooden case. I opened the door and he looked up.

"Did you find any fingerprints?" I asked

"Nary a one, if I know what you mean. Plenty of the deceased—I took his prints at the morgue. Some of yours. A lot of old ones, but you can't do anything with them."

"Any on the telephone?"

"Not a one. Somebody must have wiped it clean, probably the deceased."

"Probably." I was tired of arguing. He shut up his case and reached for the lamp and I stepped into the hall. The light clicked out and he came out the door.

"Sticky," he said.

"What's sticky?"

"The pull-chain on the lamp. Some sort of crap on it."

I heard quick steps on the west stairs and turned to see Haggerty come round the turning and trot up the last flight.

"Hello, professor. Are you finished, Sylvie?" he said. "Two bits you didn't find anything."

"That's right," Sylvie replied. "If that guy was murdered, he was murdered by a ghost and the ghost wore gloves."

"He wasn't murdered, Sylvie," Haggerty said. "Was he, professor? The girl heard him jump, she was right there, and there wasn't anybody else there. Why the hell he didn't leave a suicide note and save us all this trouble—"

"Is the main thing in a murder case to save trouble?" I said.

"For Christ's sake, are you still harping on that?" Haggerty spoke with real surprise which he exaggerated. "Better cut it, professor. Your boss doesn't like it."

"My boss?"

"I was talking to old man Galloway. He's got a peeve on you for raising a rumpus about nothing."

"Do I go home now, Sarge," Sylvie asked.

"Why not? Go ahead home. I'll stay here all night and argue with the professor about whether there's a fourth dimension. A very inaresting subject."

"Good night," Sylvie said and started down the stairs lugging his case. Haggerty stood showing his yellow teeth in a patronizing leer.

I wanted to tell him that he was acting pretty cocky for a dumb cop that didn't know one of his most important body openings from an excavation in the earth. But I also wanted his co-operation and I let him leer.

"Look, Sergeant," I said, "I'm not trying to set myself up as a detective and I'm ready to admit that you have all the apparent facts on your side. But I'm not satisfied that this was suicide, and I knew the dead man better than anyone else. If it looks like suicide, it means that Alec Judd was murdered by some very clever people."

"You're wrong." There was a whining note in his voice that made him sound tired. "My God, professor, I said I'd leave Shakespeare to you."

"If I'm wrong I'm a nuisance and damn fool," I said. "But I think I'm right. Will you help me get some information?"

"What information?"

"Information on the movements of a woman who could have killed Alec Judd."

"What makes you think so?"

"It's a long story. But all I want to know is whether she had an alibi for the time of his death."

122

"Where would her alibi be?"

"She's registered at the Palace Hotel. It should be easy to find out if she was there at midnight."

"What's her name?"

"Ruth Esch. E-S-C-H." I shifted my feet and the coins in my trousers pocket rattled. They clinked like thirty pieces of silver.

"Description?"

"Tall, red hair, green eyes, good features, thirtyish. Slight German accent—"

"You're not one of these Germanophiles, are you?" Haggerty said, squinting up at me.

"Do you mean Germanophobe, German-hater? No, I'm not."

"Galloway said something." He looked at me out of the corner of his eye as if he was playing with the notion of an idea. "Who is this dame?"

"A German refugee who just came to this country. She used to be—a friend of mine."

"Lovely circle of friends." Suddenly he spoke in a loud voice with a rasp in it, like a man who has decided that there is no risk in getting tough and is overdoing it:

"Why should I check up on your floozies for you, professor? I'm no private dick. And you better drag your face out of other people's business or you might get into bad trouble."

I said: "So you're nasty as well as stupid. I didn't know you were as complex as all that."

I left him standing in the hall and went down the west stairs to the basement and out the back door. I started home to get my car with anger tingling in my legs.

Crossing the dark campus, I saw one lighted face of the tower clock through the trees. 2:25. I felt late and old. The anger ran out of me like hot water and left my blood cold and sluggish. I thought of Ruth and my stomach felt bruised by disappointed hope. If Ruth had

123

turned her coat, I could trust nobody alive. But I had to find out about her.

There was a movement in the shadow of a tree, and I saw green eyes burning at me like metallic fire. My breath stopped in my throat and I peered into the darkness for the green-eyed woman.

I found my voice and said, "Who's that?"

A cat stalked out from under the tree and fawned against my leg. I stepped over it and walked on, restraining an impulse to kick it to death.

The back of my neck was still crawling when I got my sedan out of the apartment garage. The streets were deserted and I stepped hard on the accelerator as I circled the campus, because it helped to give me back a feeling of control over things. In less than five minutes I was parked around the corner from the Palace Hotel.

I got out and went around the corner and into the hotel. The lobby was dim and the brown leather armchairs sat in the corners like broad-shouldered, headless old men. But there was a bright light over the main desk and a young man with carefully parted fair hair sat behind it like a saint in a lighted embrasure of a dummy in a show-window. A bellhop leaning against the wall by the elevator doors stirred like a reptile at a touch of the sun when I came in the door. He saw that I had no suitcase and went to sleep again against the wall.

When I walked up to the desk, the night-clerk got up and spread his hands wide on the top of it as if it was going to be his personal gift to me.

"What can we do for you, sir?" he fluted.

"Miss Ruth Esch is staying here, I believe. I'd like to speak to her "

"It's very late. Perhaps I could take a message?"

"This is important. Will you ring her room, please."

He turned and looked at the key board and turned back to me. "I'm sorry, sir, she seems to have gone

124

out. Now, let me see, I think she went out not long ago. Yes, not very long ago."

"Did she check out?"

"No, sir. She simply went out, perhaps for a walk. She seems quite a restless young lady."

"I'll wait," I said.

"Very well, sir. But she left no word as to when she'd be back."

"Thanks."

I sat down in an armchair by a pillar where I could watch the door, and lit a cigarette. I usually smoke about two cigarettes an hour, but this was the first cigarette I had remembered to smoke since midnight. It tasted dirty and I pushed it into a jar of sand beside my chair.

There was a clang of metal behind me and I looked towards the elevator. A pair of brass doors parted in the middle and a man with a shabby purplish-brown suit, a red tie and a pink face stepped out of the lighted elevator, as if from a picture painted by a color-blind painter.

He saw me and sauntered across the carpet towards me and sat down in the chair at my elbow.

"Good evening," I said.

"Good evening," he said. "I guess it's good morning. What a life." He yawned and tapped his wide mouth with elephantine delicacy and stubby fingers. He took off his limp brown fedora and mopped his bald head with a purple silk handkerchief. He put it back in his pocket and arranged it carefully with one corner showing.

"Waiting for somebody?" he asked.

"Yes."

"It's pretty late."

"I was at a party."

"Wish I was. I spend my life breaking up parties and there's nothing I like better than a good rousing party with clean women and lively liquor. It goes against my grain always busting up parties. What a life."

"Life is very long," I said. "Are you the hotel detective?"

"That's right. At your service and at the mercy of my feet. I can't take credit for that one. That was on the wall in the office when I was a private dick in Detroit. Boy, them were the days. All the women I wanted and plenty of cash money on the side. Clean women, too. I could tear off a piece with the best of them before my heart went funny. It's as funny as hell, y'know, sometimes it goes one-two-three-stop, one-two-three-stop." He tapped on the arm of his chair to illustrate. I could see the veins on the back of his hand standing out like blue branches under the skin.

I waded into his stream of consciousness and said, "Maybe you can help me. As a matter of fact, the party's still going on and I came over here to win a bet."

"What kind of a bet?" He leaned towards me across the arms of the chairs and I could smell aniseed on his breath.

"It's a crazy kind of bet," I said, "but I stand to win twenty bucks if I can do what I'm supposed to. The idea is to trace the movements of one of the girls that was at the party. She was to come down here and register and then keep track of her own movements, the time of any telephone calls and so on, and then go back and hand in her report to the guy that's running the game. I have to trace her movements and keep my own record and if it's reasonably accurate I get a prize."

"Twenty bucks, eh?" He took out a patent nail-clipper and clipped the thick cracked nail of his left thumb. Then he started on the fingers.

I took a ten-dollar bill out of my wallet and reached over and tucked it in behind the purple handkerchief. "Do you think you can help me?"

"I might. When did she register?"

"You can easily find out. It couldn't have been much before eleven."

126

"What's her name?"

"Ruth Esch. She's got red hair and—"

"Oh, the red-headed girl?" He looked at me quizzically out of protruding blue eyes.

"You saw her?"

"Yeah. Sure. You want to wait here?"

"Yes. When she came and when she left. Phone calls. Visitors. Those are the main things."

"Especially visitors, eh?" he said, and shuffled off. I wondered what he meant.

He talked to the night-clerk first and then disappeared through a door behind the desk. I waited fifteen or twenty minutes. When he got back, I had chewed most of the skin from the inside of my upper lip.

He switched on the floor-lamp behind our chairs and sat down beside me with a small slip of paper covered with pencilings in his hand.

"Did you get it?" I said.

"Sure. Why not? Take this down if you want to."

I took a pen and envelope out of my pocket and got ready to write on my knee.

"O.K.," he said. "She registered at the hotel about eleven or a little after. Call it three minutes after. Around eleven twenty-five she got a phone call and a couple of minutes later she went out. Call it eleven-thirty. On the way out she told the desk-clerk she was just going out for a bite to eat and she asked him for the name of a good place to go. He told her the Porpoise down the street.

"She came back in about twenty minutes or so, but you can pin that down closer. She told the clerk when she went out at eleven-thirty that she was expecting a phone call around a quarter to twelve, and to hold it for her if she wasn't back by then. It came all right at a quarter to twelve and the operator held it for her about five-six minutes and she came back and took it in her room."

"What time did she get back here?"

"Ten to twelve, close as I can figure."

"Does the operator know who the call was from?"

"I asked her, just to be complete. She didn't know whether it was a man or a woman. Maybe a morphidite, eh?" He looked at me and winked and I smiled as cheerfully as I could.

"The word is hermaphrodite. The god Hermes and the goddess Aphrodite in one body blent."

"Nice set-up, eh? You from the university?"

"That's right. When did she go out again?"

"About three-quarters of an hour ago. Two-fifteen or two-twenty. Does that cover it?"

"Very nicely. You're sure that this is straight?"

"As straight as I can bring it to you. I talked to the clerk and the operator and the bellhop."

"Nice work." I leaned forward to get up but he pushed his face towards me and said in an earnest whisper:

"Listen, friend, is this girl your wife?"

"No. Just a friend."

"A girl-friend like? I mean you take her out quite a bit?"

"More or less," I said. "Why?"

"Because I won't take your money without telling you, boy. Mind you I'm not saying there's no bet, I'm just saying you take it from me that that dame's poison with a red label and you keep clear of her. She's got the skull and crossbones on her."

"What do you mean?"

"She's a dike, friend. I've seen a million of them and I know. She likes women better than men. Now go back to your party if there is any party and thanks for the easy money, friend."

I said, "Good night," in a weak voice and walked out of the hotel. The stars fell down and rattled at the bottom of the sky and the night put on shabby brown clothes.

chapter viii

I WALKED down the main street towards the Porpoise, which was a block from the hotel. Ruth Esch had an alibi all right, but I had to make sure that it was perfect before I could put her in the locked cupboard at the back of my mind and forget her for good. The blue porpoise sign over the entrance was lit, but the restaurant was closed for the night. I walked back to my car, feeling almost glad that I couldn't lay myself open to another jolt. A dream that you've slept with for six years has remarkable staying power.

The only live things on the main street were the neon signs, shining like cold fire on the three o'clock pavements. But there was a White Tower lit up across from where my car was parked, and I crossed the street and went in. My solar plexus was still numb where the word *dike* had hit me, and I ordered coffee.

The attendant filled my cup and made change without waking, moving as if his starched coat was holding him up.

I sat at the shining enameled counter, slowly burning my throat with coffee and thinking with a chilly three o'clock brain. Ruth was clear, of murder at any rate. But the Schneiders' alibi was at least as good. Maybe I was all wrong and maybe Alec had been all wrong. Maybe Haggerty and Galloway and Helen were right about suicide. Maybe I should go home and go to bed.

No. Moran the motorcycle officer could have been

bribed to protect the Schneiders. I could go and see him in the morning. I decided to hold on to the rock.

As for Ruth, why should I take to heart what a seedy hotel dick said? He wasn't my psychoanalyst. On the other hand, how could I know that his information on her movements was reliable? He could have made it up to earn ten dollars. Or he could have been bribed. He was bribable. I didn't know what to think.

I took Ruth's letter out of my inside pocket, but I hadn't the heart to read it again. I sat and looked at the envelope and saw the word 'taillour.' What had Alec meant by it? Was it an accident that 'taillour' meant 'tailor,' which meant 'Schneider'? He was a philologist, and it wasn't very likely that it was an accident. Some of his puns used to run into more than two languages.

I sat and stared at the counter and the words went round in my head until I was a little crazy. Three mad tailors ran round in my head, one talking Old French, one talking Middle English, one talking German. The Middle English tailor, who had a black beard like Schneider's, stood still and said into a dangling telephone receiver, "Middle English Dictionary office." I saw the black blood on his face.

I started. I must have dozed with my eyes open, half-hypnotized by the gleaming white counter. The three tailors were gone: my subconscious was finished with them: I had got the idea. I crossed the street to my car and drove back towards McKinley Hall. My home away from home.

I parked my car in front of the Law School. Alec had parked conspicuously in front of McKinley Hall and he had been caught in the building—I still believed that somebody had killed him, I didn't know how. If the same people were looking for me, I wouldn't advertise my arrival.

But I didn't cut directly across the campus. My unconscious was stirring like a volcano that wasn't really extinct after all, throwing up fragments of old childish fears. Fear of the dark. Fear of cats. I suppressed them as well as I could but I didn't cross the campus.

The campus was bounded on four sides by lighted streets, and I went down the street on the west side towards McKinley. The fall night was turning colder and a few fallen leaves rustled frostily under my feet. I turned up the collar of my suitcoat.

There was a taxi stand by McKinley Hall on the southwest corner of the campus, and two taxis were parked at the curb. I could see their drivers sitting in the front seat of the first one talking the time away. I knew the one behind the wheel, a dark little man called Shiny who had often driven me. As I passed his taxi he hailed me:

"Hi, professor. You're up late."

"So are you. Good night," I said, and started to walk on. He scrambled out of his seat and trotted across the boulevard towards me on short, bowed legs.

"Say, professor, what was going on in McKinley tonight?" Curiosity made his small eyes bright and seemed to enhance the curve of his central European nose. Curiosity and puzzlement were his only two emotions, and his forehead was permanently wrinkled by them.

"I don't think I can tell you, Shiny," I said like a telephone operator. "You'll read it in the papers."

"Was it a murder? Some of the boys said murder."

"I don't know."

The other driver shouted from the cab: "Hey, Shiny, it's your turn to take that call."

"I be seeing you, professor." Shiny trotted away.

I said good night again and started for the front entrance of McKinley Hall. I stopped when I saw a tall uniformed figure pacing back and forth on the steps below the pillars. He passed under a light and I saw the yellow face with the broken nose. What was his name? Sale. He must have been ordered to guard the building all night.

I went back along the street to the taxi stand. Shiny had gone on his call and the other man was already asleep in his own cab. I turned up the walk at the end of the Hall and walked quickly around to the back. The light on the corner of the building was on again and I could see dark stains on the pavement where Alec had fallen.

I unlocked one of the double glass doors that let into the basement and went in. All the lights were out. It would be better to leave them out and not bring Sale in asking questions.

With my hand moving along the wall to guide me, I went down the basement corridor to the elevator, the least obtrusive way to get to the fourth floor. I unlocked the elevator door and pushed the button. It clanked once and started down towards the basement. While I was waiting, I noticed that there was a light under a door on the other side of the corridor.

I knew the door. It opened onto a concrete stair leading down into the steam-tunnels which branched all over the campus like arteries in a body, carrying steam from the university powerhouse to heat the buildings. One of the janitors must have left the light on. I crossed the hall and unlocked the door to turn out the light, but I couldn't find the switch. I left the door open so a janitor would see it in the morning.

The elevator was waiting and I got in and went up to the fourth floor. All the lights were out but the door of the Dictionary office was still open. I had the air-raid warden's flashlight, and I switched it on and entered the office, closing the door behind me.

The making of a historical dictionary is a long process. For five years Alec had been co-editor of the *Middle English Dictionary*, with a dozen people working under him. One thing his death meant was that the Dictionary would have to find a new editor. I had never had anything to do with the Dictionary directly, but Alec had given me a general idea of it.

It was intended to put in print for the first time, in ten handy volumes weighing about fifteen pounds each, all the meanings of all the words written in English between the death of William the Conqueror and the time of Caxton, the first English printer. This meant that the editors and sub-editors and infra-editors had to read all the books and manuscripts remaining from four hundred years of English writing. They had to keep a file of every word read and examples of every use of every word. That is the first half of the process of making a historical dictionary.

The second half is the actual writing of the dictionary, listing every meaning of every word and at least one example of each meaning.

Since the reading in the Midwestern Dictionary office had been going on for a mere seven years, and not more than a dozen people spent only six or seven hours a day reading, the first half of the process was not yet complete. But there was already a roomful of tall steel filing cabinets filled with examples of the uses of Middle English words filed in alphabetical order.

I went into this inner room to look up 'taillour.' My throat was constricted with excitement. For the first and last time in my life, I knew how philologists must feel when they're on the track of an old word used in a new way.

If the word meant anything, it could mean that Alec had hidden his evidence against Schneider in the Dictionary office, filed under 'taillour.' A philologist like Alec would think of something like that.

But Schneider was a philologist, too. I remembered with a tremor of misgiving that I had given the word away in front of him. Perhaps he had already been here.

I flashed my torch on the black cabinets standing along the walls like coffins on end. None of their doors was open. I swung the light along the letters of the alphabet which were painted on the cabinets in white. A had two cabinets because so many words began with A. B had one. I found the white T on the door of a cabinet and opened it. The cardboard boxes on the shelves looked undisturbed.

I pulled out the first box on the top shelf and put it on the table and removed the lid. Turning the light on the stacked cards filed upright in the box, I found the tab marked 'Taillour.' I put the torch on the table shining towards me but it rolled and I fixed it in place with a heavy horseshoe paperweight. Then I pulled out the cards behind the tab. The thing I was looking for dropped out from among them and rolled on the table.

It was a tiny oilskin envelope rolled into a cylinder no bigger than a .22 shell and tied with tape. I tore off the tape and unrolled and opened the envelope. It contained a closely folded sheet of very thin paper. I unfolded the paper and saw at a glance what it was: I had seen it the week before: the schedule of the new A S T Program.

Schneider could explain the copy as an indiscretion, I thought, but he'll have a hard time explaining the trimmings. Maybe I've got him.

I heard a faint sound of friction against the composition floor of the outer office and reached for my light to douse it. Before my hand touched it, the lights flashed on over my head and I straightened up blinking. Dr Schneider dropped his left hand from the light switch beside the door, stepped forward a pace, and closed the heavy door behind him without turning.

His right hand stayed where it was at chest level, holding a Lüger pointed at me like a long thin finger with an empty, questioning tip.

I tried to palm the yellow envelope and the paper but he said, "Put it down, Dr. Branch. Evidently you have found what I was looking for. I was about to examine the T file when the noise of the elevator disturbed me."

"Yes," I said, putting it down, "you mingle philology with homicide and espionage, don't you?" I hoped the light would bring Sale upstairs if I could stall the Lüger long enough. I looked at the windows. All the blinds were drawn. I could have used the ceiling lights myself.

"I am not a spy, Dr Branch. Nor am I a homicide."

"Nor is this anything but a game of cops and robbers."

"This is not a game, sir. I refuse to allow my enemies to persecute me. You are forcing me to inflict death upon you in order to protect my personal honor."

It sounded like the kind of nonsense a man talks when final disillusion has deprived words of all meaning for him, but his gun was as steady as part of the building. Yet he sounded faintly regretful, like a mosquito-lover who has to kill a mosquito.

To prolong the conversation I said, "Your personal honor seems to be extraordinarily flexible. Have you thought of offering it to the government as a substitute for rubber?"

"I have heard more dignified last words, Dr Branch. I fear that your nature is essentially trivial. Your imagination seems unable to embrace the fact that I am on the point of shooting you." His face and eyes and voice were very weary, as if he had lived past the love of life and the fear of death.

I hadn't. He was standing nearly ten feet away from me, but I felt the cold iron of his gun in the pit of my stomach.

Tell him to give it to W.P.B., one part of my brain piped in hysterical glee, and another part said calmly, You've got twenty-five years on him. If you don't move now, you'll never move again.

"You can't mean it, sir," I babbled. "Don't kill me, sir, don't kill me. I'm sick." I rolled up my eyes and gasped, "I feel faint."

I fell to the floor and he took three steps towards

135

me and I rolled under the table onto my hands and knees. He shot and splintered a leg of the table in front of my face. I dived for his legs with chips in my eyes and he shot again and the bullet tugged at the padding in the left shoulder of my coat.

I got his legs and he went over backwards. The gun flew out of his hand and his head smacked very pleasingly against the doorjamb. I picked up the gun and stood over him. He didn't stir.

I examined the Lüger and saw that it was empty except for the two used shells, and looked around for another weapon. There was the gilded horseshoe paper-weight on the table. I picked it up and hefted it. It would do. I put the gun on the table and, with the horseshoe in my right hand in case he was shamming, kneeled down to examine him.

He was breathing stertorously and the whites of his eyes showed. I touched one eyeball with my finger. He wasn't shamming and I put the horseshoe down.

I left Schneider as he was and went down the central stairs to get the policeman with the broken nose. I met him on the first floor coming in. Sale had a gun in one hand and a flashlight in the other. He pointed both at me.

"Hands up," he said. His face gleamed yellowly, like wax, above the flashlight beam. I put up my hands.

Then he recognized me. "So it's you, professor! I thought I heard a noise like a shot. What's up?"

"The murderer," I said. "On the fourth floor. I laid him out." I lowered my arms.

"No kiddin', professor! Show me."

He followed me up the flight of stairs to the fourth floor and down the corridor to the Dictionary office. At the end of the hall I thought I saw green eyes glaring at me from the darkness at the top of the west stairs. I pointed Sale into the office and went to the end of the hall to turn on the corridor lights. Nothing on the stairs, not even a cat.

I turned out the lights and went back to the lighted

office. Sale met me at the door with his gun in his hand and his broken nose poised like a hammer.

"This guy is dead, professor," he said. "I got to put you under arrest."

"Dead? Are you sure? He was just unconscious when I looked at him a minute ago."

"He's dead, professor. His brains are leaking out."

"Let me see him, will you?"

"If you like it. But put up your hands."

He circled me in the hall and walked behind me when I went into the office. I saw the top of Schneider's head in the doorway. It had a deep hole in it, bleeding red and white onto the floor.

"My God, I didn't see that," I said.

"You see it now. He's dead. Murdered." He was still behind me and I couldn't see his face but he smacked his lips over the last word.

"Murder, hell," I said. "It was self-defense. He shot at me."

"You'll have a chance to prove self-defense," Sale said. "Now I got to take you to the station."

"Just a minute. I've got proof here that this man was a spy."

"Go and get it and give it to me," Sale said. I looked at him over my shoulder. He was standing three feet away with his gun levelled at my kidneys. My kidneys are important to me.

I stepped over Schneider's head and shoulders into the inner room. The oilskin envelope and paper and the Lüger were gone from the table, but something else was there that made me feel sick. The gilded horseshoe was lying on the table. One end of it was splattered with red blood flecked with white. And the rest of it was covered with my fingerprints.

I thought of the green eyes in the stair-well at the end of the hall. I hadn't been quick enough. Ruth Esch was very quick indeed. Perhaps she was as quick as Peter Schneider. My stomach heaved and I was sick on the floor.

137

Sale stood and watched me silently with his gun on me. When I had finished he said:

"Where's your evidence, professor?"

"It's gone."

"Is that what you used to kill him?" He pointed at the horseshoe.

"Somebody used it to kill him," I said. "I didn't kill him."

"That's right," Sale said. "You just laid him out and he died naturally."

"Better take it with you," I said, and picked it up.

"Put that down, you bastard," Sale yelled. "Fingerprints!" He started towards me. I was facing him with the horseshoe in my right hand, my back against the table. I leaned to the left as if to replace the horseshoe on the table on my left side.

When it was nearly touching the table, I threw the horseshoe backhand at Sale's gun. The two pieces of metal clanged and the horseshoe ringed his wrist. The gun went off and dropped to the floor and I dropped after it.

Sale got me in the side with the toe of his boot but I got the gun. He put up his hands as I stood up with it.

"Nice work, professor. Just an old horseshoe pitcher, eh? But you're crazy, professor. You can't get away."

I wasted three words, "I've been framed."

"Sure, sure. We'll get you, professor."

The conversation bored me and I picked up the flash and locked him in the inner room, which had a heavy oaken door. I had to move Schneider to do it.

Before I reached the head of the stairs, I heard a police whistle.

I was a fool. He could whistle out of the window. But what could I have done to him? Tie and gag him? Sure, and suffer for it later. But I had his gun.

I ran down the steps to the basement as fast as I could in the dark. If Shiny was at the corner, I might get away in his cab before the police arrived. I didn't know where to.

I ran out the door at the back and around the corner of the building. No cabs in sight. Far down the street, I saw two policemen running towards McKinley Hall.

I thought of the open door leading into the steam-tunnels and ran back into the building. When I got to the door it was closed and the light behind it was out. Could there be a janitor here this early? Maybe Sale closed it and turned out the light.

The door wasn't locked and I opened it. Nothing but darkness. I still had the flashlight and turned it on and flashed it down the steps. The concrete basement room at the foot of the stairs was bare and the door in the grey wall which led into the tunnel was closed.

I heard a sound of running feet behind and above me on the first floor of the building and put out my light. The bulb which lit the stairs from the first floor into the basement corridor was switched on. I stepped inside the door and closed it except for a crack through which I could watch the lighted stairs. A bareheaded man with a gun in his hand came down the stairs two at a time.

I recognized the wide grey shoulders and the sullen Indian face. He paused at the foot of the stairs and looked up and down the basement corridor, his gun following his glance. Then he turned and ran out the back of the building.

Christ, was Gordon after me already? I thought of following him and throwing myself on his mercy—he was probably more intelligent than the local police—but I dropped the idea as soon as I picked it up. I was in a box that it would be hard to argue myself out of. The only way to get out was by running.

There was a pounding on the double doors at the west end of the corridor, and then the crash of glass. The police. I closed the door quietly and went down the concrete stairs into the steam-tunnel.

chapter ix

THE basement was hot—perhaps the steam was on: it was just past the equinox and the weather was turning cold. As soon as I opened the second door, I knew the steam was on. It was like opening the door of a moderate hell. The air rushed out to take me like black flames. I closed the second door behind me and switched on the flashlight.

The two huge steampipes, green-painted, hung before me like twin segments of impossible serpents glowing with impossible energy. To my right and left they were lost in darkness in the endless man-made cave. I chose the left at random and started down the tunnel, the flashlight beam dancing before me like a wild hope. Then I remembered the closed door I had left open and the dark light I had left on.

Somebody might be waiting for me at the first turning. I put out the light and, with the unlit flashlight in my left hand and the gun in my right, went on in darkness. The concrete roof nearly brushed my hair as I walked and I left the whole building above me like a weight on my neck. The sweat ran down in my eyes from the heat and I couldn't stop to take off my coat.

I went faster as my senses grew used to the darkness. At least I heard no one following. I half-turned my head to listen and walked into a wall. The clang of my flashlight against the concrete sounded like a gong.

I switched it on—it wasn't broken—and saw that the tunnel jogged to the left. Something on the tunnel floor caught my eye, a shining object. I picked it up and looked at it. It was a small metal cylinder, a lipstick. Women go everywhere nowadays, I thought. I put the lipstick in my pocket in case I should meet a woman, and held my gun cocked for the same reason as I went on.

I turned out the flash and went on in the hot darkness of the forest-floor of the twentieth-century jungle. The forest that bears no fruit, the rivers of steam and brooks of sewage that quench no thirst. I remembered something Alec had said about the carnivores creeping on rubber tires in the urban valleys. The blessings of civilization, I thought.

Not that I couldn't have done with a small armored motorcycle. Or even my car would do. If I could get to my car, I could get away into the country. But my car was parked on the campus and I didn't dare try to reach it.

I barely raised my feet and my leather soles hissed along the concrete. I walked with my hands held out to protect my face, like a blind man in an unfamiliar room. I felt as if I had walked a mile; the hot air was palpable and seemed to resist movement like water.

I switched on the flash for a moment and saw a dark open arch in the left wall about fifty feet ahead of me. I walked to it with the light on and the gun ready.

There was a sign stencilled on the wall in black letters at the side of the opening: Natural History Museum. It was nice to know where I was but I hadn't gone as far as I thought. Hardly more than a quarter-mile. At least the museum wasn't on the campus, which might now be surrounded by police. It stood in its own grounds across the street from the campus on the north side. It was a chance to get away.

I found the door out of the tunnel and beyond it the stairs leading up into the museum. I mounted them cautiously and opened the door at the head of the stairs. No light and no noise. I stepped out into the hall.

Across and down the hall from where I stood, there was pale light like moonlight falling through a great arched doorway. I tiptoed to the doorless arch and looked in.

Fixed lights from outside, street-lights probably, shone through the high windows into a huge hall that seemed to have no ceiling. Impossible monsters, one of them twenty feet high, watched me from every side. You've got the jungle on the brain, I said to myself. Out of one jungle into another.

I recognized the room. The tall monsters were the mounted skeletons of prehistoric saurians. I could see the light shining bleakly through their ancient ribs.

There was a slight rustle on the other side of the room and I stepped out of the doorway and sidled along the wall into dark shadow. I heard no other sound. Probably the noise was a prehistoric mouse no more than five feet tall.

I shifted my position and looked along the opposite wall. In a dark corner, almost facing me, four human figures crouched. I huddled down against the wainscotting like a six-foot mouse. Then I remembered the exhibition in that corner of the room, several life-size dummies painted and dressed like Neanderthal men, holding stone weapons and squatting over a cold fire in an imitation cave.

But I didn't remember *four* dummies. I leveled my gun and walked to the roped enclosure where the cavemen sat on their heels. They didn't move.

I stepped closer and looked down at the bushy papier-mâché heads. The light was weak, but I could see that two of the heads were black and one was lighter and one was almost white. I felt as if I jumped a foot but I didn't move. My back was to the windows and my face was in shadow.

I lingered a moment, reining the wild horses in my legs, and then moved away. As I moved I saw with the edge of my retina that the caveman at the end was looking at me from under tousled red locks, out of live green eyes. He held a stone hatchet shaped like a gun.

I sauntered back to the other side of the room, feeling I had a fifty-fifty chance of not being shot. Peter and Ruth could have shot me then, but I was their scape-goat for Dr. Schneider's death. And they didn't know I'd seen them.

I stepped into the striped shadow of a brontosaurus skeleton, drew a quick bead on the head at the end of the roped enclosure, and fired. I must have missed because two flashes answered my shot simultaneously and two shadows came over the ropes towards me.

I turned and ran through the arch and heard two more shots as I turned the corner. I clattered down the tiled hall and found another corner to turn and then another. The feet behind me were light and quick like cats' feet.

I ran into a door with a bar across it like an exit and it flew open under my weight. I staggered out onto a concrete loading-platform at the back of the museum, slammed the door behind me, and jumped to the ground.

The corner of the building was quite near and I turned it as I heard the door spring open. I sprinted across a lawn, keeping in the shadow of bushes and trees, towards the circular building surrounded by cages, where the museum kept its live animals. I put this building between me and the cave-dwellers, but I heard their light feet running towards me on gravel.

I passed a fox curled up asleep behind his wire netting, and I envied him his nice, safe cage. I wanted one of my own. I could have one if I could get into it before the feet came around the animal-house. Across from the fox-cage there was a pit perhaps four feet deep where the snakes and turtles were kept. I vaulted the iron fence around it and landed on my hands and knees on the gravel floor. I scuttled against the concrete wall like a frightened crab and a black snake slithered away from under my hands. I crouched there trying to control my panting, and heard the running feet go by above my head.

When the sound had ceased, I climbed out of the pit like an ambitious turtle and ran back to the museum. The back door was still open and I scrambled up on the loading-platform and went in, leaving the door open behind me. The corridor I had dashed through three minutes before seemed longer on the way back. I found the door at last and went down into the tunnels again. They wouldn't come back to the museum. Someone must have heard the shots and the police would soon be here.

I flashed my light in the sub-basement and saw a chart on the wall. McKinley Hall, the Little Theatre, the Women's Building, the Graduate School, the Natural History Museum circled in red. A network of black lines crisscrossed the chart. It was a map of the steam-tunnels.

The university powerhouse was about as far from the museum as McKinley Hall, but in the opposite direction. I got my bearings and went into the tunnel. As I closed the door behind me, I heard loud feet like policemen's feet on the floor of the building above me, and a sound of voices. I set out for the powerhouse. Powerhouses have always interested me.

My shirt was still sopping and my coat began to get wet. My heart was beating hard from the sprint and the darkness swelled and contracted around me like black blood in an artery. It slithered like a snake past my sightless eyes. Suddenly, I noticed that I had no gun. I must have left it in the reptile-pit.

As soon as I bumped into a wall and turned a corner, I used my flashlight. There could be no one in front of me now until I reached the powerhouse. I quickened my pace and trotted along on the left side of the green pipes, sweating like a wrestler. My feet clattered on the paved floor and I let them clatter.

I heard feet behind me far down the tunnel and I stopped for an instant and looked back. There was a faint light on the wall where the tunnel turned and shadows like grey fingers reached out towards me. I switched out my light and ran on blindly in the dark with heavy footsteps reverberating behind me.

Something struck me across the chest like a falling tree and I leaned against it gasping for breath. I felt searing heat against my body: it must be the steam-pipe. I crawled under the pipes where they turned into the wall and ran on with one hand scraping the wall, feeling for the door that must be there.

Flashlights came around the corner on pounding feet a hundred yards behind me. I saw my shadow leaping ahead of me like a frantic mimic of my fear. And I saw a door.

A man's voice shouted, "There he is," and a gun went off with a sound like vessels bursting in my brain. The bullet ricocheted from the wall behind me and passed me like a droning bee. I have always hated bees.

I dived for the door and it opened under my hand. I ran out on the floor of a great concrete vault lined on one side with black iron boilers. By the light of the few unshaded bulbs that hung in the furnace-room I could see no one, but the footsteps sounded through the door at my back like pounding fists. To my right were windows and an iron ladder leading up to a door in the wall.

I dropped my flashlight and scrambled up the ladder and got the iron door at the top open. The door from the tunnel sprang open below and I slammed the iron door shut. Two bullets rang flatly against it like the knocking of iron knuckles, and I jumped onto a black hill which loomed outside the door.

I was halfway up the side of the university coal-pile. Anthracite is not good to run in but there was no-where to hide and nothing to do but run. I leaped and scrambled down the side of the coal-pile towards a railway track which gleamed faintly in the starlight.

I heard the iron door open behind me and the sound of another shot but I didn't look back.

When I reached the track it was easier to run, and there were buildings on each side which helped to shadow me. I heard scrambling and cursing behind me but I ran straight on down the track to the end of the buildings. By now the feet behind were ringing on the ties and I turned to my left and jumped down the embankment.

There was a board fence in front of me and beyond it the clotted darkness of a clump of trees. Before the flashlights behind me reached the end of the buildings, I flung myself over the fence and landed on my side in weeds.

I got to my feet crouching low and ran into the patch of trees. When I reached the other side with my face scratched by low branches, I stopped and listened. There was no sound behind me, but I had to get away from there. I remembered newspaper stories of police cordons thrown around trapped killers. To the police, I was a killer. But I wasn't trapped yet.

The grove was in a valley, and on the hillside opposite me there was a huge dark building punctured with a few lighted windows. I knew the building—it was the hospital—and it helped me to get my bearings. Helen Madden lived near the hospital. If I could get to her she would help me.

Keeping close to the edge of the trees I ran along the valley, stumbling over hummocks and rubbish. With the lights of the great hospital above me, I felt more than ever like an outlaw, and I felt self-pity that other men should make me run like an unwanted dog among rubbish-heaps. But I felt pleasure, too, in running for my life. My two enemies were running in the same darkness.

I skirted the base of the hill beyond the hospital and climbed through underbrush and saplings to the old house where Helen Madden had an apartment. It had been made over into an apartment house which stood on a spur of hill overlooking the uncleared hillside I was climbing. When I got out of the woods I saw that a light was on, on the ground floor where Helen lived.

She was sitting at a lighted casement window looking out, with a cigarette in her hand. It's smoke rose straight up and she did not move. I tapped on the window and showed my face in the light. Her face changed when she saw me but she did not start. The line of smoke wavered once and was straight again.

She stared at me for a moment and then her eyes contracted and I knew she recognized me. She flung the window open and said, "Bob, what is it?"

I put my finger to my mouth; there were other people in the house.

I whispered, "The police are after me. Schneider has been killed and they think I killed him."

"Did you?" she said without changing expression.

"No. I was framed. But I have to get away."

"Who killed him?" Her voice was very light and dry.

I said, "Ruth Esch and Schneider's son."

Her whisper hissed, "His son!"

"Yes. I caught them escaping and they tried to kill me."

Helen said quietly and seriously, "You're not crazy, are you, Bob? If I let myself go to-night, I'd be crazy."

I said, "I'm not crazy. Will you help me?"

"How?"

"Go and get my car and bring it to me."

"Go to the police, Bob. Tell them the truth and stick by it. They can't convict an innocent man."

"They seem to have orders to shoot me on sight," I said.

"Let me call them on the phone. This is fantastic."

"It's fantastic, yes. But they have evidence of murder against me."

"Bob, did you kill him?"

"I almost wish I had. But I didn't."

For a quarter of a minute she said nothing. Then she said, "Have you your car-keys?"

I gave them to her.

"Where is the car?"

"Parked in front of the main entrance of the Law School. You can't miss it."

"Shall I bring it here?"

"No, not here. I've got to get away from here. Bring it to the Slipper." The Slipper was a roadhouse a mile or so out of town where we had danced together.

"Can you get there?"

"Look, drive past the Slipper about two hundred yards, straight down the road, and park. I'll be there as soon as I can."

"I wish you'd let me call the police," she said.

"I'll let you when I get Alec's murderers," I said, but I had very little hope of that.

"I'll be there," she said.

She closed the window and moved away into the room and I started down the hill on the other side of the house. From the streets beyond the hospital, I heard a police siren rising like the terror behind my eyes.

There was a scattering of houses along the crest of the hill, on the side of Helen's house away from the hospital. None of the houses was lighted but I went down into the lightly wooded ravine behind them and headed for the open country. I avoided the roads, which might already be patrolled, and ran in the fields. This meant uneven footing and barbed wire fences to crawl through, but the cows and horses I saw carried no guns.

Most of the fields were of stubble or dying grass. I saw no people or lights. I could have been the last man, running from nowhere to nowhere across the dry skin of a played-out world.

I came to a railway embankment paralleled on both sides by board fences. I climbed the fence and the embankment and crouched by the tracks, trying to see and hear any sounds of pursuit. There were none. Behind me I could see the lights of the city, and far beyond them to the north, the reddish reflection of the lights of Detroit hung in the sky like the glow of a giant fire.

I crossed the tracks and descended the embankment and ran along beside the board fence on the other side. I was very tired, so tired I was no longer sweating, and I went more slowly now that I was away from the city. It would take Helen some time to get my car and drive out to the Slipper.

I had to cross a main highway to reach the side road where the roadhouse stood, and I travelled in the shadow of the railway embankment until I saw the highway. A car went by and I saw its headlights shine on the concrete. Down the road they scudded out of sight and there was no other car coming from either direction.

I crossed the highway on the railroad tracks and took to the fields again. So long as it was dark I felt safe from the police in the open country. So long as they were alive I couldn't feel safe from Peter Schneider and Ruth Esch, but they had no way of tracing me here. If they didn't have dogs' noses.

Dog and bitch. A mad dog and a ravening bitch. I didn't like to think about Ruth. The moral insanity of a friend is worse than a friend's death.

I crossed more fields and reached the road I was looking for. Walking on the edge of the fields near the road, I headed for the Slipper.

I heard a car coming behind me and lay down behind the wire fence in the grass. Headlights came down the road between the trees like controlled lightning. I saw the car approaching—it wasn't going very fast—and the orange light above the windshield. It was a taxi.

As the taxi went by, I saw a hooked nose and black eye above the steering wheel—Shiny! I had no time to hail him and it was just as well because there was somebody in the back seat. A head with a man's hat on it was outlined in the rear window for a second before the car went out of sight.

I got up and walked on a quarter of a mile to the driveway which led into the Slipper. I could see the long low building dimly through the trees, with no lights showing. Still no sign of Helen.

I heard another car coming and flopped to the grass again. As it came nearer I could see the lights sliding along the gravel road, and recognized the sound of my engine. So she had done it, and done it quickly! I began to plan a back-road route out of the country, but I lay where I was. Maybe the police were trailing her.

My sedan came in sight, going very slowly, and suddenly stopped. But I had said the other side of the Slipper! Then I understood. Two men got out of the car and climbed into the back seat. I couldn't see who they were in the reflection of the headlights, but one wore a policeman's cap and they both carried guns.

I lay still where I was, feeling angry and betrayed. The car started again and went slowly past me. I saw Helen's white face behind the wheel, but nobody was visible in the back seat. She was helping the police to catch me. She thought I was either crazy or wrong. Christ!—the thought numbed my throat—perhaps she thought I was a murderer, too.

I had to get away from the Slipper. I couldn't go back towards the highway because there would be more policemen waiting there. When I didn't appear for my appointment with Helen, they would start searching the country around the Slipper.

I had to keep on going. I got up and ran away from the road until I came to the fence on the other side of the field. It was a rail fence and I climbed it and moved along behind it in a half-crouch. Two hundred yards across the field I could see my car parked on the road with its headlights shining steadily. Nobody

150

moved in it or around it. Keeping well away from the road, I headed in the direction Shiny had taken.

There was a chance that I might find him and get him to drive me somewhere or let me use his taxi. Perhaps he had been driving a late partygoer to his house in the country, and would drive back on the same road with an empty cab. In that case I'd better get back to the road so I could hail him if he passed.

When the headlights of my car were out of sight behind the trees, I went back to the road and walked along beside it in the ditch. A car's headlights and engine would warn me in advance and give me a chance to hide if it came from behind me. If it came from the other direction, it might be Shiny.

I walked nearly a mile—to my tired legs it seemed farther—but no car came from either direction. The night was still very dark.

At last I came to a lane leading down a slope under dark arched trees. At the end of the lane there was a red light glowing. Maybe the tail-light of Shiny's taxi. But any car would do if the keys were in it.

I turned down the lane walking as silently as I could in the fallen leaves. When I got closer to the red light, I saw that it wasn't the tail-light of a car. It was a small red bulb hanging in the front window of a house. All the blinds in the windows were drawn but there was light shining around the edges and through the cracks.

I passed an old barn on a hillock beside the lane. It hung sideways against the darkness like a tired old man leaning on a wall. Half its boarding had fallen off and I could see the stars through it.

When I had walked past the old barn, I could see the lower front of the house. There was a patch of bare ground in front of it and two cars were parked there with their red tail-lights burning. Before I reached the cars, I saw that one was Shiny's taxi.

The dashboard lights were on and I looked for the

ignition key. It wasn't there. None in the other car, either.

There was a burst of music from the house, shrill clarinets and drooling saxophones. *Sugar Blues*. I looked at the red bulb in the front window, hanging between the pane and the drawn blind. The music had stopped pretending to have a tune and was pumping rhythmically at a single theme.

I moved around to the side of the house. The dingy white paint was peeling off it and the windowsills were rotting. The blinds were drawn in the side windows, too, but I stood on tiptoe at the window where the music seemed to be and looked past a torn corner of the blind.

There were several people at tables in the room, three men I didn't know and Shiny. He was sitting at a round table by himself with a glass of beer in front of him. Two young men sat at another table with whiskey-glasses, and an old man in shirtsleeves was in the far corner beside a record-player, tapping his knee with a finger in time to the music.

I heard the high giggle of a woman from an upstairs room. The music went on pumping. Finally, it went out with a whine and the old man got up with difficulty and turned the record.

Shiny sat over his beer, moving only to smoke and drink. The two young men were arguing with drunken extravagance, as if something mattered very much and they knew what it was. One turned to the old man and said, "Bring us another, pop," very loudly. The old man hobbled over and took their glasses.

I went back to the front of the house, climbed the porch, and knocked on the front door. There was a sound of dragging steps and the door opened six inches. I saw a porous, red-veined nose and drooping eyes like an old hound's.

The old man whispered, moving his stubbled lips like an elocutionist, "What you want?"

"A drink," I said. "And a fried egg sandwich if you can make it."

"You got us wrong, friend, this is a private house."

The woman's voice came from upstairs in a high, thin scream which fluttered down into a giggle, "Stop it."

"There's a friend of mine in here. Shiny."

"Shiny? Say, you ain't one of the boys from the university that got us knocked off last year?" He was still whispering.

"Do I look it?"

He opened the door wider and looked at my face. "Who scratched your face?"

"My wife."

"What happened to your clothes? You're all mud."

"I fell down," I said. "I was walking along in a field and I fell down."

"Drunk?"

"I'm always drunk. When I have the money."

"Well, come on in." He opened the door wide for me. "You look kind of tuckered out."

His breath as I passed him was like alcohol spray. He closed the door and shuffled down the worn, brown-painted hall. A narrow staircase rose from the hall to the second floor and I saw a light at the top.

The old man pointed to a door opposite the staircase. "Just go in and sit down. Shiny's in there. What'll you drink?"

"Bring me the egg sandwich first. Empty stomach."

"We don't usually serve vittles," the old man whispered. "It'll cost you thirty-five cents."

"All right. And a glass of beer."

He looked at me suspiciously. "I thought you said you drank."

"I alternate beer and whiskey," I said. "When I can't get grain alcohol."

"I got grain alcohol," he whispered proudly.

"That's great," I said. "Bring me some with my sandwich."

He hobbled off down the hall to the back of the house and I opened the door and went in. The young men were still arguing, "—I tell you she's frigid—"

Shiny looked up and saw me and half-rose from his chair. "Professor! What are you doing here?"

"Shut up, Shiny," I said. "I came here for a drink." Before he could say anything else, I walked over and sat down opposite him and whispered, "If you want to talk, whisper. Everybody's doing it."

"What's the matter with your face?"

"A cat scratched it. One of my many cats."

"Jeez, professor, you're a mess." He hadn't heard that I was wanted for murder.

"I'm in a mess," I said, still whispering. The men at the other table went right on arguing. "The people who killed Alec Judd are after me. I've been running across country."

"You look it. Jeez, why don't you get police protection?"

"I can't," I said. "The police are after me, too."

"Why? Whatja do?"

"Nothing. But they think I killed a man."

"Who?"

"A Nazi spy," I said. "But they don't know it."

"Christ, did you kill Mr. Judd, professor?"

"Do you think I did?"

"No."

"Then drive me into Ohio. I'll pay you double rates."

'I can't do that, professor. I'm on a call."

"Call another taxi for your call. I'll pay for it."

"Hell, I can't drive a fugitive from justice, professor."

"Then give me your keys. Tell them I stole your car. I've got to get away."

"I can't do that." His whisper was getting hoarse with fright and I couldn't afford to frighten him.

I said, "All right, Shiny." I was too tired to run much more—my legs were thirty years old and felt sixty—and if I was caught running away I'd probably be shot. Maybe if I stayed here and gave myself up to the police in the morning, I'd be able to talk myself out of a murder charge. Maybe more evidence would turn up.

The room was battered and dirty and run-down, but it was warm and bright. I didn't want to leave it for the dark fields.

Shiny was sitting, watching me with some suspicion and more curiosity. One of the young men said, "Yeah, but when I went into the bedroom she was in bed and this guy was standing there with just the tops of his pyjamas on. That's gotta mean something."

The other said, "They're all whores. Especially the frigid ones."

The first wept brokenly in a high drunken voice, "She's a whore. She's a whore. And I loved her so truly." He sobbed gustily and added, "And I'm a low-down bastard myself."

Shiny said to me, "Who else got killed? You said the police thought you killed somebody."

"Where have you been since I saw you in front of McKinley?"

The old man came in and put a large fried egg sandwich on a cracked plate in front of me. He stood there until I gave him thirty-five cents, and shuffled off.

"Bring me whiskey," I said. "Two whiskeys."

"I thought you said grain alkie," he whispered in a disappointed way.

"Make it whiskey." I ate my sandwich.

Shiny said, "Hell, I've been driving this call all over and gone trying to find a dame for him. He's got no nose and none of the hookers in town will take him. He said he only had seven dollars."

"Where is he now?"

"Upstairs with Florrie. She takes anybody. The funny thing is, though, he said he lost his nose in an industrial accident. Clipped right off." He illustrated with his hands.

"Who's Florrie?"

"The old man's daughter. We call him the Tube."

"The Tube?"

"Yeah, he eats through a tube. Cancer of the throat. You oughta see him pour whiskey down that tube."

He remembered his curiosity and said, "Who got killed?"

"Schneider," I said. "Dr. Schneider. He was a spy."

"Who killed him if you didn't?"

"Nobody you know. His son, and a woman called Ruth Esch. Listen, Shiny."

"Yeah?"

"When you get back into town, tell the police to start looking for them. They probably won't believe it but tell them anyway. This is, if I get away."

"Not me. If you killed him that makes me a accessory or something. Listen, professor, you better get out of here. I won't tell anybody I saw you."

"I didn't kill anybody. The same people killed Schneider that killed Alec Judd. A blond man and a red-headed woman."

"A red-headed woman?" Shiny's eyes snapped. "What does she look like?"

"Red hair with a permanent. Green eyes. About thirty. Pretty good-looking and painted to kill."

"Jeez, professor, I had that dame on a call to-night. From McKinley down to Main Street. German accent?"

"Yes. When was this?"

"Around midnight."

"When around midnight?"

"I don't remember. Sometime before midnight."

"Have you got your call-sheet?"

"Yeah." He pulled the pad out of his pocket and turned a page. "Quarter to twelve. I drove her from McKinley downtown at a quarter to twelve."

"Are you sure about the time, Shiny?"

"Yessir."

"Will you swear to this in court?"

"Why not? It's the truth."

"Then I'll drive into town with you until we see a policeman and give myself up."

"Best thing for an innocent man to do, professor. That call should be down soon. He certainly takes his time."

The old man brought out whiskey and I drank mine at a gulp. Shiny sipped his.

I heard a car in the lane. Probably the police. I was ready for them: I had at least one piece of evidence to give them.

"Look out and see who that is, Shiny. Will you?"

He went to the window and pulled aside the edge of the blind.

"Coupe," he said. "Two people in it." I heard the car stop. "They're getting out," he said. "Say, professor, there's your red-headed friend."

I ran to the window and looked out. The headlights of the car cast light enough to see Ruth Esch and Peter Schneider walking towards the porch with casual right hands in the pockets of their natty sports coats.

chapter x

I TURNED to Shiny and said, "Have you got a gun?"

"Nope. What would I want with a gun?"

"Don't tell them I was here," I said. As I started
across the room I heard knocking on the door. I went
through the door at the back of the room into the
kitchen.

The old man was sitting at a wooden table with a
half-gallon can and a glass of colorless liquid in front
of him. He had a rubber tube in his hand which
seemed to grow out of the shirt-collar.

"More whiskey?" he whispered, and began to get
out of his chair. There was a louder knock on the
door, and he started.

"Who's that?" he said.

"The police."

"So you got me knocked off, you—"

"Don't be crazy. Don't let them in. And don't tell
them I was here."

The two at the door began to shake the knob. I had
no time to ask the old man if he had a gun, and I went
out the back door. I closed it quietly behind me and
jumped off the railless back porch into a yard over-
grown with weeds. I waded through the rank growth
and stepped over a broken-down wire fence into a
field. I could hear voices from the front of the house.

Avoiding the beam from the headlights of Schneider's car, I ran crouching down the slope of the field
into a gulley where a patch of trees hid me from the
house. There was a small stream tinkling in the gul-

ley and I followed its course because it was something to follow. It seemed I had been running for days, but the night was still dark.

The stream led me out of the woods into an open field. It was a field of turnips. The turnips stuck out of the ground like human heads in rows and made it very hard to run until I turned away from the stream and followed the turnip-rows.

When I had crossed the turnip field I had to climb another fence, and beyond that the ground started to rise under my feet. I climbed the hillside and stopped to look back.

I could see the dim outlines of the house I had left across the valley, and the headlights of the coupe still shining fixedly. As I watched, the headlights moved and I heard the sound of the distant engine. The headlights went up the lane way from the house and disappeared.

Perhaps Shiny and the old man had convinced them that I hadn't been there, and they had given up the chase. Perhaps not.

My heart was pumping like a racing engine and I was beginning to sweat again. Moving more slowly, I climbed to the top of the hill. A horse standing on the other side of the hilltop shied away from me and galloped off down the pasture. I had a wild idea of trying to catch him and ride away on his back.

I ran down the hill to the end of the pasture and the horse circled me and ran uphill away from me. I climbed another fence and crossed another field of stubble and went up another hill. From the top I could see lights across the next valley, and the wind brought me the sound of music. I went down the hill and across the fields towards the lights. They were hidden now by a shoulder of hill but as I got nearer the music became louder. It sounded like a violin, and I wondered if shock and terror had affected my mind.

I climbed across another wire fence into a lane which ascended the hill. As I went up, the violin-music came clearer and I recognized the piece. *Turkey in the Straw,* played on and on and on. I walked up the hill in time to the music and heard the shuffling and stamping of feet.

Then I saw the lights again. A huge barn on the other side of the hill was blazing with light through every window and crack. The wagon-doors at one end were wide open and threw a sheet of white light over the barn hill. The music stopped and there were howls and squeals and the stamping of feet.

The music started again and a whining insistent voice chanted rhythmically:

> "Now swing your ladies round by the right,
> Swing 'em round, roll 'em round."

There was the sound of feet again, trampling in unison on the wooden floor. The fiddle played on and on like a mechanical fiddle.

Somebody must have built a new barn and the barn-dance celebrating it was still going on. But it must be nearly dawn. I pulled out my watch and looked at it in the light from the barn. The crystal was smashed and the watch had stopped at about 3:45.

It must have been broken when I ran into the steampipe in the tunnel. I thought of the tunnel, and shivered. I had never been a lone wolf or a cat that walks by itself, and my lack of a gun and the weariness of my legs made me feel more gregarious than ever. If Ruth and Peter were going to find me again, I wanted people around me. Any people would do.

Then I thought of the cars the people must have come in. I climbed the fence into the field and circled the barn, keeping outside the rectangle of light thrown through the barn door. Inside the barn, brilliantly lit by a dozen gasoline lamps hanging from the rafters, I could see shirt-sleeved men and girls in bright dresses going through the figures of a square dance.

There were a dozen cars parked under trees on the other side of the barn and I climbed over the fence and walked towards them. I looked in the front window of the first one to see if the ignition key was there and a bass voice from the back seat growled, "Pull in your neck, buddie, or I'll twist it for you."

I glanced into the back seat and saw the glimmer of a girl's white thighs, and delicately withdrew. The cars were not for me.

I turned around and walked into the barn as if I belonged. Nobody questioned my right to be there. There were a dozen kegs of beer in tubs of icy water standing on trestles along one wall, and I moved through the dancers towards the beer. None of them paid any attention to me, but a large hairy man sitting at the end of the row like a thirteenth keg stood up and stuck out his hand to me.

"Greetings, stranger," he said above the sound of the fiddle and the shuffling feet. "Have some beer?"

I said I would and he drew me a foaming mug. "Here you are. Drink it up. Plenty more where that comes from. I buy so much I get a wholesale price on it."

"You're lucky," I said.

"Of course I'm lucky. Always have been lucky, always will be lucky." He belched voluptuously and wiped his mouth with the back of his thick hand. "Luckiest thing ever happened to me was when my old barn burnt down. Needed a new one for years and now I've got it. Gift of the insurance company. Lucky as a rabbit in clover."

A man and a girl drifted away from the dancers and came over and asked for beer. The lucky man drew it for them and said, "Drink up. Build up your energy. Look at me. Always been energetic, always will be. Why? A gallon of beer a day keeps the doctor away, that's why."

The couple laughed and drank up and went back to

dance some more. He sat down beside me again and said, "Say, how'd you get here?"

"I walked," I said. "Ran out of gas and lost my way."

"Where you from?"

"Arbana."

"Hell, stay with me and I'll drive you in, in the morning."

"Thank you," I said. "Any rabbits around here?"

"Millions of them. Trillions of them. Swarm all over, eat me out of house and home. Why?"

"I thought now that I'm out here I'd try to do a little hunting before I go back to town. Have you got a gun?"

The big man threw his left leg over his right knee, bent over with a grunt and began to unlace his left boot.

"I said have you got a gun."

He said, "Ha! Ha!" and pulled off his boot and sock and pointed triumphantly at his bare foot. The big toe was missing.

"I said a gun, not a big toe."

"That's correct." He laughed uproariously. "No big toe, no gun. I used to have guns, dozens of them. A whole arsenal. Then one day, about five years ago, I was out hunting rabbits and crawled through a fence with a shotgun and the damn thing went off and shot off my big toe. After that no more guns for me. If I lost a few more toes or a whole foot, I'd be a damn cripple. Won't even look at a gun. Stranger, don't ever come trying to sell me a gun."

"I won't," I said.

"Let the damn rabbits eat up everything I've got. If you were the president of the United States, I wouldn't let you *give* me a gun." He bent over and put on his sock and boot.

"Have you a telephone?" I asked.

"No *sir*, no telephone for me. They attract lightning. When I want to talk to the next farm, I just go out on the barn hill and holler. Like this." He hollered. Nobody paid any attention.

"I see. Have they got a telephone at the next farm?"

"Yeah, I been telling them for ten years they better watch out, the lightning'll get 'em sure as shooting. But the damn fools haven't had it torn out yet. They'll be sorry when the house burns down around their ears and—"

I cut him short. "How do you get to the next farm?"

He waved his arm. "Right down the lane past the house. Just follow the lane. You can't miss it."

"I think I'd better go and try to get in touch with a garage to pick up my car," I said. I got up and thanked him and said good night.

"Good night," he yelled. "Too bad you can't stay."

The music stopped and the dancers headed for the beer. I walked around them along the wall to the open doors and saw a car coming down the lane. The light was very dim but it looked like a coupe.

I turned and ran back across the deserted floor to the other end where the fiddler was drinking his beer. A small door in the end wall was open and I ran through it and found myself running in air.

I only fell a few feet but it seemed like a hundred. I landed in a soft pile of manure that squished up around my ankles and my wrists. I got up and crossed the barnyard and ran around the house to the lane. A pale blue neon light was creeping up two sides of the sky and I could see another farmhouse and a barn a quarter of a mile down the road. There was a light in the house, and I ran for it as hard as I could go.

Before I got there I heard the car behind me on the road and looked back and saw it coming. I ran like a rabbit hypnotized by headlights straight down the centre of the road to the farmhouse. I ran through an open gate into the front yard and saw a light in an outhouse in the yard and somebody moving inside.

The car drew up at the gate—it was a coupe all right—and I ran for the outhouse. An old woman working over a cream-separator heard me coming and came to the door of the outhouse. She had a hard, bright face with a long nose in the middle of it.

I ran up to her and said, "Call your men. There's a murderer after me."

She sniffed and said, "You've been drinking. Are you one of the friends of that O'Neill man on the next farm? Look at you, you're all covered with cow-dirt." She sniffed again in disgust and her long nose pointed at me like the finger of scorn.

"Call your husband," I said. "Tell him to bring a gun." I looked behind me. Peter was walking across the lawn towards us with his right hand in the pocket of his coat.

"Why should I bother my husband on a drunkard's say-so?" the woman said. "He's out in the barn milking. He's a respectable man. If you got yourself a steady job you wouldn't be running around early in the morning smelling of liquor and trying to frighten hard-working people. The Devil finds things for idle hands to do."

Peter Schneider was at my shoulder. He said very respectfully as if butter wouldn't melt in his mouth, "I quite agree, madam. I apologize to you for my friend's drunkenness." I felt his gun pressed hard against my buttocks.

"*He* should apologize," she said, bridling with justified virtue. "Is he a friend of yours?"

"He was at one time," Schneider said. "I still feel some duty towards him. I've been looking for him all night to take him back to the hospital."

"The hospital! Is he sick?"

"Not exactly. After a week of steady drinking he succumbed to delirium tremens. The poor fellow is out of his head. He even imagines that I want to kill him."

"You're a true Good Samaritan, young man."

"He's a German spy," I said. "He killed his father tonight and now he's trying to kill me."

He caught the woman's eye and laughed infectiously. They laughed together.

"Mercy me, I shouldn't laugh at him," the woman said. "Drink is such a horrible tragedy. But I'm so glad you found him before he destroyed himself."

"So am I," Schneider said. "He needs a nurse's tender ministrations. I'll take him back to the hospital now."

"Before you go," the woman said, "will you wait a minute? I have something for him. It may help him."

"A gun would help me," I said. "Nothing else would." She threw up her hands and eyes and bustled off to the house.

"You are excessively naïve," Schneider said to me. "I have no intention of shooting you. You are much more precious to me alive."

"How you cheer me," I said. I turned and faced him and saw his unlined, complacent face and the bulge in his pocket. "But you'd better kill me quickly. Otherwise I'm going to kill you."

His laugh sounded flatly against the roof of his mouth. The woman came back from the house and handed me a little printed pamphlet. In the growing light I could make out the title *The Horrors of the Demon Drink*.

"Thank you very much, madam," I said.

"We must go now, Freddie," Schneider said. "The doctor will be worried."

I turned to the woman once more, "I'm a murderer," I said. "The police are looking for me. My name is Robert Branch. Phone the police in Arbana and tell them you saw me escaping. This man's name is Peter Schneider."

"No more wild tales, Freddie," Schneider said.

"Good heavens, he's out of his mind," the old woman said. "Delirium tremens is a terrible thing."

"Lips that touch liquor shall never touch mine," I

said and turned towards the car. Peter Schneider followed close behind me.

I passed through the open iron gate outside of which the green coupe was parked with the engine running. The woman was still standing watching us. He couldn't shoot me in front of a witness. Or could he? I took the chance.

I slammed the iron gate hard against him as he passed through and he staggered back with a cry.

"Goodness gracious," the woman shrieked, "he's getting away again."

I ran towards the road and around the corner of the barn. The road was no good to me; he had a car. Across the road were willow-trees and beyond that an open pasture. I heard running feet behind me. I put the trees between me and Peter, and headed straight across the pasture.

He came across the pasture fifty feet behind me, but I didn't look back. I had to get away from him before we were out of sight and earshot of the house, or he would be free to shoot me. There was a deep woods on the other side of the pasture, its half-turned leaves becoming gorgeous in the dawn. I tried to lengthen my stride, but tiredness hung around my thighs like iron hoops.

A shotgun roared from the woods and a rabbit came running out into the pasture towards me dragging a leg. It saw me and moved floppily aside like an old hat in a wind. Then it fell on its side and kicked once.

I ran towards it and picked it up and stood holding it by the ears with the blood dripping from it. Peter came up beside me with his chest heaving. "You can't shoot me here, you bastard," I said. "The man that shot the rabbit is coming."

There were cracklings and rustlings among the trees and two men came out of the woods with shotguns under their arms. They saw me holding the rabbit and broke into a trot. They were young men in bright plaid shirts with smiling faces. One of them held out his hand for the rabbit and I gave it to him.

"Will one of you fellows lend me his shotgun for one shot?" I said. "Just to shoot at a tree. I haven't shot a gun for—"

Peter Schneider broke in, "Don't give him a gun. This man is an escaped murderer."

The young men stood and watched us with blank, smiling faces. One of them took a card out of an inside pocket and handed it to me. It was an old dirty card bearing print which said:

> "John Maldon,
> Speech Institute, Arbana.
> Please excuse me. I am a deaf-mute."

I found a pencil in my pocket and wrote on the back of the card: "I'll give you $40 for your shotgun and some shells. Now."

I took two twenties out of my wallet and handed the card and the bills to the young man. He read what I had written and looked at me in smiling surprise. Then he turned to the other hunter and talked to him on his fingers. The other man's fingers began to talk.

The first young man smiled more intensely than ever and nodded and handed me his gun. It was a single-barreled twelve-gauge shotgun and I broke it to make sure it was loaded. It was. The young man handed me a cardboard box of shells.

I felt very good. A shotgun can blow a man's head off at close quarters. Peter had begun to move away. I held the gun at the hip so that it pointed at him and said:

"Stand still, Schneider."

He edged behind the two deaf-mutes and, using them for cover, ran for the woods. I stepped around them, brought the gun to my shoulder, and fired quickly. Too quickly. He plunged into the woods and disappeared, and I heard his receding footsteps crackling in the underbrush.

The young men stared at me aghast and ran away across the pasture making little bleating noises.

I broke the gun and reloaded and emptied the shells into my pocket. Then I ran into the woods after Peter. It wasn't a wise thing to do, but I was very eager to kill him. He had hunted me all night and now I was hunting him.

It was a maple-woods, probably sugar-maple, and well thinned out. I ran on a thin carpet of fallen leaves, sallow and brown and blond and blood-red, between trunks like black pillars. Far ahead of me I could hear the running feet, and I caught a glimpse of him between the trees. I lost sight of him again and kept on running. The shotgun hampered me but I ran hard. I was so angry I forgot to be tired.

I leaped a stream and came to a rail fence with open fields rolling beyond it. The fields were empty. There was a sound along the fence a hundred feet away from me and I turned and fired and reloaded on my knees behind the fence. There was a shot and a bullet spatted into a tree behind my head. He broke from cover and ran across the field in front of me and disappeared behind a little hill.

I climbed the fence and walked up the hill with the gun at my shoulder. From the hilltop I saw him running across dry grass in a shallow valley, dragging a leg like the rabbit. On the next hillside there was a tumbledown barn beside the grass-grown foundations of a house that had probably been razed by fire. He was running uncertainly towards the barn.

There was a splash of bright new blood on a white boulder halfway down the hill. It went to my head and I felt like laughing out loud. I had winged him.

He fell once before he reached the old barn, and got up and dragged himself in through the gaping door. A thin, dribbling trail of blood led down the hill from the boulder where the blood-splash glistened, and I followed it across the field.

I walked towards the barn with the gun at my

shoulder, expecting a pistol shot. There was none. There was a low moaning from inside the dark barn, and then silence.

I tiptoed to the door and looked inside under floating cobwebs. I could see nothing but old chaff on a floor of loose, rotting boards.

I forgot I wasn't hunting rabbits and stepped across the rotting doorsill. A noose came over my head from the side and jerked me off my feet. My gun went off with a roar that shook the barn and killed nobody.

The noose drew tighter and burned my neck and I could feel congested blood swelling my face. I was flat on my face and he had one foot between my shoulder blades. It felt as if he was leaning back on the rope around my neck. I tried to get onto my hands and knees.

"Don't struggle, Dr. Branch. It will do no good and will only force me to shoot you."

I turned my head sideways and tried to see him but he drew the rope tighter. My eyeballs threatened to burst and the light seemed tinged with red. I heard a click like a box closing or opening and he kneeled on my back holding the rope tight. He pushed up the sleeve on my right arm and I felt a prick near the elbow. I tried to struggle and he drew the rope tighter. Swarming blackness dipped down at my consciousness and I relaxed. He loosened the rope a little and the black cloud receded.

"What a child you are, Dr. Branch. You Americans know nothing of war. I cut my arm and left a little trail of blood for you, and you followed it as a donkey follows a carrot. You must fancy yourself as a hunter, Dr. Branch."

My right arm felt numb and my head began to go around in stately circles, humming like a distant motor.

"Relax, Dr. Branch." His voice came from the other end of a dark tunnel. "You'll go to sleep very shortly. Then I shall have the pleasure of hanging you."

The rope was looser now and I tried for the last time to get my knees under me. I couldn't raise my head. The black cloud had come back and rested on my head and it was as heavy as tons of coal.

Schneider's voice droned on like a doctor's soothing a patient going under ether, "Hanging is a fitting end for a murderer, is it not? Self-slaughter. Homicide and suicide. No one will guess that you did not hang yourself. In fact, you will hang yourself. I shall make that possible for you, Dr. Branch.

"So fortunate that this rope was here in the barn. Otherwise I might have had to shoot you. So fortunate."

With the idiot speck of consciousness I had left, whirling in the midst of blackness, I felt soothed and delighted by the good fortune. How lucky we both were, and how pleasant it was to be going to sleep with a gentle voice droning in my ears.

The speck of consciousness flickered and went out, and I turned on great black wheels in an infinity of humming wheels.

chapter xi

AFTER the wheels had completed several 365-day jour-
neys around the sun they stopped rotating, but the
universe went on humming like an engine in neutral.
I was lying on the rim of a wheel so big that it seemed
flat to my back. The university coal-pile was on top
of me and pinned me to the wheel so that I could
not move my arms or head.

There was something in my right hand and I
squeezed it and discovered that it was my left elbow.
The coal-pile pressed down on my upturned face and
there was something tight around my neck. I blew out
and drew in a deep breath which whistled through
my flattened nose. At least I was still breathing.

I stuck out my tongue and it came against a hard,
rough surface that tasted familiar. Wood. Old wood.
That was it, it was the lid of a coffin. I was buried alive
in a tight coffin that pressed down on my face and
folded arms. A wild claustrophobia seized me and I
kicked out. My legs were free to kick but the lid of
the coffin pressed down painfully on my stomach and
groin.

I pressed out with my bent arms and the lid shifted
slightly but the thing around my neck began to choke
me. I felt like crying at the unfairness of being buried
alive with something around my neck to choke me.

To choke me. I remembered Schneider and his
promise to hang me. Was this how it felt to be
hanged? Anger surged through me and I pushed
frantically at the heavy lid of the coffin. It rose

171

slightly and I saw light, but the rope was unbearably tight now and I moved my head sideways to ease the pressure.

I freed my right hand and got hold of the coffin-lid at the edge and pushed and it rose higher. But the rope had pulled my head over the edge of whatever I was lying on. I was going to give the lid a final desperate shove when I heard running feet somewhere below me.

A man's voice, a voice I remembered from somewhere, shouted, "Branch, don't move, and don't let go of that beam."

I tried to speak but there was no hole in my throat to speak through and the blood swelled in my head. As the black cloud bellied down at me again, the heavy lid lurched sideways but I held on with my right hand. Quick footsteps came up from somewhere and the weight was taken off my hand and arm. The pressure on my neck was released and the black cloud swooped up and away from me like an escaped balloon.

A hand raised my head where it dangled in space and I lay panting on a hard, narrow surface with somebody's arm around my shoulders. As my vision cleared, I saw a face above me, a sullen Indian face that I remembered.

Wild ideas rushed through my mind like leering mimics of truth. He's no F.B.I. man, he's another spy. The president is a spy. And the old woman with the hard, bright face.

I struggled against the arm around me and tried to get up. The dark face said, "Take it easy, old boy. You'll be all right in a minute. I'm Gordon, remember?"

I lay back and took it easy and my mind came back a piece at a time and fitted together like a jigsaw puzzle, with cracks in it. My neck was sore and my Adam's apple felt as if Eve had taken a bite out of it. My arms were stiff, and my head and groin throbbed like a toothache. In five minutes I wasn't all right, but I was fairly sane.

Gordon didn't look particularly friendly, but he didn't look like a spy either. Spies put ropes around your neck. I was still wearing a thick noose, with its end severed, around my neck like a necktie. Gordon had loosened it and I worked it over my head and took it off.

"A highly ingenious arrangement," he was saying. "And so simple. Truly Attic in its simplicity."

"What?" I said. "The Parthenon?" My voice scraped my throat like sandpaper and sounded like a crow cawing.

"Feeling better, Branch?"

"Yes, thanks. But my neck is somewhat chapped. Bring me my honey and almond cream. Also my bow of burning gold. I'm on a hunting trip."

"You were, but you're not," Gordon said. "You're going to be too busy explaining to play hare and hounds for a while. Can you get up now?"

"With excruciating ease," I said and sat up. My head seemed to linger where it was and then got up by itself and jumped onto my shoulders with a jolt. In a minute it stopped vibrating and I could use it again for elementary purposes.

I was sitting astride a two-foot beam running along the top of a wooden wall twelve or fifteen feet above the floor of the old barn. The wall divided the wagon-floor, where Schneider had snared me, from the hay-mow, which still had some old grey-green hay in the corners. Gordon was sitting beside me on the beam supporting me with one arm, his feet on the top rung of a ladder which ran down to the wagon-floor.

The beam that had pinned my face and arms and that I had mistaken for the lid of a coffin lay on the beam in front of me. One end of it was between my legs, and I could see a rope knotted around its middle. The rope passed over a rafter above my head and hung above the floor of the barn a few feet out of my reach.

"Do you see it?" Gordon said. "Study it as an object-lesson in the inadvisability of going on extra-legal spy hunts. Delayed-action murder fixed to look like suicide."

"I don't get it," I said. "I'm feeling dull this morning. It's still morning, isn't it?"

"It's not seven yet. But you appear to be rather dull in the evening, too, if last night was typical. Dull is putting it mildly."

"Go to hell," I barked, but my throat regretted it. "A man was killed, and somebody had to do something."

"Such as kill another man?"

"Nonsense. What happened to you after Galloway's hothouse-liberal fiasco?"

"I tailed Dr. Schneider to his home. But the more interesting question is what happened to you? And what happened to Dr. Schneider?"

"All right," I said, "I'll tell you. But not here. I'm grateful to you for saving my neck, but I don't have to submit to cross-questioning on a two-foot beam forty feet in the air."

"Fifteen feet is a better estimate."

"So what? While we sit here chatting, the man who put me here is probably on his way out of the state. Did you ever hear of Peter Schneider?" The ironic rasp I forced into my voice made me cough.

"The police are after him," Gordon said. "They're after you, too."

"I thought you were the police."

"That's right. Can you climb down by yourself or do I use the fireman's lift on you? Or do you want to stay up here and hang yourself some more?"

I remembered what Peter Schneider had said before I passed out. "What do you mean?"

"I mean that when I came into this barn you were in the act of hanging yourself. The rope around your

174

neck was slung over the rafter, pulled tight, and tied to this heavy loose beam. The beam was then placed on your face so that when you pushed it off it would fall and jerk the rope. The rope would then jerk you off the beam by the neck and either break it immediately or strangle you."

"So I suppose you're going to book me on a charge of attempted suicide." Watching the fixed snarl on his face, I wouldn't have put it past him.

"Don't be childish, Branch. I told you we're after Peter Schneider."

"Is it childish to ask why he went to all this trouble with ropes and beams? Why didn't he just give himself the pleasure of hanging me by hand?"

"He went right back to the farm and told the old lady you had tried to kill him but he got away. The deaf-mutes confirmed the story in writing. She had already phoned the Arbana police about you. Schneider said he was going to get help, and drove away."

"I get it," I said. "If you found my body soon enough, you'd be able to establish that I killed myself after he left. 'Slayer Suicides after Killing Father and Attempting to Kill Son.'"

"I'm glad you feel able to joke about it," Gordon said with a certain nasty primness. *"Did* you kill Dr. Schneider?"

"I'll answer questions on terra firma," I said. "Go ahead and I'll follow you down."

Gordon went down the ladder like a cat, and I climbed down after him holding on tight. He went to the door and I followed him into the shaft of sunlight that came through it. I saw the shotgun lying in the chaff beside the door and stooped down to pick it up, balancing my head carefully.

"Drop it," Gordon said, his hand inside his left lapel.

I straightened up in surprise. "For Christ's sake. I paid forty dollars for that gun."

"And it looks as if you intended to get your money's

175

worth," Gordon said. "It was a trail of blood that led me to this barn. And I notice that you're not bleeding anywhere."

"You're damn right I used it. Unfortunately, I didn't hit him. He cut his arm and used the blood as bait for me. Like a sucker, I followed him to the barn and got a noose around my neck."

"Stick to rabbits, Branch." Gordon picked up the shotgun and broke it to see if it was loaded. It wasn't, and he handed it to me.

I didn't like his attitude. "Mr. Gordon," I said, "I admire the bloodhound instincts which just saved my neck. But now you're barking up the wrong tree. If you arrest me for murder, I'll sue you for false arrest."

Gordon's teeth gleamed in the sun as if he was proud of them, but he wasn't smiling. "You've got a lot of explaining to do, Branch," he said. "And you can start now. Why did you follow Schneider into McKinley Hall this morning?"

"How do you know I followed him in? Or do you hesitate to reveal the secrets of your fascinating trade?"

"It's not your business, but I'll tell you. After the War Board meeting, I tailed Schneider on the chance that he'd go looking for this evidence you were talking about. He went home in a taxi and his son met him at the door. They had an argument in German and finally the old man gave in. They came out to the green coupe parked on the driveway and drove into Arbana."

"All very interesting," I said. "But all it proves against me is that I was right."

Gordon clipped me off. "Not quite. They parked near the campus and the old man got out and crossed the campus to McKinley Hall. I couldn't follow him in because I had no key, so I stood in the shadow of a tree and watched all the back doors. A few minutes after Schneider went in, you came around from the front of the building and entered by the west door. I want to know why."

"I'm not ashamed of my reason," I said. "I got the idea that Judd had hidden his evidence in the Middle English Dictionary office, and I went to look for it. Old Schneider had the same idea. I found it and Schneider tried to hold me up. I knocked him out. But it's obvious to me now that I should have let him shoot me."

The irony was lost on Gordon. "Did you knock him out with a horseshoe?" he said. "And have you got the evidence you found?"

"Listen, Gordon," I said. "I'll answer questions after you find Peter Schneider, if you still want to ask them. Didn't you see anybody else enter the building?"

"Just before I heard the shots I saw a man and a woman go in at the east end. The man looked like Peter Schneider and—"

"I knew it," I said. "Peter Schneider and Ruth Esch killed the old man. I left him unconscious on the floor —*without* a hole in his head—and went down to get the policeman. While I was gone, they killed him and ran away with the envelope."

"What envelope?"

"An oilskin envelope with information about the new A S T Program in it. Judd told me he found it in Schneider's office. Schneider and his son were both spies, and Peter made off with the evidence."

Gordon kept on looking like a stolid redskin. "You say that the two Schneiders were spies working in cahoots, and you also say that Peter killed his father. It doesn't hang together."

"Doesn't it? Peter couldn't get his father out of the building. Maybe the old man was weakening and Peter was afraid he'd talk to the police. He had no deep filial affections, I happen to know. And it was a chance to frame me for murder."

"You're good at explanations, Branch. But there's no evidence."

"What happened to Schneider's gun? He had a Lüger which he tried to use on me. Even if I had killed him, it would have been in self-defense."

"So you say. Did you assault a police officer in self-defense?"

"That was a mistake. I saw I was being framed for a murder and it made me mad. I guess I was a little crazy. Anyway, I thought I had to get away and I got away."

"For a while," Gordon said. "You'd have been better off in jail. Don't attempt another getaway. I can shoot, and I can run."

"And you can swim," I said. "What a list of accomplishments! Go practise the aquatic art in some convenient lake."

"I can also be unpleasant, if necessary."

"You've convinced me."

He snarled silently one last time and jerked his thumb towards the door. I stepped outside into sunshine that hurt my eyes, and he followed me. We left the barn with nothing dangling in it but the rope.

I felt good about that and about the bright sun on the autumn fields. But I resented his suspicion and the crack about being better off in jail. It implied that all my bones were sore for nothing.

As we started across the field, where Peter had pretended to stagger and fall, I said, "If I had spent the night in jail I wouldn't have found out who killed Alec Judd."

"So you know that, too," Gordon said.

"I know that Ruth Esch left McKinley Hall about a quarter to twelve last night."

"Twenty minutes before Judd was killed, according to your own story."

I said with heavy irony, "No doubt delayed-action murder sounds fantastic to the literal ear of the law, but I recently acted as guinea pig in a little experiment intended to prove its feasibility."

Gordon turned to me with a glint in his sombre eyes. "You've got something there, Branch. I'll have to examine that room."

"There's another possibility, too," I said. "At least it may not be an impossibility. The receiver of the telephone in Judd's office was hanging down when I went up there after he fell, and it seems he put in a phone call shortly before."

"He did? Who to?"

"I don't know. I tried to find out from the university operator, but she wouldn't tell me what she had heard. She probably told Sergeant Haggerty—I know he was talking to her."

"I'll ask him," Gordon said. "Who is Ruth Esch?"

"A German woman who just came to this country. Peter Schneider's fiancée."

"Red-headed?"

"And green eyes. About thirty."

"Is that the woman the taxi driver saw at the bootlegger's?"

"Shiny? Yes. Did Shiny tell you?"

"He recognized this woman as the passenger he had driven downtown just before midnight. She recognized him, too, and left the bootlegger's immediately. That's suspicious in itself."

"Where did she go when she left the bootlegger's? Peter was alone when he caught up with me at the farm."

"She hasn't been seen since," Gordon said. "Two drunks left at the same time, according to the taxi driver, and maybe she went with them. They haven't been found, either."

We passed the white boulder stained with Schneider's blood. The stain was darker now. I remembered my exultation when I first saw it, and felt humiliated. Better stick to rabbits, Branch, half my mind said; but the other half said, you'll get them yet.

We climbed the rail fence where Schneider had taken cover and entered the maple woods. It was pleasant to walk between the two levels of color, on the trees and on the ground, and have nothing around my neck. Not even skin.

Even Gordon was taking on some of the attributes of a human being. I said to him, "May I assume that you are beginning to be willing to toy with the hypothesis that I am not a murderer?"

His smile was so much like a sneer that it left me guessing. "If you're innocent you have nothing to fear." He added heavily as if he was by Jehovah out of the goddess of justice, "The law exists for the protection of the innocent and the apprehension of the guilty."

He couldn't even be friendly without riling me. "Don't be so impartial," I said. "I pay my income tax, and I haven't killed anybody yet. Why didn't you follow those two into McKinley Hall when you saw them, and apprehend the guilty and protect the innocent?"

"They had a key and I hadn't. I should have jimmied the door sooner, but I didn't do it until after I heard the shots. By the time I got in they were gone. I still don't know how they got out."

"I do," I said smugly. "They got out through the steam-tunnel the same way I did. I met them later in the museum and we exchanged a few well-chosen shots." I said nothing about seeing him in the basement of McKinley Hall. He wouldn't have liked it.

"Have you any further information?" Gordon said. "It will be best for you if you tell me everything you know."

"Nothing I can think of at the moment. Except that somebody is hitting me over the head with a hammer."

"Your humor is excessively tinny this morning." I couldn't argue.

"I need breakfast."

We emerged from the maple woods and crossed the pasture. I had chased Peter Schneider farther than I thought at the time, and I began to wonder how Gordon had got to the barn when he did.

"How did you happen to get here in the nick of time? Or is that just an old Federal Bureau of Investigation custom?"

"I'm glad you feel happy enough to joke about it," Gordon said.

"After all, it was my own personal lynching party," I said. "But it was pleasant to have you drop in. I'll never resent the withholding tax again."

"They don't deduct it in jail," he said, and I felt less chipper. He went on:

"I was at the Slipper with Haggerty when the taxi driver came tearing down the road, and we drove over to the bootlegger's right away. Haggerty had a police car with a radio and when the old woman phoned the Arbana police about you, they got in touch with Haggerty at the bootlegger's and I came over here with a couple of policemen. After a fairly lengthy correspondence with the deaf-mutes, I got the idea that you might be over there in the woods, so I went over. I finally worked over into the field and found the trail of blood, and that led me to the barn."

"I'm glad Schneider cut his arm," I said. "But it should have been his throat."

We passed under the willow trees and around the corner of the barn. There was a long black sedan parked at the gate.

"Is that the police car?" I asked.

"No, it's mine. I sent the police after Schneider."

He opened the gate and said: "I want to phone. They may have caught him."

The old woman came out of the front door of the farmhouse. She took one look at me and yelled to Gordon:

"That's the man! Don't let him get away!"

I have many of the aspects of a gentleman. I wear

sixty-five-dollar suits. I am a member of the Modern Language Association. I speak pure English, at least in the lecture-room. I am generally chivalrous in my attitude to women. But I raised my right hand, pressed the thumb to my nose, and wiggled the fingers. The old woman groaned righteously and raised her eyes to heaven.

Gordon frowned at me. "Sit in the car, Branch. I trust you won't try to run away again."

I said I wouldn't. I put the shotgun in the back seat and climbed into the front. Gordon followed the old woman into the house. I noticed he hadn't left the ignition key in the car.

I caught a glimpse of myself in the driver's mirror. There was chaff in my hair, my nose and cheeks were scraped, and I needed a shave. But what interested me most was my eyes. The pressure of the rope had broken some of the small vessels and suffused my eyeballs with blood. I looked like a pulp-magazine illustration of a homicidal sex-fiend whom any jury would convict on appearance alone.

I moved out of range of those horrible glaring eyes and saw that there were radio-dials on the dashboard. I turned on the radio in the hope of getting some news. My hope was not disappointed.

After listening to several numbers on a program of prewar recordings, I got an early news broadcast from Detroit. The Allies were advancing in Italy and the Russians were advancing in Russia, as usual.

"News of the state," the announcer said breathlessly as if Atropos was standing at his shoulder. He was wrong, she was standing at mine.

The staccato words crashed into my consciousness like machinegun bullets: "Arbana: In the early hours of this morning, a member of the faculty of Midwestern University was murdered, allegedly by a colleague on the university staff. The victim was Dr. Herman Schneider, well-known refugee from the Nazis and head of the German Department at the university. Professor Robert Branch of the English Department, who quarreled publicly with the murdered man earlier in the evening, is now being sought for questioning by police.

"Hearing the sound of gunshots from McKinley Hall, the main building of the university, shortly after 3 A.M. this morning, Constable Sale of the Arbana police force rushed into the building and apprehended Professor Branch, who was running downstairs from one of the upper floors. In an office on the fourth floor the officer discovered the body of Dr. Schneider, his skull smashed by a blow on the head from a horseshoe paperweight.

"Shortly after this discovery, Professor Branch overpowered the police officer and made his escape through the steam-tunnels underneath the campus. He is now being sought by local and state police and by the F. B. I., who expect further developments within a few hours. Detectives report that there is possibly a connection between the brutal murder of Dr. Schneider and the death earlier in the evening, apparently by suicide, of Professor Alexander Judd, chairman of the War Board of the university. The president of the university, Dr. Galloway, could not be reached for comment. Lansing . . ."

The announcer went on to something else and I switched off the radio. I sat perfectly still for a minute, numbed by shock. Then the panic that had driven me through the tunnels and across the fields came back and walloped me in the stomach. I flung open the door and jumped out of the car, ready to run.

Gordon came out of the farmhouse and walked across the lawn watching me alertly. I saw his long legs and remembered his shoulder-holster. I said, "I wonder if I could get a drink of water."

He went to the dairy and brought me a brimming dipper. I emptied it and felt better, but my stomach was knotted and my knees were weak.

"Did they get him?"

"Not yet," he said as he got into the driver's seat. "They're still after him. He went around Arbana on the back roads and apparently headed for Detroit."

He started the engine and I got in beside him. He turned up the road in the direction of the barn where the barndance had been.

I felt irrational resentment against Gordon. He hadn't let me know how serious my situation was. He had saved me from one noose, only to lead me into another. Then I remembered the serious warnings I had laughed off. I had been so glad to get out of the frying-pan that I didn't believe in the fire. Probably I should be grateful to him for not putting handcuffs on me.

We passed the barn and the dancers were gone and the fiddler had stopped playing.

"Where are we going?" I asked.

"To the bootlegger's."

"The whisperer?"

"Yes. I'm going to trace the two drunks who left when Ruth Esch did."

"What if you don't catch them? Do I stand the chance of being convicted of Schneider's murder?"

Gordon avoided a direct answer. "We'll catch them. Every policeman in the state will be on the lookout for them. And I'm going to telegraph their descriptions to every police station in the Middle West."

"Don't omit Canada. They just came from Canada and may try to go back."

"Where in Canada?"

"Ruth Esch wrote me a letter three days ago from Kirkland Lake, Ontario."

"Have you still got it?"

I felt in my pockets. The letter was gone.

"No, I must have lost it. Or Peter took it."

"You say the Esch woman wrote you a letter. Is she a friend of yours?" He shifted his black eyes from the road for a moment to glance at me.

184

"She was. In Germany, years ago. Not anymore."

I told him what he needed to know about Ruth Esch, including a complete physical description. Like Gordon, I wanted to catch her, but I dreaded meeting her again. There is a story in the *Heimskringla* about a Norse king who married a witch. She died but her body remained warm and beautiful. The king went mad and kept vigil by her beautiful body in the belief that she was sleeping and would come back to him. After years of vigil, he awoke from his madness and the body was crawling with worms.

I dreaded meeting her again. But I was going to have to travel a long way before I met her again.

I said to Gordon, "I heard a news broadcast on your radio. The police are after me for Schneider's murder."

"I told you."

"Yes, but not so vividly as the newscaster. Are you going to turn me in?"

"I have to," Gordon said. "In any case, it's the safest place for you."

"Because Michigan doesn't inflict the death penalty? I want to know whether it can be proved that Schneider was a spy, even if you don't catch the other two."

"Maybe it can. He hasn't been investigated yet."

"What have you got on him?"

"Everything you've given us, but that isn't enough without evidence. Naturally we'll investigate him thoroughly now. Have you any further leads?"

"I've told you everything I know. At least I think I have." Something was struggling towards the surface of my unconscious. I could feel it moving but I couldn't see what it was. Probably a duck-billed platypus, I thought, and tried to relax.

It was farther to the bootlegger's by road than it was on foot. We had to follow the side road until it reached the main road and then turn back towards the old house.

Before we reached the main road we passed a patch of woods on the right side of the road, and I saw something that made me suspicious of my unconscious again. Two men wearing bright plaid blankets around them and colored leaves in their hair came running out of the woods towards the car, yelling and waving their arms.

Gordon stopped the car and we sat and watched them climb over the fence and jump across the ditch to the road.

"Can you give us a lift to town?" one of them asked. He stuck his head in the open window on my side and I saw the tear-stains on his face and recognized him.

I said to Gordon. "These are the two men that left the bootlegger's when Ruth Esch did."

"Get into the back seat," Gordon said and they climbed in, clutching their blankets around them.

"I've got to get to the police," the weepy one said. "My car has been stolen."

Gordon turned around in his seat and said, "I'm a police agent. Where have you been?"

"In the woods, sleeping," said the other babe in the woods. I turned and looked at them. Their eyes were like boiled Brussels sprouts and their faces were sicklied o'er with the pale cast of a hangover.

"On a camping party, boys?" Gordon said. "I was just going to start looking for you."

"Hell, no," said the man who wept, beyond irony. "Our clothes were stolen. And my car." His eyes glistened with unshed tears, and I reached for a handkerchief.

"By a red-headed woman?"

"How did you know? Say, did you catch her?"

"Not yet," Gordon said. He started the car and in a minute we turned into the main road.

"Well, you better get busy. I want to see that dame put away for a good long time. She asks me for a lift and she looks like a lady and naturally I give her one at that time of morning. But after we drive down the road a piece, she pulls a gun on us and makes us get out of the car and take off our clothes and drives away with the car *and* the clothes. First time a hitch-hiker ever fooled me and, by Jesus, it's the last—"

Gordon cut him off. "Why didn't you report this theft sooner?"

The other man spoke, "Well, Johnnie here was awful broken up, and when she took his car he went off in the woods and was sick."

"No, I wasn't," Johnnie said, "I was just sad. My dear wife, and then my dear car—"

"Yes, he was," the other man said. "I went to find him and he had passed out. I couldn't wake him up so I covered him with leaves and let him sleep. I couldn't leave him in that condition, so I kept guard over him—"

"You passed out, too," Johnnie said.

"Oh, I did not. I—"

"I'm taking you to the local police," Gordon said. "They'll ask you to swear out a warrant for the woman's arrest."

"Nothing I'd like better," said Johnnie. The tears of things were not affecting him so strongly now, and he seemed to have given up the idea of weeping.

A minute later I felt like weeping myself.

Gordon turned down the lane under the trees, and I saw the old barn and the dingy house. The barn looked even worse by day, like a corpse in sunlight. The sight of the house with the paint peeling off was not improved by the black police car which stood in front of it.

As we drew up behind it, a sharp-nosed man in plain clothes came out of the house and let out a combination of a whoop and a sneer.

Haggerty came down the porch steps with the speed of a weasel and said to me, "Get out."

I got out.

187

He said, "Hold out your hands."

In a dazed hope that he might be going to give me something to eat, I held out my hands. He snapped handcuffs on my wrists.

chapter xii

THE blanket boys goggled and Johnnie whined, "Say, he was in here just before that woman came in. I bet he's one of the gang."

I said, "Have a good cry about it," and turned to Haggerty: "if you arrest me, sergeant, I'm going to sue you for false arrest."

Haggerty pushed his face at me as if he intended to stab me with his nose. "Yeah? What do you mean, professor, false arrest?"

I said, "I didn't kill Schneider. He was killed by his son and a woman called Ruth Esch. The same woman that stole this man's car. Take these things off me and go and catch them." Go and catch a falling star, my mind chattered. Go and catch whooping cough.

"I know about her," Haggerty said. "Shiny told me. And maybe you didn't kill Judd and Schneider. Maybe you did. While I'm finding out, I'm going to book you for larceny, aggravated assault, and obstructing an officer in the performance of his duty."

"Obstructing, hell." The handcuffs saved me from another charge of aggravated assault. They were better than a rope, but they pinched my wrists.

I turned to Gordon, who had got out of the car. "For Christ's sake, tell this—detective to take these handcuffs off me."

Haggerty burst out, "This isn't a Federal matter. Damn it—"

"Better take them off," Gordon said. "Dr. Branch has had a bad night of it, and he needs medical attention. Less than an hour ago, Peter Schneider tried to murder him by hanging."

"I can't run the risk of letting him get away again," Haggerty said.

"Take them off," Gordon repeated. "You'll have other chances to display them."

Haggerty turned a delicate amethystine color but he produced a key-ring and took the handcuffs off my wrists. Encouraged by Gordon's support, I said, "What time do they serve breakfast at the jail?"

Haggerty threatened me with his nose again. "It'll pay you to be respectful, professor. You're going to learn respect for the law."

Gordon said, "Has the woman been found?"

"No," said Haggerty. "Every main road is being watched. And we have men at the airport and the station."

"This man wants to report the theft of his car." Gordon jerked his thumb at Johnnie, who was still staring at me. "It was evidently taken by Ruth Esch. She also took their clothes."

Haggerty motioned to Johnnie to get out of the car and said, "License number and description?"

"Just a minute, sergeant," Gordon said. "I have to get away."

"Yeah?"

"Any sign of Peter Schneider?"

"He hasn't been caught. His car was seen by a gas-station attendant on the other side of Arbana, at least it was a green coupe with one man in it."

"Headed where?"

"Direction of the Bomber Plant."

"You can take these men into town."

"O.K. Especially this one." Haggerty jabbed a thumb towards me.

"Treat him kindly, Sergeant," Gordon said, with just enough condescension to make me want to kick him. "Oh, yes, there's another thing I wanted to ask you, Haggerty. Did the operator tell you anything that was said on the line into Judd's office last night?"

"Yeah, but it didn't make any sense."

"I'll decide that," Gordon said sharply. "What was it?"

"Don't get your shirt-tail in a knot. I was just trying to remember the exact words. I think it was: 'Get up, old man, get up. You can't stay there all day.' Something like that."

"I see. Perhaps I'd better talk to her myself. What was her name?"

"Hilda Kramm, I think," Haggerty said. "They can tell you at the U exchange."

"No doubt they can," Gordon barked. "But it's your duty as an officer to keep accurate records. In a murder case, they are precisely a matter of life and death."

"Murder! My. God, are you going off the deep end—"

Gordon delivered a look that shut Haggerty off in mid-sentence, and slid behind the wheel of his car.

Three separate things were jostling in my mind, which the terror and exhaustion of the night had already pulled apart at the seams. One was the intense pleasure of hearing Haggerty rated for incompetence by a professional superior. One was a wild guess about the meaning of Alec's telephone conversation. I thought of Poe's Valdemar, and the Wizard King who could hypnotize people at a distance. Could Alec have been hynotized and commanded over the telephone to *get up* on the windowsill and jump to his death? The idea seemed fantastic, but I had a friend in the Psychology Department who had shown me what hypnotism could do.

The third was the duck-billed platypus who was still swimming around in my unconscious, very near the surface. As Gordon's car started to move, he came up for air and my conscious mind got hold of him. His name was Rudolf Fisher.

"Gordon!" I yelled. "Wait a minute!"

He braked the car and leaned his head out of the window. "What is it, Branch?"

"A possible lead on Schneider. Alec Judd suspected a man named Rudolf Fisher of being Dr. Schneider's contact man with the Detroit ring. Your Detroit office has investigated Fisher and they should be able to tell you where to find him. Rudolf Fisher—I think he's a naturalized German."

"Right. I'll look into it." He waved his hand and threw out the clutch. The whine of his engine mounted like a small siren as he went up the lane.

Haggerty climbed the stairs to the porch and yelled through the open door, "Hey, Joe! Let's go!"

A policeman in uniform emerged from the house and Haggerty said, "Stay away from that tart if you don't want syph. Her last customer didn't have any nose."

"You should give him some of yours," I said under my breath so he wouldn't hear me. "A nose-transfusion."

Haggerty put me in the front seat beside the policeman and got into the back seat with the Indian braves. As we drove away, I could feel his eyes on the back of my neck.

I said over my shoulder, "If you won't tell me when breakfast is served, will you tell me whether there are any beds in the jail?"

Haggerty said, "There are. But don't be so cocky, professor. They're not comfortable."

The policeman behind the wheel said, "Want me to shut him up, Sarge?"

"Don't touch me, officer," I said, "until you have a Wassermann test."

"Leave him alone," Haggerty said. "He nearly got hanged. And I think he's nuts. He talks nuts."

"My sleep was strangely troubled last night," I said. "Mind if I snooze?"

Haggerty began to question Johnnie about his car

and paid no attention to me. I rested my head against the back of the seat and went to sleep. I was sitting in a dentist's chair with my head back saying, "It's the tooth in my throat that troubles me, doctor." He reached into my throat with a pair of gilded tongs which he drew from his beard, and when he pulled them out they were spattered with blood. Then I saw that he had green eyes and long hair like a woman, made of twisted hemp. He curtsied to me and I saw the hole in the top of his head and the announcer said, "Arbana station."

"I said wake up, Branch," Haggerty said. "We're at the station."

I opened my eyes and blinked and got out of the car, balancing my head on top of a stiff neck. Haggerty took me by the arm.

He said to the driver, "Better take these guys home to get some clothes on," and the police car moved away.

It was just eight by the electric clock in the hallway of the police station. Lieutenant Cross was going off duty but he stayed to help question me. They took me into a bare back room and asked questions for nearly an hour while a policeman took shorthand notes.

I could have refused to talk or demanded a lawyer but I was too tired to bother. I answered all their questions and told them everything I knew.

When they had finished, Cross said to Haggerty, "I'm going to put this man in the hospital, sergeant. Under guard. He looks as if he needs a doctor."

"I need a cook," I said. "And an oculist. I don't think my neck needs setting."

"They'll feed you at the hospital," Cross said.

They did. Coddled eggs and toast that retained its shape no matter how you bent it. Before that I had to take a bath and the nurse wondered how the patient got so filthy and I said I didn't know, I'd have to ask him, but I thought he was preparing to write an article on barnyard imagery in Shakespeare.

After that they x-rayed my neck and an oculist put drops in my eyes. He took my broken glasses to have the lenses reground, and left me alone with a policeman. Policemen had begun to bore me, and I wriggled my toes between the sweet, clean sheets, turned over and went to sleep. Those whom the gods wish to go to sleep, they first make sleepy.

I was awakened for lunch, which began with a bowl of chicken broth and ended with cornstarch pudding. "You must keep your strength up," the nurse said, and I didn't laugh because my laughing apparatus had congealed. Also, because they'd probably put me in jail if they found out that I wasn't an invalid.

While I was still inflicting cornstarch on my palate, an orderly brought me my mended glasses. I polished them on a corner of the sheet and put them on and looked around. They let me see things more clearly but the new lenses didn't filter out the policeman. He was still there sitting inside the door, moving his jaws scissorwise like a camel.

"Have you got a cigarette?" I asked.

"Not me, professor." He exhibited a wad of tobacco between his teeth. Then he moved to the window to spit.

I noticed that the window was the same as those in McKinley Hall: the heavy steel-sashed lower pane swung outward from the top, supported by steel arms at the sides. I remembered that the hospital was a university building, built at the same time as McKinley, by the same contractor. I also noticed that my room was on the ground floor of the hospital, and that the window was only a few feet above the lawn of an inner courtyard.

I said to the policeman, "Would you get me a pack of cigarettes? The booth is just down the corridor, I think."

"Sorry," he said. "My orders are to stay here."

"You don't think I'm going to run away in a night-shirt that barely covers my navel, do you?"

"A guy ran away from this hospital once without anything on at all," the policeman said. "He was coocoo."

"Listen, I haven't had a smoke for twenty-four hours. I'll give you two dollars for twenty cigarettes."

"Where's the money?"

"At the station. What's your name? I won't forget you."

"Stevenson," he said. "Robert Louis Stevenson."

"You're looking better, R.L.S.," I said. "Will you do it?"

"Well, I hate to see a guy suffer. What brand?"

"Something mild," I said. "My throat needs kindness."

He spat out of the window again and sauntered out of the room.

The window had given me an idea. I got out of bed and opened the lower section wide, so that the pane was horizontal, with two-foot spaces below it and above it. Across the courtyard in another wing of the hospital, a window-cleaner was cleaning the upper pane of another window like mine. He had opened the lower pane wide and was sitting on it as he worked. When I saw the window-cleaner, my idea became a momentary obsession.

I climbed onto the sill and sat on the pane like the window-cleaner, with my feet on the sill. I raised my feet and swivelled on the cold, smooth glass, keeping my weight on the inner end of the pane. When my feet were pointing outwards, I leaned back and slid forward until my legs were hanging over the outer edge and my shoulders rested on the steel sash at the inner edge.

I felt like somebody's sweetie laid out on a table in St. James Infirmary, and I wondered what an unconscious man would do if he came to in that position.

There was a bellow from the room behind me,

"Hey!" and I sat up startled. The window partly closed under my weight and I tobogganed into air. But it was a drop of only four or five feet and I landed on all fours in the grass without hurting myself.

Haggerty stuck his nose and a gun out of the window and said, "Stay where you are."

I said, "Throw me a sheet then. My knees are naked to the blast. As well as my—"

"I said you were nuts," Haggerty growled but he threw me a sheet and I disguised myself as Julius Caesar. He clambered over the sill, dropped to the ground, and seized my togaed arm.

Feeling unpleasant and at the same time unaccountably gay, I said, "Et tu, Haggerty? Then die, Caesar."

"Jesus," Haggerty said to himself, looking at me with the awe policemen reserve for rich men and lunatics. "He really *is* nuts."

He spoke to me in dulcet accents, as to a little child, "C'mon, professor, let's you and me just go inside eh? What are you doing out here anyway, eh?"

"Reconstructing the crime," I said.

"C'mon, professor, that's all right, forget it. Don't bother your head anymore with that awful tragedy. You've had an awful night."

He twisted his face into what he thought was a smile of kindly solicitude, and led me gently but firmly towards a side door, babbling lines from Grade B movies:

"Everything's going to be all right, professor. You just have a nice, long rest and everything's going to be jake. President Galloway's here to see you and we're going to drop our charges against you."

"You mean I can get out?"

"You don't have to run away, professor. Nobody's going to hurt you. You just stay in bed and have a nice, long rest."

"Like hell I will. Bring me my clothes."

Haggerty led me into my room and urged me towards the bed with friendly grimaces. The policeman with the camel jaws was standing by the bed, looking sullen and betrayed. He said:

"I just went down the hall for a drink of water, and when I came back this bastard is out the window."

"Where's Galloway?" I said. "If you won't bring me my clothes, bring me Galloway."

"You just get in bed now," Haggerty said, "and I'll bring you anybody you want. Then you can have a nice sleep and forget all about this awful calamity."

I sat down on the edge of the bed as a concession and said, "You damn fool, I think I know how Judd was murdered."

Haggerty looked at me and it began to dawn on him that I wasn't crazy after all. I could see the sun rising in his eyes. Midnight sun. He said:

"None of that talk now, professor. You can't talk like that to an officer of the law. I could be pretty nasty about you trying to escape again."

"I wasn't trying to escape. I was going to tell you how Judd was killed. Now I'm not going to give it to you."

"He wanted to confess, sarge," said the ship of the desert. "Want me to take it down?"

"Bring me my clothes," I said. "And take me to Galloway."

"Listen, professor." Haggerty's personality shifted again but it was still deficient. "If you know something, it's your duty to tell us. Come on, professor, let's have it."

I thought of the handcuffs and the thought left me feeling unpleasant and not at all gay. "I wouldn't trust you with an old menu. I want to talk to a detective who isn't moribund above the coccyx. Bring me my clothes."

Then I remembered that the clothes I had been wearing would make a good tail for a kite.

A nurse opened the door and said to Haggerty, "Does the patient seem able to receive visitors?

President Galloway is waiting in the office to see him."

"It depends upon the visitors," I said. "These gentlemen, for example, irk me. Please take them away and bring the president."

Haggerty turned red and said, "You'll have to talk at the inquest to-morrow morning." He went out and the other policeman followed him, shaking his head over my treachery.

After covering my legs with a sheet so as not to arouse her, I called in the nurse:

"Will you do something for me, nurse?"

"It depends on what it is," she said, as if I looked capable of anything. I remembered my eyes.

"Will you call up the janitor of the Plaza Apartments and tell him to bring me some clothes?"

"I can't do that," she said. "You have to be released by a doctor."

"Is Dr. Meinzinger, in Surgery, here now?"

"I think so."

"Bring him here. He'll release me. And then call Max Simon at the Plaza and tell him to bring me a complete outfit in a taxi as fast as he can. Suit, shirt, tie, shoes, socks. Underwear. From my apartment."

"Yes, sir, if Dr. Meinzinger releases you."

"Tell him that if he doesn't, I'll remove his thyroid gland without benefit of ether. And please tell President Galloway I'll be very glad to see him."

"Yes, sir." She crackled off down the hall.

I got up and put on my toga and looked out the door. There was an office across the hall with an open door and a telephone on the desk. So far as I could see, there was nobody in the office.

I ran across the hall, closed the door behind me, and sat down at the desk. I dialed the police station and asked to speak to the motorcycle officer who had interviewed Dr. Schneider about his automobile accident. I couldn't remember his name.

"Who is speaking, please?"

"Beaumont Fletcher," I said recklessly, "of the F.B.I. Quickly, please."

"Yes, sir."

The motorcycle officer came to the phone and said, "Yes, Mr. Fletcher? Moran speaking."

I said, "When you interviewed Dr. Schneider last night, did he do any phoning? Or did his son do any phoning?"

He thought a moment and said, "No, sir. None of them did any phoning while I was there."

"You're sure?"

"Yes, sir."

I said, "Thanks," and hung up.

Then somebody else must have called Alec and told him to get up. Ruth Esch? I didn't see how she could have, because she hadn't got back to her hotel until ten to twelve. And when she got there, she had had to take a phone call herself. The call on Alec's line had been put in soon after 11:30, the operator thought. Did Peter and Ruth have a third accomplice?

But according to my reconstruction, Alec was unconscious until five minutes after twelve; otherwise, he'd have heard Helen Madden at the door and answered her. How could anybody have telephoned him if he was unconscious?

I couldn't work it out. I remembered where I was and got up and went into the hall. The nurse was coming down the hall towards me with President Galloway. I pretended to be a lost sheet blowing idly in the wind and scampered inconspicuously back into my room.

I was in bed when the nurse opened the door and said, "Naughty, naughty, Mr. Branch. You haven't been released yet. But I've brought you a visitor."

"Thank you. I was just testing my legs. Now bring me Bill Meinzinger and my clothes. Max Simon. Plaza."

She went away again and Galloway came across the room with his hand out. I shook the hand that had shaken the hands of governors and penetrated the pockets of wealthy alumni.

"How are you, Robert, how are you?" Galloway intoned with the extreme urbanity of embarrassment. "You've had a fearful ordeal."

"I feel all right, thanks. A bit stiff, but I needed exercise. I understand the police are letting me out of here."

"Chester Gordon and I talked with Garvin, the county prosecutor, this morning. Gordon found the marks of Schneider's bullets in the Dictionary room. Garvin decided that—this—was all a mistake and he took immediate steps to rectify it. Perhaps you acted a trifle—er—indiscreetly, Robert, but the rest of us were decidedly obtuse. I feel very badly that you should have been—forcibly detained."

"I had a good sleep. There's nothing like a police guard to keep people away from you—and you away from people. Has Peter Schneider been caught?"

"Not yet. But they're hot on his trail, I understand."

"Where's Gordon now?"

"At McKinley Hall, I believe. After we spoke with Garvin, he said he was going to make a thorough examination of Alec's office. He may very well be there still."

Bill Meinzinger put his long, intelligent Savonarola face in at the door and said:

"Hello, Bob. I hear you want to see me."

"Pardon me," I said to Galloway. "Do you know Dr. Meinzinger? President Galloway."

They shook hands and I said, "Did you see my x-ray pictures?"

"Yeah," Bill said. "Your neck's O.K." He reached over and dug his fingers into it. It hurt and I threw up my hand to ward him off.

The sleeve of my hospital gown fell down and exposed my forearm and he shifted his attention to it.

"What's the matter with your arm?" he said. "Intravenous? Whoever did it bungled it."

I looked at my arm and saw the blue circular bruise as big as a nickel just below my elbow. As soon as I looked at it, I was conscious that it hurt slightly. I remembered the sharp stab I had felt in my arm when Peter Schneider had me hog-tied in the barn.

"I guess that's what it is," I said. "I was drugged this morning when I—"

"I heard about that," Bill said. "You don't know what drug it was, do you?"

"No."

"What were your subjective symptoms?"

"I just went out like a light, it felt like floating away. Like sudden death. When I came to, I had a hangover head."

"How long were you out?"

"I don't know. It couldn't have been so very long. Perhaps half an hour."

"It sounds like sodium pentothal to me," Bill said.

"What's that?"

"One of the barbiturates. Nothing to worry about; in fact, we've been using it a couple of years for bone-setting and the like. I understand they're using it in the army now for battle fatigue. 20 c.c. will put a man out in about ten seconds, and keep him that way for twenty minutes to half an hour. No ill-effects, except that it leaves him feeling as if he's been on a jag." He stopped lecturing and looked at my arm again. "Your man knows the latest in *materia medica*, but he's no hell at giving an intravenous."

"He's good enough," I said. Suddenly I thought of something: "Would this drug—sodium pentothal, is it?—show up in a post-mortem?"

"Probably not, unless death occurred immediately after the injection. It's excreted very rapidly. The mark of the needle would show, of course. It usually bruises the tissue a bit. But if you had succeeded in hanging yourself, there'd likely have been no trace except the mark on your arm, that is if it was sodium pentothal."

"Watch those eyes," he said. "I'll give the nurse some drops for you."

"Can I get out of here now?"

"If you want to. Don't you want more sleep? Or have you decided to break off the sleeping habit?"

"I have a date with the F.B.I."

"Take care of yourself. Alec is going to be missed."

"He certainly is," Galloway said.

I said to Bill, "Tell the nurse I'm free, will you?"

"O.K. So long. Good day, Dr. Galloway."

Bill went away and I turned to Galloway, who had sat down in a chair beside the window. "Have they captured Ruth Esch?"

"No, they haven't." After a pause, he said as if he were contemplating a newly-discovered department of the university:

"It's something I can't understand, how scholars like Dr. Schneider, devotees of the humanities, can sink to such a level."

"Pro patria. They're Germans. One-third of the officers of the Nazi party are school-teachers, or used to be. But I can't understand the Esch woman." I tried to think and talk about her as impersonally as I could. "When I knew her in Germany she was liberal to the core."

"Schneider, too, seemed to be a genuine liberal," Galloway said. "He had taken out his American papers, you know. I've rarely been so mistaken in a man."

"I hardly took Alec's suspicions seriously at first, yesterday." Yesterday seemed very remote, something seen through the wrong end of a telescope. "I was trying so hard to be liberal and tolerant that I couldn't see straight. Alec himself tried too hard to be fair. If he had gone to the police right away, he'd be alive now. But he gave Schneider an even break, and it cost him the best years of his life."

"He was a good and useful man," Galloway said. "We shan't be able to replace him."

The nurse opened the door, and Max Simon followed her in with my clothes over his arm. Everybody went out and I put them on in a hurry, cursing Max's ideas of color-harmony under my breath.

Galloway drove me to McKinley Hall and left me on the first floor to go into his own office. I started up the stairs two at a time. Halfway up to the fifth floor, I met Gordon coming down. He looked tired and strained—he couldn't have had any sleep yet—but more friendly than he had been.

"Hello," I said. "I'm a free man, thanks to you."

"Good. How do you feel?"

"Better than I look. I want to talk to you, Gordon."

"Make it fast. I'm on my way."

"Then you've figured it out?"

"How Judd was killed? No, I haven't. I read the police reports, and the record of your testimony, and went over the room. But it doesn't come clear. The autopsist found the marks of an intravenous injection on his arm, so it's fairly certain he was drugged. But that doesn't fit in with his being conscious when he fell. Are you sure about that?"

"Yes, and so was Helen Madden. It fits in. Come up to the office, will you? I think I can show you how it was done."

He stopped straining at the conversation like a whippet on a leash and came along quietly to Alec's office. Nothing had been changed in it since I saw it last the night before, except that the telephone-receiver had been replaced and the window closed.

I opened the bottom pane wide, swinging it out to a horizontal position. Then I lifted the dumbbell shaped receiver-transmitter from the telephone on the shelf beside the window, and hooked the receiver end over the inner edge of the sash so that it hung there precariously.

"What are you doing?" Gordon asked, with a resurgence of impatience in his voice.

"I'm reconstructing a delayed-action murder. The principle is much the same as that of my own hanging-party. It's the principle of the booby-trap, which is arranged in such a way that the victim destroys himself by his own efforts. It's a clever idea but Schneider made the mistake of applying it twice. The repetition of a phenomenon leads to generalization."

I deliberately adopted the dry and impersonal manner of a lecturer, partly because it was the easiest way to talk about Alec's death, partly because Gordon had been too condescending in the morning. He took it very well:

"I think you're right. I had the same idea but I couldn't make it fit the circumstances. As a matter of fact, I found out from Schneider's housekeeper this morning that Peter had been trained in the German army as a booby-trap expert."

"Did you find out anything else?"

"Nothing important, except that Peter almost never came home because he got on badly with his father. The old woman's either completely ignorant and innocent, or devilishly clever. Go on with your reconstruction, Branch."

I took the chain of the wall-lamp beside the window, which was still sticky at the end, and fastened it to the inside corner of the open pane with the piece of adhesive which was still there.

"That's all," I said. "I'm not sure of all of this but I'm sure of most of it: Peter drove the Esch woman down to the hotel, where she registered about eleven. Meanwhile, Alec found his evidence against Dr. Schneider and hid it in the Dictionary office. On the way home, Peter spotted Alec's car in front of McKinley and followed him in here—he must have had one of his father's keys. Alec heard somebody in the building and phoned me, but before he could finish, Peter surprised and overpowered him. He gave Alec a shot of sodium pentothal or some other quick-acting drug to put him to sleep. Then he phoned Ruth at the hotel, because he needed help. She must have come up here by taxi in a hurry.

"They carried Alec up here, opened this window wide, and laid him out flat on it. Then they called up an accomplice on Alec's telephone, and hung the receiver on the window like this. They didn't leave anything to chance. The accomplice kept on saying, 'Get up,' or something of the sort over the telephone—"

"That's right," Gordon said. "I talked to the operator. The exact words she heard were, 'Get up, old man, get up!'"

I went on: "That was the unintelligible voice Helen Madden heard through the door. When Alec came to, he heard the insistent voice telling him to get up. He didn't know where he was, his mind was dazed and confused by the drug, and he said, 'I don't feel like it, but I will if I have to.' Helen heard him. He sat up, the window partly closed under his weight, and he fell to the pavement. The person on the other end of the wire hung up."

"Why do you assume an accomplice, Branch? The principle of scientific parsimony—"

"There must have been one," I cut in brashly. "Peter did no telephoning after he got home. When Ruth got back to the hotel, she had a phone-call waiting for her to establish the time of her alibi, and she couldn't have done it. They couldn't have called Alec anyway: an unconscious man can't answer the telephone."

Gordon didn't look tired any longer. There were tiny candle-flames of excitement in his black eyes. He said:

"Ruth Esch called *herself* at the hotel before she left this office. Then she wiped the receiver—or more likely she wore gloves—and hung it on the window and rushed down in a taxi to take the call at the other end. Certainly, it helped to establish her alibi, but it meant as well that she could sit down in her room and listen to his every movement over the telephone. She could persuade him to get up and make sure that he died. Perhaps she heard him cry out as he fell, perhaps the fall of the receiver when the window closed was all she waited for."

I had a clear, ugly vision of the woman sitting in a chair in her hotel room listening to a man die by telephone, with bright concentration in her green eyes.

"Look," Gordon said, stealing my thunder. "When the window closed under Judd's weight, the receiver would be knocked off."

He closed the pane to an angle of thirty degrees with the vertical, and the receiver was knocked off by the bottom sash of the upper pane. He caught it as it fell. "The sound of the jar and the fall would be enough for her. If Judd had somehow got back into the room, he'd have tried to phone the police and she'd have heard him."

When Gordon closed the window, the chain attached to the upper corner jerked the wall-lamp on and broke loose from the adhesive tape.

"That explains the light going on," I said. "They couldn't leave the light on when they left him on the window for fear he'd be seen from outside. They unscrewed the bulb on the corner for the same reason. They arranged for the light to go on when he fell, because a fall from a lighted room would look more like suicide."

"A suicide in the dark is a rare thing," Gordon said. "That Nazi pair is well informed—not that I ever thought the democracies had a corner on intelligence. The light was one of the things that puzzled me, and the window was another. I didn't think he could have been lying on the window, I didn't think it would bear a man's weight."

"These windows are heavy glass," I said, "and the

sashes are steel. The Buildings men sit on them when they clean the upper panes. I just tried lying on one of them at the hospital about an hour ago." I didn't go into the details. "It worked all right."

Gordon surprised me by holding out his hand. "I owe you an apology," he said. "Frankly, I thought you were a bit of a damn nuisance this morning. I don't think so now."

"I have my uses," I said. "I made a good guinea pig for Schneider to experiment with and give himself away. But he still has to be caught."

"He still has to be caught," Gordon agreed. "The woman has disappeared completely, but Peter has been traced as far as the Bomber Plant. I'm on my way there now."

"Take me along."

The sullen shadow passed over Gordon's face and drew down the corners of his mouth. For five seconds he said nothing.

Then he said, "Let's go."

chapter xiii

I PICKED up a trench coat I had hanging in my office and we went down to the president's office on the first floor. Gordon went in to report to Galloway and I remembered that I had no money in my pockets and went down the hall to the Business Office to cash a check.

On the way out I met Helen Madden in the hall. She was walking slowly and meticulously like a woman learning to walk again after a long illness. She was very well groomed, as if she had had nothing else to do all night. She came up to me and put a kid-gloved hand on my arm and said:

"I'm sorry, Bob. I thought I was doing the right thing but I made a mistake."

"I make hundreds. I made a dozen last night—"

"I thought you'd gone off the deep end. I was the one that had."

I said: "We're all in this together. Death is the least rational thing there is, and it affects everybody whether they know it or not. When a man is murdered, everyone gets a little irrational."

"Was he murdered, Bob? I was sure he killed himself, but I didn't know why he should."

"He was murdered." I told her because any spoken word is better than newsprint. "Peter Schneider and his woman drugged him and left him on the window to fall out when he came to. He came to and fell when you were at the door."

"Why did they kill him? They didn't even know him."

"To cover up for Dr. Schneider. Three hours later they killed Dr. Schneider to cover up for themselves. It's the Nazi principle that killing people is less complicated than living with them. If they were allowed to carry it to its logical conclusion, the world would be populated by the 6,600,000 members of the Nazi party and their women and children and some slaves."

My little lecture sounded *gauche* in my own ears but I thought it might help Helen to see Alec's death in perspective. Then I realized that it would take her years. Perhaps it would take me as long.

She said, "Have they been caught?"

"No, but they will be. The F.B.I. is after them and they can't get away. I'm going to Detroit now with the F.B.I. man, Gordon."

She said, "Kill them," through jaws so tense that her teeth chattered.

After a pause I said, "I'd like to talk to you tomorrow or so. You'll be around?"

"No," she said. "I hate this city. I'm going away as soon as we bury Alec. I applied at the Red Cross this morning. It's funny how a city can change overnight. I loved it yesterday and today there's dust over everything."

I had nothing to say. I couldn't even say, "You'll get over it in time," because I didn't think she would.

I said, "I hope I see you before you leave."

She gave me her hand and said, "I hope so, too." My eyes followed her down the hall. Something in the way she moved made me think of a naked woman in a cold place.

I went back to the president's office and sat down in the anteroom to wait for Gordon. Through the closed door to the inner office, I could hear him telephoning.

Galloway's secretary, a faded blonde who had every department of the university filed and classified in her mind and was always looking for new items to file, stopped typing when I sat down, and started to pump me.

While she was still priming me with rumors, Gordon came out of the inner office and overheard the conversation. He closed the door behind him and said:

"We're keeping this thing out of the news for the present. It will help us to catch them if they don't know we're looking for them, or how hard. So the less talk about it the better."

The faded secretary faded some more and went back to her typing, jabbing at the keys as if they were hostile eyes.

Gordon said, "Ready, Branch?" and I followed him out to the black sedan. We got in and headed for Detroit.

On the outskirts we passed a police patrol and I said, "There's been no sign of Ruth Esch?"

"No. Nor Schneider. I've just been talking to the Detroit office. They've telegraphed their description to police all over the Middle West."

"What about Kirkland Lake?"

"And Kirkland Lake. All the leading cities in Ontario, in fact. We're going to send out circulars if they're not in our hands by to-morrow."

"Has the Detroit office gotten hold of Rudolf Fisher?"

"Not yet. We've got a man watching his house. When he comes home he'll be picked up. I want to question him myself."

"And that's where we're going now, is it?"

"Eventually. I'm going to stop at the Bomber Plant on the way. The green coupe answering to the description of Schneider's car was last identified turning in at the Bomber Plant. I've got an idea about that."

I had asked too many questions and I said nothing, but my silence hung question-marks in the air. Gordon went on talking with his eyes on the road ahead:

"Schneider's car hasn't been seen on the other side

of the Bomber Plant. It may have been missed, but it's more likely that he turned into the plant to throw off pursuit. The entrance guards insist that he couldn't get in without an employee's badge. But his name's not on the list of employees. For that matter, he hasn't a car license under his own name either."

"Is it your idea that he may have been working at the Bomber Plant under another name?"

"Yes. If I'm right I don't think I have to look any further for the saboteur we've been hunting."

"Galloway said something about your being at the Bomber Plant last night."

"I've been there every day for a month," Gordon said, "pretending to be a maintenance man. Half the time on the night shift. We've had a man in every department—I don't have to tell you to keep this to yourself, Branch. We didn't catch anybody, but there's been no sabotage for a couple of weeks."

"Peter Schneider went to Canada a week or two ago," I said. "Maybe the coincidence isn't fortuitous. And when he was in Kirkland Lake according to Ruth's letter, there was a mass escape of German prisoners from a prison camp near there. It could be that he's a very active and versatile young man. He's a bungler, though. He sets his hand to too many things. He bungled my execution, and all the prisoners have been caught or killed."

"Not all," Gordon said. "They killed or recaptured all the Bonamy prisoners but one. A certain Captain von Esch is still at large."

"*Captain von Esch!* What's his first name?"

"I don't know. We're looking out for him, of course, but he hasn't been seen in the United States. I could find out, if you think you know him. Do you know the whole German nation, Branch?"

"I know Captain von Esch if he's Ruth Esch's brother. I met him once. Her name was originally von Esch before she dropped the von. Her brother's name is Carl."

"I'll check on it," Gordon said. "This thing may have greater ramifications than we realized."

Ruth Esch had greater ramifications than I realized, I said to myself. She must have gone to Kirkland Lake to help her brother to escape. A woman doesn't travel five hundred miles north to a country of forests and bare rock on a pleasure jaunt. Yet even when I condemned her to myself, there was a residue of my old feeling for her in my mind, an irrational hope that she would escape or die or dissolve into thin air before she was caught. Peter Schneider was the one I wanted to see again. He had taken me in three rounds and I was waiting for the fourth. It was getting to be a long time between rounds.

The highway curved up over a rise and the Bomber Plant came in sight ahead and to the right. It lay low on the horizon in the afternoon sun like a walled city in a wasteland. For a mile or more the road followed the high net fence, supported by steel posts and crowned by barbed wire, that surrounded the plant. Then we came to the wide entrance gates and turned in.

A fat uniformed guard, with Auxiliary Military Police on his left shoulder, stepped into the path of the car and stopped us. Gordon took out his wallet and showed the guard his credentials: "Is your group leader around? I'd like to speak to him."

"Yeah, he's over at the Exit gate. I'll go and get him. You better swing your car in over there." He pointed to the back of the new red-brick building marked Employment Office, and waddled away with his holster swinging against his hip.

When we turned the corner of the building, I saw the green coupe parked at the curb.

I whispered to keep from shouting, "That's Peter Schneider's car."

"It looks like it," Gordon said.

He parked and we got out and looked at the coupe. It was a 1938 Ford V-8, an ordinary enough car but I didn't like it. It had chased me down a dirt road at dawn. Now it sat at the curb, quiet and dead, like an empty green beetle shell.

Gordon searched the back of the seat and the dashboard cupboard. The ignition key was in place but there was nothing in the car. He got behind the wheel and started the engine. It started smoothly enough but I noticed that the needle of the tank gauge pointed to Empty. Gordon saw it, too:

"He may have seen that he was running out of gas and left his car here so he wouldn't have to abandon it on the road."

"Maybe he ran out of coupons," I said.

Gordon said unsmilingly: "He must have got here this morning about when the shift changes. That would give him a good chance to take a bus to Detroit without being observed."

The engine coughed and Gordon switched it off. A weather-beaten man in a blue uniform with wide shoulders and a narrow waist hugged by a black Sam Browne belt came round the corner.

"My name's Killoran," he said. "You're Mr. Gordon, isn't that right?"

"Yes. Where did you pick up this car?"

"We went over the parking-lots when you phoned us and found this over behind the Bomber School, and we brought it here. I don't know if it's the one you want but it answers the description."

"You keep a file of the employees' license-numbers, don't you?"

"Yeah, only this crate is listed under a guy called Ludwig Vlathek."

"It is, eh?" Gordon looked at me and I looked at him. "I want your complete file on Ludwig Vlathek."

Killoran turned to the fat guard, who had trailed him around the corner at a distance. "Raym, get the file on Ludwig Vlathek. V-L-A-T-H-E-K. If there's more than one Vlathek, it's the one with the California birth-certificate I want."

Raym heaved himself out of sight. I wondered about the birth-certificate, but remembered that they can be forged.

"What's this guy wanted for?" Killoran asked.

"Read it in the papers," Gordon said, "if it's the right man. Was there anything in the car?"

"Not a thing. Just a jack and crank under the seat. Oh, yeah, and an old newspaper. I swiped it to take home. I don't often get to see a Canadian newspaper."

"Give it to me," Gordon said. "And in future leave things as you find them."

Killoran produced a wooden, "Yessir," and brought the paper out of his inside breast pocket.

Gordon unfolded it and I looked at it over his shoulder. It was the Toronto *Globe and Mail* of the day before. He riffled through it hurriedly, scanning it page by page. Near the top of page eight, directly below a picture of Wendell Willkie, there was a piece torn out.

"It would be interesting," Gordon said, "to know what our friend tore out of a Canadian newspaper."

"Our good friend, Bonamy," I said cryptically because Killoran was standing beside us with his ears perked up. "I can find out, the university library takes it. Let's see, third column on page eight."

"I'll have a man check it in the Detroit Library," Gordon said.

Raym appeared with a heavy paper folder under his arm. He handed it to Killoran and Killoran handed it to Gordon.

"It's all here, is it, captain?" Gordon said. "Thanks for your co-operation. Hold the car until you hear from us, will you?"

"Yeah. Good luck." He went away with Raym at his heels.

Gordon and I climbed into the black sedan and he opened the folder. Attached to one of the sheets there was a small photograph, hardly bigger than passport size, of a man's head and collar.

"Do you recognize Ludwig Vlathek?" Gordon said and handed me the picture.

Vlathek's hair was dark and curly but his skin looked very fair. The eyebrows on the prominent eye-ridges were long and thin and curved, like a woman's eyebrows which have been plucked and lengthened with a pencil. The eyes were pale behind rimless spectacles and the general impression of the face was one of almost grotesque earnestness, emphasized by the sharp triangular chin and thick straight nose.

I knew the eyes under their bulbous ridges, but the last time I had seen them they were set under eyebrows so faint they were almost invisible.

"This is Peter Schneider, with a dark wig and eyebrows and glasses."

"I never got a good look at Schneider," Gordon said, "but I'd have my doubts of Vlathek if he looked like a typical Rabbi. Now we've got two versions of Schneider to look for."

"I don't like either of them. I'd like Peter best as a bare skull that had been dead a long time. Alas, poor Vlathek."

Gordon started the car and we circled the Employment Office and went out through the Exit gates. Killoran saluted as we passed.

We turned into the expressway and headed for Detroit at a speed that wasted rubber.

"What was Vlathek's job?" Gordon said. "Can you find it in the folder?"

I picked it up from the seat between us and went through it. Born in California—the certificate *must* have been forged. Experience at the Skoda works in Czechoslovakia. That was possible, but the Nazis had controlled the Skoda records for years. I found what I wanted:

"He's an inspector in the machine tool division."

"No wonder they've been having production trouble. Where does he live?"

I found the address and told him, "215 Pequegnat Street, Detroit."

Gordon said nothing, but the speedometer climbed so that the wind blasted the windshield.

"Does that mean anything to you?" I said.

"Uh-huh. Something," he said with painful smugness. "215 Pequegnat Street, eh? A small world."

"Well?" I said not with a bang but a whimper. Gordon smiled secretly. The car was whistling down the expressway like a long, black bullet. I looked at the speedometer again. The airblast on the windshield was a ninety-mile-an-hour hurricane now. When we hit the top of a rise the wheels soared off the road for a fraction of a second.

Gordon flicked an eye at the speedometer and said, "We'll hold her there—no use taking risks."

"Of course not," I said. "That would be foolhardy, indeed. Why the warm, mysterious glow about Vlathek's address?"

"Rudolf Fisher lives at 215 Pequegnat Street."

Pequegnat Street was in a lower middle-class residential section near Gratiot and Seven Mile Road, the kind of section where people are neither high-class nor low-class enough to know their neighbors. The houses were all the same, middle-sized frame buildings too old to be smart and too new to be interesting, each with a patch of lawn big enough to turn a somersault on.

There was nobody turning somersaults on Pequegnat Street when we got there after breaking all the speed-laws of the County of Wayne and the City of Detroit. Except for a few parked cars, the street was empty as far as I could see. The houses had a blank, closed-up look like the secretive look of a woman who has no secrets. The house with 215 painted on its glass number-plate had venetian blinds which gave it a more secretive look than the other houses, but it had the same number of windows of the same size and shape in the same positions.

Gordon drove past the house without slackening speed and I said, "Hey! We passed 215."

"That's right."

He turned the next corner, parked fifty feet from the intersection, turned off the motor, and waited. In a minute a blue Ford roadster which I had noticed when we passed it on Pequegnat Street came around the corner and parked behind us. A burly young man who looked like an insurance agent got out of the roadster and came up to our car on Gordon's side.

"Mr. Fenton," Gordon said, "I'd like you to meet Professor Branch. Professor Branch is a public-spirited citizen who has been very helpful in the Schneider case."

Fenton smiled a quick, public-spirited smile and said, "I'm pleased to meet you, Branch."

Before I could answer him he was talking to Gordon: "Fisher came home about half an hour ago. He's there now."

"Anybody with him?"

"No. He came by himself on foot. Do I go and get him?"

"We'll both go."

Gordon started to get out on his side of the car and I started to get out on mine. He said:

"You'd better stay here, Branch, if you don't mind. This Fisher may be dangerous."

"Not this boy." Fenton smiled a contemptuous smile that turned down the corners of his wide mouth. "Unless you're afraid that Professor Branch will be seduced."

"Eh?"

"I interviewed Rudy a couple of weeks ago. His element is the boudoir. He wants to grow up and be beautiful like Hedy Lamarr. He intimated to me in his subtle feminine way that he could really go for me because I'm such a masculine type, if only I weren't so coldly professional in my attitude." Fenton twisted

217

his mouth sideways, rubbed his blue-black chin with a thick rectangular hand, and spat in the road.

"I see." Gordon got out of the car and I followed him. On the way back to Fisher's house, Gordon told Fenton about Ludwig Vlathek in a hundred words.

"I underestimated Rudy," Fenton said. "I thought he was baring his soul to me but the little bastard had this up his sleeve. I guess I don't understand women."

When we turned up the narrow concrete walk, I saw a movement behind the venetian blinds.

"Stay out here, Branch," Gordon said. "If nothing happens I suppose you can come in."

Fenton had climbed the porch steps and was knocking on the door. Gordon mounted behind him and stood at his shoulder. The door opened immediately. I couldn't see who had opened it but I heard a soft contralto voice with a German accent say:

"Hello, Mr. Fenton. This *is* an unexpected pleasure. *Won't* you come in. And your friends, too, of course."

Gordon looked at me and I followed them in. Rudolf Fisher held the door for me and I got a good look at him.

His makeup was tastefully applied but it couldn't stand white daylight. His lips were rich and red like fresh liver. The rouge on his cheek-bones was carefully tapered-off but it was too gaudy against the chalky whiteness of his powdered face. The shadowing around his gentian-blue eyes made them seem ridiculously large and insanely sombre. But the hand-set wave in his light brown hair was a masterpiece, as shiny and as precisely corrugated as a glass washboard.

He said: "Won't you come into the den, gentlemen? It's cozier in there."

He drew his Tyrian-blue dressing-gown closer about his willowy form and tripped ahead of us into the den. He turned on a table-lamp with a scarlet silk shade and a porcelain base decorated with droopeared Chinamen. I could see the room now: the

218

ivory baby grand with the black fringed drape, the two Persian rugs piled one on the other in front of the ivory mantel, the dead black linoleum on the floor, the ivory-framed Van Gogh reproductions on the ivory walls like windows into a new intense world, the white satin divan with its black and gold and crimson cushions.

Fisher fluttered a white hand towards the divan, said, "Won't you sit down, gentlemen?" and sat down on a red leather hassock with his black silk ankles crossed in front of him. In the red light, his face looked quite healthy, like any other young *chatelaine's*.

Fenton said: "We'll stand, Rudy. We won't be long. Where's Vlathek?"

Fisher's shoulders came closer together under the purple gown, as if a wind had risen in the room. "He left me. I told you two weeks ago my friend left me. He was an awfully fine person but he just couldn't stand it when you suspected me of those things. He was terribly disgusted with me." His lower lip trembled and he touched it with the long pink fingernails of his right hand.

"Peter will be terribly, *terribly* disgusted now," Fenton said.

The ivory fingers clenched in the purple lap. "Why do you call him Peter? My friend's name is Ludwig." The contralto voice had a soprano range.

Gordon said: "Peter killed his father last night. And he killed another man who told us about you before he died. Talk about Peter."

The red mouth opened as if gun-barrels had glinted, but the scream that tortured the white face was silent. The red mouth closed and opened again and closed again. Then it said in a babble of words:

"I hate him, too, I don't like him a bit, he treated me horribly. Peter took my car this morning and all the gasoline coupons that I've been saving up to go to Chicago to see the Post-Impressionist exhibition and when I tried to stop him he *slapped my face*. I used to think he was an awfully nice person but now I don't like him at all anymore, he's not a fine person at all."

"You'll talk then," Gordon said.

Fisher got to his feet and shook his clasped hands in front of him. "I most certainly will, I'll tell you all about Peter. Why, I was tremendously fond of Dr. Schneider, he was really a *dear* man. And I just *hate* Peter."

"Where did he go?"

"I don't know, he wouldn't tell me a thing. I haven't had anything to do with him for weeks and weeks. He was never a true friend of mine. But I'll tell you everything that I know about him—"

"Not here," Gordon said. "You can come down to the Federal Building with us and give a full statement."

"Get your wraps, Rudy," Fenton said. "It won't take long."

It took long enough. An hour later I was still sitting in the black sedan on Lafayette, waiting for Gordon to come out. He had refused to let me enter the field office on the grounds that the agent in charge chewed small change, distrusted superfluous laymen, and spat nickel-plated bullets.

For the first half-hour I went from newsstand to newsstand trying to buy the Toronto *Globe and Mail* of the day before, but there was none to be had. Then I went back to the car for fear of missing Gordon, and sat and thought with a brain whose contents were as strange and kaleidoscopic as Rudolf Fisher's den.

Obviously Rudolf's attitude to Peter was that of a deserted wife. Did Ruth Esch know her lover was such a versatile amorist? Or didn't she care? Maybe women in the Third Reich were trained to like that sort of thing. I thought of Roehm, the homosexual chief of the S A whom Hitler murdered with his own talented hands in the blood-bath of 1934. I thought of the elegant Nazi boys I had seen in the Munich nightclubs, with their lipstick and their eye-shadow and their feminine swagger, and the black male guns in their holsters. I thought of the epicene white worms which change their sex and burrow in the bodies of dead men underground.

Something wriggled away from my mental censor and hopped into my consciousness: the name that the hotel detective in the shabby brown suit had called Ruth Esch. White fluorescent light flooded a deep pit in my mind where the albino serpent and the red-headed toad grappled with each other in a nest of worms. The whole thing seemed tragically clear. Nothing real, nothing outside of imagination is ever as real or as painful as that image was. I closed my mind against it for a strange reason: I felt such pity for Ruth.

"Still waiting?" Gordon said. I hadn't seen him come up but he was standing at the curb beside the car. "We just got a telegram from the Kirkland Lake police. There's a woman answering to Ruth Esch's description in the hospital there. She's badly injured and can't be moved so they put a guard on her. It must be a bum steer, though."

It took me a moment to grasp what he said. Then I said, "Why? She probably went back there because she thought it was the last place you'd look for her."

"Figure it out," Gordon said. "It's about four now. She's had nine hours at most to get there from here, and it's over six hundred miles."

"An airplane could do it."

"It's remotely possible that she went there by plane. But we checked the airports, and we've been watching all private planes closely since the war broke. Also, she'd have had to fly over a guarded border. I think it's a bum steer."

"It's a hell of a coincidence then. I don't believe it's a coincidence."

"No time to argue," Gordon said. "I've got to catch the Chicago plane. There's a lead there that isn't bum.

221

Captain von Esch was recognized in Chicago this afternoon. Pardon me, I've got to go and get Fenton to bring my car back from the airport."

He crossed the sidewalk and re-entered the Federal Building. By the time he disappeared I had decided to go to Kirkland Lake. I followed him into the building and found a pay-phone. The airport told me that I could get a plane to Toronto within an hour—somebody had cancelled his reservation. The New York Central station told me I'd reach Toronto in plenty of time to catch the northbound train. I had a hundred and fifty dollars in my pocket and that was enough to go on with.

I went out and climbed into the back of the car and a minute later Gordon and Fenton climbed into the front.

"Where can I drop you, Branch?" Gordon said with a shade of impatience in his voice.

"I'll go along to the airport, thanks. I'm taking the Toronto plane."

"What the hell for?"

"I'm going to Kirkland Lake. I want to see if the woman in the hospital is Ruth Esch."

"You're wasting your time," Gordon said, but he started the car and headed out Jefferson. "Even if it is the right woman, she's injured and under guard. She can't get away."

"I like travelling," I said. "I've heard that Kirkland Lake is quite a charming town in its crude way."

Gordon shrugged his shoulders without looking around. "It's your time and your money. There's a faint chance that she went by plane. But we can leave her to the Canadian authorities for the present. Her brother is our responsibility."

"Captain von Esch *is* her brother then?"

"His name's Carl, and he even seems to bear her a family resemblance. Same features, same coloring. We got a complete description of him from the Canadian War Department. How he got from northern Ontario to Chicago I don't know. But I do know that he's not going to get out of Chicago."

"Did Fisher tell you anything about the Bonamy prison-break?"

"No, he didn't know anything about that phase of Schneider's activities," Fenton said. He half-turned in the seat and hooked a grey herringbone arm over the back. "He claimed he never heard of either of the Esches. He may have been holding out, but I don't think so. He was scared green."

"Verbal diarrhoea," Gordon said. "He dictated over three thousand words in a little over an hour. I could hardly get a question in edgeways."

"Three thousand words about what?" I said.

"It's a long story the way he told it," Fenton said. He turned to Gordon: "Is it all right to tell him, Chet?"

"Hell, no," I said. "I'm just a public-spirited citizen. Read me some selections from Proust instead."

"Tell him," Gordon said. "Branch literally risked his neck on this case. God knows he must have learned to keep mum by this time."

"Well, keep it to yourself until it breaks in the papers," Fenton said. "If it ever does. According to Fisher, Herman Schneider was a spy in spite of himself. He left Germany in the middle thirties for honest liberal reasons. The Nazis couldn't risk concentrating him then because too many people in Germany and outside of Germany knew his name. So they let him go, but they kept Peter. Peter was only a kid then, but he was in the Hitler Youth and he didn't want to leave. He stayed and grew up into a hundred percent Aryan superman with bells on.

"By the time Germany invaded France and the Low Countries, Peter was an officer of Engineers in the regular army. He showed such aptitude for sabotage and psychological warfare that they shifted him to Intelligence and trained him to work here in the United States. They knew they'd be fighting us soon

223

and they were ready for it, they thought. They looked a long way ahead but they didn't see the right things. For one thing they over-estimated the strength of native fascism in this country. Anyway, Peter was slated for the job of engineering adviser to the Gauleiter of Michigan. It sounds crazy, doesn't it? It wasn't as crazy as it sounds now, before Russia held the Germans and Pearl Harbor gave us the shock treatment.

"After a year of working with English phonograph records and studying at the Skoda Works and the Ford plant in Belgium and a few other places, Peter was ready to graduate to America in the summer of 1941. We weren't at war with them yet and it was easy enough for them to get him into this country, but they made it hard for the sake of an added advantage. The Nazis are experts in making everything pay off double—"

"Including trouble," I said. "Double, double, toil and trouble."

"That's true, too," Fenton said. "Peter contacted his father through a Gestapo stooge in the Free German underground. He said he had had a change of heart and all that crap and he was just dying to get out of Germany but the nasty Nazis wouldn't let him go. Old man Schneider fell for it and went to the German Consulate in New York. They agreed to let Peter out of Germany and save him from Stalin and the steppes, for a price. If the Herr Doktor would provide them with a certain piece of information— The Herr Doktor had a moral conniption fit and gave them what they wanted. They released Peter, and old man Schneider went to the State Department and got the prodigal son into the country before you could say Heliogabolus Schwartzentruber.

"Ever since then the prodigal has been blackmailing Dr. Schneider for more information, and getting it. But that was just a sideline for Peter. In two years he's worked in at least six of the important war plants in the Detroit area, under different names with stolen birth certificates. He's had a hand in psychological sabotage, too. He's been helping to direct the activities of the native fascists in Detroit, the fanatical anti-Jew anti-Negro anti-labor boys. Fisher didn't say, but I suspect Peter Schneider played a part in inciting the race riots."

"Where does Fisher fit into all this?" I said.

"He's Peter's friend," Fenton said with heavy irony, curling his lip as if friend was a four-letter word. "They met at a pansy drag soon after Peter came to this country, isn't that romantic? Rudy's a weak willie—at least he's trying like hell to act like one—and Peter used him for little errands like contacting old man Schneider. That's Rudy's story: if it's not true we'll break it down. But it's pretty clear that when we cracked the Buchanan-Dineen circle, Peter dropped his Vlathek alias and cleared out for Canada, leaving Rudy holding the bag with his lily-white hands. I only hope he didn't leave our Rudolf with child."

"Have you ever thought of helping to solve the sewage problem by converting your imagination into a septic tank?" Gordon said.

Fenton grinned and said to me, "Chet's the last Puritan, Mr. Branch. Santayana's boy was only the second-last. I trust I haven't offended your delicate shell-like ears with my coarse talking."

I said, "I teach a course in Swift and Fielding. Compared with them you're mealy-mouthed."

"My God, Gordon," Fenton roared, "did you hear that? I'm mealy-mouthed."

The mid-afternoon traffic was light and we were already in the suburbs. When we reached the airport, the Chicago plane was landing. Gordon had just time to give Fenton a few instructions and to say to me:

"If you find out anything let us know. Call the Detroit or Chicago field office and reverse the charges."

He shook my hand and walked up the ramp and ducked into the plane. A ground attendant lifted the ramp and shut the aluminum door behind him. I stood with Fenton and watched the great plane change from an incongruous winged turtle on the ground to a bird in the sky.

Fenton shook hands and said, "See you again, Branch." He went back to Gordon's car and drove away.

I picked up the ticket I had reserved and went into the waiting-room to wait for the Toronto plane.

chapter xiv

Early twilight hung over the city like a thin, grey haze and made the lake a sheet of striated lead, stretching to a leaden horizon, when I landed at the Toronto Airport. I took a taxi to the Union Station. Down the long, drab streets the neons trembled in the gathering air, glowing blue and red and green with a quiet, inhuman lustre.

At the station a ticket-clerk told me I had nearly five hours to wait. The next train that would make the Kirkland Lake connection at Churchill left Toronto at 11:30 that night. I wouldn't get to Kirkland Lake until two o'clock the next day.

I found a phone-booth and called the airport, but there was no seat available on any plane going anywhere. I went back to the ticket-clerk and bought a coach ticket, which was the only kind I could buy. That meant I had to sit up all night.

I went through the tunnel from the station to the Royal York, ate a quick dinner in the grill, and hired a room to sleep in until my train left. I was hatless and suitcaseless and wild-eyed, and the desk-clerk looked at me suspiciously. I mollified him by paying in advance.

"I'd like to be called at 11:10," I said. "I have to catch the North Bay train."

"Yessir, you shall be called," he said, and signalled to a bellboy.

I followed the bellboy across the huge lobby to the elevators, but before I got to them something took

227

hold of my attention and stopped me in my tracks. It was a newspaper folded inside out and left by someone on the seat of a leather armchair. At the top of the page that was showing there was a picture of Wendell Willkie.

I picked up the paper and saw that it was yesterday's *Globe and Mail*, opened at page eight. I scanned the columns. It was the third column from which Peter Schneider had torn the clipping. Where the empty space had been in Peter's copy there was nothing but a patent medicine advertisement offering solace to those undergoing change of life.

The bellboy was waiting by the elevators with a blank, intolerant expression on his sharp jockey's face. I was just about to throw the paper down and follow him, when I thought of something that made me realize what a hell of an amateur detective I was. It was the simple staggering fact that newspapers are printed on two sides.

I turned the page and the heading I was looking for blazed black in my eyes. The bellboy kept on waiting while I read:

> Unidentified Woman Regains Consciousness
> Injured Woman in Kirkland Lake Hospital
> Unable to Remember Name.

Kirkland Lake, Sept. 22 (C.P.):—The unidentified woman who two days ago was found, suffering from exposure and concussion, on the outskirts of this Northern Ontario mining town has regained consciousness. Although hospital authorities state that she has every chance of complete recovery, she is suffering from temporary amnesia as a result of her injury, and is unable to identify herself.

The injured woman, an attractive red-head in her late twenties, was undoubtedly a victim of foul play according to police. She was found unconscious in an old mine shaft south of the city on the night of September 20, by a group of boys who were playing there. She had not been assaulted, but her appearance suggested that she had been struck on the head with a blunt instrument and flung into the shallow shaft. She was dressed in men's clothes of good quality but there were no personal effects or money on her person when she was found.

Police assign robbery as the motive, but have been unable to apprehend the author of the brutal attack. Sergeant Norris E. Collins, of the R.C.M.P., has advanced the theory that one of the prisoners who escaped from the Bonamy prison camp on September 20 may have been responsible for the vicious attack on the unknown woman. The Bonamy camp is only a few miles from the scene of the crime. (See p. 3 for an account of the capture of the German escapees, only one of whom is still at large.)

According to Dr. R. A. Sandiman, resident physician at Kirkland Lake Hospital, the injured woman speaks English with a slight German accent and frequently lapses into German as if it were her native tongue. Anyone who can supply information which may help to identify her is asked to communicate with the Royal Canadian Mounted Police at Kirkland Lake.

I stood and looked at the date on which she had been found. September 20. It twisted in my mind like a key, but no door opened. This must be the woman that the Kirkland Lake police had put under guard. My first thought was that Gordon was right and it couldn't be Ruth after all. After the night and day I had gone through, insane coincidence seemed more probable than any kind of luck.

I noticed that the bellboy was still waiting and told him to leave my room-key at the desk.

He saw the look on my face and said, "Is anything wrong, sir?"

"Plenty. But there's nothing you can do about it."

He started away and I said, "Yes, there is. Where's the tavern?"

"Right this way, sir," and he led me to the copper-gleaming tavern on the basement floor.

I sat down at a corner table and ordered a quart of

229

Molson's Ale. Despair was dragging me down by the heels but the hot fingers of hope had me by the nape of the neck. The ale ballasted me but the wild pulling in two directions went on. A graph of my feelings for the next few hours would have looked like the Manhattan skyline.

One question I could not get around. If the woman wasn't Ruth, why had Peter Schneider torn out the clipping about her? If the woman who had been in the Kirkland Lake Hospital for three days was Ruth Esch, it was not Ruth I had seen trading blows and kisses with Peter Schneider. Somebody else had helped him to murder Alec Judd and Herman Schneider.

After a while the ale slowed down the alternating swing of my feelings and I went up to my room to try to sleep. The two-hour sleep I got was a restful as a surfboard ride. Finally, the beetle-green motorboat that was dragging me over the dream-waves of hope and despair stopped with a grinding of gears and I answered the telephone.

The switchboard girl said it was 11:10 and I had twenty minutes to catch my train.

I put on the rest of my clothes over the underwear I had slept in, went down to the desk and checked out, and walked quickly through the brightly lighted tunnel to the station. I had time for a cup of coffee at the lunchbar before the train left for North Bay.

It took eight hours to get to North Bay, which was just a little better than halfway to Kirkland Lake. The dusty red plush seats of the old coach were crowded with civilians who looked as sleepy as I felt and soldiers who laughed and sang all night. Nobody got any sleep but I achieved a partial coma that made the trip unreal enough to bear. Farms and forests and dimly shining lakes slipped past the window for hours and merged with the images of my half-conscious dreams.

When the mind is held awake on the point of sleep, an imagined face will take a hundred shapes, changing like a movie fadeout and fadein from beauty to ugliness, from gracious intelligence to idiot evil and back again to virtue and beauty. A goddess, a leering devil, a Victory of Samothrace, a sexless imbecile, a sweet young girl, a gross hag. The obscene amorphous masks changed constantly behind my eyes and cold sweat ran down the back of my neck. I sat and watched Ruth's face change all night.

When daylight came it was better. I could see trees that seemed thicker as we went north, the rock ribs of the country bursting from the earth, still lakes like wide, innocent eyes mocking the bright blue sky. At dawn my brain felt drained and chilly but it gradually drew heat and energy from the sun. Breakfast was better still.

When I got back from the dining-car, a soldier had taken the seat beside me and we talked all morning. He was going home on sick leave after service in the Middle East and Africa, to his parents' farm in the Clay Belt. I asked him what ailed him and regretted it. He tapped his left leg with his brown walnut knuckles and the leg rang with a metallic sound.

I felt like a child frightened by bad dreams.

At Churchill, a wooden hamlet like an angular fungus on the railway line, I changed to another train. Half an hour later I got off at Kirkland Lake and took a taxi to the hospital.

We went down streets of wooden buildings that looked new and jerry-built. Between and beyond the packing-case buildings I could see the peaked hills of exhausted grey-black earth thrown up by the gold-mines. In atmosphere, Kirkland Lake was like a western boomtown, but there were restaurants and drug-stores with shining plastic fronts and electric signs, and faces on the streets from every race in Europe.

The hospital was a brick building standing in its own grounds. When the taxi took me up the drive and let me out at the main entrance, I noticed a man in plain clothes in the vestibule. He gave me a quick,

231

hard look as I mounted the steps, and then turned away.

I passed him without shying, though I was still leery of plain-clothesmen, and walked up to the information desk. The nurse on duty was a middle-aged woman with a brittle grey permanent. Her face was white and starched like her uniform, and her voice when she spoke was very hygienic:

"What can we do for you, sir?"

"My name is Branch, Robert Branch. I—"

"Oh, are you Professor Branch?"

"Right. Has somebody—?"

Her sharp voice amputated my sentence like a sterile knife: "Do you know a man called Gordon?"

"Chester Gordon? Has he been here?"

"No, he has not been here. He called you this morning by long distance."

"Where is he?"

"The call was from Chicago."

"What did he want? Did he tell you?"

"No, he told me nothing. When I told him that we had never heard of you, he asked to speak to the policeman on duty here." She sniffed, as if all policemen were typhoid-carriers.

"Nurse, will you do something for me?"

"What is it? We have rules, of course."

"Of course," I said. "This is obviously a well-run hospital. Would you be allowed to put in a long-distance call for me, to Chicago?"

"This is not a telephone exchange."

"No, but the call has to do with one of your patients. And it's very important."

"What patient?"

"The unidentified woman with concussion."

"She has been identified," the nurse said with the satisfied click of a mousetrap shutting on a mouse.

"She has?"

"Her brother was here this morning. She is a Miss Vlathek."

I stopped breathing. When I started again I said, "Did you see him? What's his first name?"

"We did not exchange first names." But I knew what hers was. Gorgon.

"What does he look like?"

"Black curly hair. Spectacles. Rather pale in the face. A most courteous young man." Unlike me.

"Where is he now?"

"Nor did we exchange addresses," she said frigidly. "You can't really expect me to answer all these questions. Are you a detective?"

"No, not exactly. But I'm assisting the F.B.I." I hoped I was.

"Then the police will answer your questions." She began ruffling papers.

I handed her a ten-dollar bill. "Look, put in that call for me, will you? This will cover it."

"This is American money," she said.

"I know, but it's still good. Will you put in the call? It's a matter of life and death." I didn't know then that it was, but I hoped she would recognize the phrase.

"Really?" Interest warmed her eyes almost to freezing-point. "Whom do you wish to speak to in Chicago?"

"The man who called me, person-to-person at the Chicago office of the F.B.I."

"You *are* a detective," she said, and even began to flutter a little. I was careful not to deny it.

"Is that the policeman that Gordon talked to this morning?" I pointed towards the vestibule.

"Yes."

"Before or after Vlathek was here?"

"After, I think. Yes, it was after Mr. Vlathek left. He was here quite early. He said he drove up from Toronto overnight, as soon as he saw the newspaper account of his sister's accident."

"How is she?"

"Very weak, but much better. She's suffering more from shock than concussion. She's not allowed visitors, of course."

"How did Vlathek identify her if he didn't see her?"

"Oh, he saw her. A nurse took him in for a moment when she was sleeping. There was no doubt in his mind that she was his sister."

"There wouldn't be," I said. "May I see her?"

"You'll have to ask the police. I'm sorry." Her thin mouth arranged itself in a facsimile of a smile.

"All right. Thanks very much for your trouble. And you *will* put in that call right away?"

"Yes, sir. Chester Gordon, F.B.I., Chicago."

I did my best to devastate her with a grateful smile and went out to the vestibule. The officer in plain clothes, a brown hulk of a man whose straight back must have worn a uniform most of his forty years, was rolling a cigarette between fingers like Polish sausages.

"My name's Branch," I said.

"What can I do for you, Mr. Branch?"

"Perhaps you can give me some information. If you'd be good enough."

"Perhaps."

"I'm assisting the F.B.I.," I said, wondering if that was enough to convict me of impersonating an officer.

"Credentials?"

"I have none. I'm a private citizen. But an agent of the F.B.I. has asked me to obtain some information."

"Sure, but how do I know that?" He raised one thick eyebrow and lowered the other so that he was scowling and looking superior at the same time.

"I'm calling Chester Gordon in Chicago now. The man you talked to this morning. You can ask him about me."

"That's all right. He said something about you. I just had to be sure you were the right guy."

His low eyebrow went up and joined the high one

and he drew in and blew out smoke. "What do you want to know? I'll tell you if I can."

"How long has—Miss Vlathek been in the hospital?"

"Three days. But her name's not Vlathek."

"What is it?"

"You tell me."

"Ruth Esch," I said.

"That's what Gordon thinks."

"What did Gordon tell you?"

"Plenty." He inhaled deeply and expelled smoke through wide nostrils and wider mouth.

"Did he tell you to arrest Vlathek?" I asked.

"That's what I'm here for. He said he was coming back. He tried to take the woman out of the hospital this morning but they wouldn't let him. She was still under guard and the doctor wouldn't let her be moved, anyway."

"Will you let me see her?"

"She can't have visitors. Doctor's orders."

"I just want to see her. Vlathek saw her this morning. If it's Ruth Esch I can identify her."

The big man opened the inner door of the vestibule and spoke to the nurse behind the information desk. "Will you get somebody to show Mr. Branch here where Miss Vlathek's room is?" She pressed a buzzer beneath the desk.

"Miss Vlathek?" I said in a lowered voice. "Doesn't she know there isn't anybody called Vlathek?"

"What people don't know won't hurt them," he said. "We want to get Vlathek."

"Vlathek-Schneider. Gordon told you about Schneider?"

"Yeah. Don't worry, Bud, we're combing the whole region for that guy. All I ask is to get in sight of him." He clenched a fist like the end of a knotted club and fondled it with his other hand.

I saw a nurse coming down the hall and left him in the vestibule.

"Did you put in that call?" I said to the nurse at the desk.

"Yes. The operator said it would take a few minutes." She turned to the nurse who had come up behind me silently on rubber soles. "Is Miss Vlathek sleeping?"

"Yes," the nurse said from behind a white starched bosom like a barricade.

"Take this gentleman to see her, please. He is on no account to speak or disturb her in any way." She looked at me as if she suspected that I had a noisemaker in my pocket.

"This way, sir." I followed the nurse along the hall to a rear wing of the hospital. Her starched posterior was immobile as if she moved on wheels. I had to hold myself steady to keep from running ahead of her down the corridor.

We turned into another corridor and she led me to a closed door and stood with a finger on her lips. My heart seemed to reverberate in the quiet wing like a muffled gong. She half-opened the door and I looked over her shoulder into a cool, dim room smelling of the hospital neutrality between life and death. The shade was almost completely drawn but I could see a mass of roses burning darkly on a table by the window and on the pillow a pale sleeping face beneath a helmet of bandages.

The nurse whispered, "She's sleeping. Don't make any noise. Can you see her from here?"

"Not very well. May I go in if I'm quiet?"

"Just for a minute."

I tiptoed into the room and across to the head of the bed. It was Ruth, but not the Ruth I had seen with Peter Schneider. Though the face on the pillow was faintly hollowed by time and pain, it was as fair and smooth as a child's face. Even in sleep and illness, her lips and chin held the curve of gaiety and courage.

Her lowered lashes shadowed her cheek delicately,

and I bent to kiss her closed eyes. Then I remembered that I must not wake her and stood still with my head bowed over her. She must have felt my breath on her face. She raised her eyelids and her clear eyes looked at me.

Something hovered in her eyes, circled wildly and hovered again, like a lost gull over moving grey-green water. The lost thing plunged and her eyes focused and took hold of the meaning of my face.

Her lips fluttered and her voice seemed to come from a distance: "Bob Branch!" Something glittered in her eyes and two tears fell across her temples into the pillow. I touched her face with my hand.

She said in German, "My name is Ruth, *nicht wahr?* I am Ruth Esch."

"Yes."

"I remember now—You got my letter?"

"Yes, I came here to find you."

"My brother," she said. "Peter Schneider came to me in Toronto and told me my brother was no longer Nazi. He said Carl was sick in the prison camp and calling for me. I came here with Peter and waited to see Carl for three days. Then he took me to a dark field and Carl was there and they struck me—I did not know after so many years my brother could hate me so terribly—"

"Forget your brother. I love you. I came to take you home with me."

The nurse came across the room and hissed, "You must leave now. You must not disturb her."

Ruth said, "Don't go." Her hands moved under the sheets, beating against them feebly like caught birds.

I said, "I won't go away, darling. I'm going to stick around. But you've got to rest some more."

She smiled and two more tears fell. I kissed the bright track on her temple and felt the steady, heart-breaking tremor of the pulse that beat there. I went out of the room with sweet salt on my lips.

The nurse shut the door behind me and turned accusingly. "You said you wouldn't disturb her."

I felt like laughing in her face and weeping on her shoulder. "What would you do if you loved somebody and lost him for six years and found him again?"

She looked at me for a moment. Then she smiled and patted my arm. "I know. My husband's been in England since 1940. I'd turn handsprings, I guess."

She frowned and opened the door quietly and looked in. When she had closed it again I said, "What's the matter?"

"Oh, nothing. I thought I might have left my bundle in there this morning, but I guess I didn't. You didn't see it, did you?"

"What kind of a bundle?"

"A big paper bundle of laundry. You know, caps and uniforms. Maybe I left it in the Residence."

"No, I didn't see it."

Another nurse came tripping silently down the corridor. "Professor Branch?" she said. "Your party is on the line."

I went back to the front desk and the grey-haired nurse got up from her seat and handed me the phone.

"Hello, Branch speaking," I said into it.

"Mr. Gordon is on the line," the operator announced above the electric murmur of the wires.

I said, "Gordon? This is Branch."

His voice clear and crisp over a thousand miles of wire. "Hello, Branch. Have you seen the woman?"

"I've seen her. It's Ruth Esch, and she's been here for three days."

"You're quite sure? You were wrong once."

"My glasses were broken and I don't see so well without them. But there's no mistake this time. She recognized me even before I spoke."

"Would you swear to her identity?"

"I'm going to marry her. Does that convince you?"

"I have to be sure," Gordon said. "But I figured she must be there."

"What do you mean, you figured? You thought it was a bum steer."

"I was wrong. I mean that's what I figured this morning after we captured Carl von Esch."

"So you got him."

"We had to shoot him a little, but he'll live to stand trial. Did you ever see him, Branch?"

"Once."

"He resembles his sister, doesn't he?"

"No. Yes. I don't remember very well. I didn't see much resemblance at the time, but he's not a big man, is he?" A door in my mind opened on whirling vistas of possibility and another door clanged shut for good on a dark, ugly place. "Listen, Gordon, he knocked out his sister and left her for dead in an old mineshaft here. *Was he disguised as a woman?*"

"When we caught him," Gordon said, "he tried to ditch a bundle he was carrying. I've got the bundle here. It contains a set of women's clothes, a woman's red wig, and a pair of rubber breasts. He had Ruth Esch's passport and visa on his person, and her Department of Justice permit to enter the United States. Incidentally, he entered this country from Windsor the night of September 21—the day before this whole thing started. Peter Schneider must have driven him down from Kirkland Lake this morning. He had on a man's suit, but he was wearing women's underwear under it. I got the suit identified over long-distance by the man that had his car stolen, you know, the little man in the blanket. All in all, I think we've got enough to convict von Esch of murder."

"Is he homosexual?"

"He has some of the mannerisms. Good female impersonators usually are pansies; they like pretending to be women. Why?"

"I saw Peter Schneider kiss him. That's what buffaloed me from the first, more than my bad eyes, I think. I've seen men in women's clothes in Paris, in the hole-in-the-wall dancehalls around the Place de la Bastille. But I forgot there were such things."

"You'll never forget again. They haven't got Schneider yet, have they?"

"No. At least I don't know. There's still a policeman here."

"Sergeant Cummings? Let me speak to him, will you?" I was laying down the receiver when Gordon said, "Just a minute. How badly hurt is she?"

"Pretty badly. Concussion and shock. She seems to be recovering—her memory has come back—but she'll be in bed for quite a while."

"If I can get permission, I'm going to come and talk to her when she's able. Are you staying?"

"I'm going to stay here until I can take her back with me. There's nothing on the books against her?"

"Not on our books. It's pretty clear that her brother and Schneider sapped her and stole her clothes and papers and identity so that Carl could get away to this country. It not only got him across the border but it provided him with respectable shoes to step into, with very little danger of our investigating him. You were the nigger in the woodpile, Branch. You know now why they tried to kill you."

"I know now all right. The irony is that when I did see Carl I was taken in. Herman Schneider wasn't taken in, though. I doubt if they tried to fool him. He saw the whole thing and couldn't stand it, even if he was working for the Nazis. They probably told him he had to co-operate or else. He co-operated to save himself, but he was cracking. They must have seen that he was both useless and dangerous to them, and had no qualms about killing him. They could get around whatever political morality he had, but his sexual morality was too strong to curb, stronger even than his vanity. Besides, he was a friend of Ruth's and so far he knew they had killed her."

"They may try to yet."

"What?"

"Look, Branch, she's got to be guarded. I'll talk to the police but you see that they're not niggardly with protection. Her life is in danger."

"From Schneider?"

"Why else would he go back to Kirkland Lake? Fenton checked that item in the *Globe and Mail*. He must have been in a hurry, to leave the paper in his car. The item he tore out—"

"I know. I saw it in Toronto."

Gordon spoke with a harsh sincerity that made the telephone vibrate: "She's got to be guarded twenty-four hours a day as long as Schneider is at large. They must have thought they killed her and that she wouldn't be found. Now that he knows she's alive, he'll try to finish the job. So far as he knows she's the only one that can put the finger on him."

"Do you want to talk to the mountie?"

"Right. I appreciate your calling back right away. I'll have the charges reversed."

I called the man in the vestibule to the phone and listened to him asking and answering questions. Then he asked a nurse to get the resident physician, and she fetched a stout man in a white coat.

I heard him tell Gordon that Ruth should be able to talk to him in a week, perhaps sooner if necessary. He hung up.

The plain-clothesman called headquarters and asked for another man to help guard the hospital. When he finished phoning I said:

"Are you going to put a man in her room?"

"What do you think, Dr. Sandiman?" he said to the stout doctor. "The F.B.I. thinks there's going to be another attempt on her life."

"They do?" Dr. Sandiman's chins shook. "We must do everything possible to protect her, sergeant. Of course. But he'll have to be very quiet, as inconspicuous as possible. A sudden shock to the patient could have very serious repercussions."

"Could it?" I said.

"Very serious, indeed."

"And Schneider was in her room?"

"Yeah," Cummings said. "I only wish I'd known it sooner."

"Did he leave those roses by the window?"

"Yeah. But I examined them. They're O.K."

"The point is that they're there, visible from outside. He could have put them there to mark her room."

"I didn't think of that."

I turned to Sandiman. "I have a suggestion, doctor. Miss Esch should be protected against the danger of shock as well as other dangers. Could you move her to another room without disturbing her?"

"Yes. Yes, of course. I think that would be very sensible."

"Then why not do it now?"

He gave orders to the nurse. As she started down the hall I said to her, "Leave the roses where they are."

Sergeant Cummings went back to the vestibule. I said to Sandiman:

"Will you let me have the room that Miss Esch is vacating?"

"What on earth for? Are you ill?"

"Not especially, though you might have a look at my eyes. It's just that if a certain visitor comes to that room I wouldn't want him to be disappointed."

"You'd do better to leave it to the police." There was officious disapproval in his bulging blue eyes.

"The visitor I expect murdered my best friend. Yesterday he tried to hang me." I showed him the marks on my neck.

He clucked like a sympathetic hen, but he said, "All the more reason for leaving it to the police."

"Look, doctor," I said, "I am leaving it to the police. He'll never reach that room. But if he does I don't want him to be disappointed."

"Have you a gun?"

"No."

"You'll need a gun. Come along."

He took me down the hall to his office. On the white wall above his desk there was a photograph of a young man in army uniform who looked like Sandiman's son. But it was a uniform of the First World War. I looked at his face and saw the unchanging bones under the fat. He was the young man in the photograph.

He opened a drawer and laid a Colt .45 on the desk. "Keep this under your pillow. It's loaded."

"Thanks. Now how about bandaging my head. My concussion is paining me something terrible."

He glanced at me sharply and gradually smiled. "Good idea. What reason shall I give for admitting you? It's imperative to have a reason."

"My eyes. Make it my diabolical eyes."

"By the way, what happened? Hemorrhage?"

"Yes, the hangman's noose—"

"I see. We'll put some drops in them while we're about it."

I took off my glasses and he put drops in my eyes and covered my hair with bandages. He handed me the Colt and led me down the hall to the room that Ruth had left. "We put her at the other end of the wing," he said.

"Good."

"Well, I've got work to do. Good luck." He waved a pudgy hand and closed the door.

I got into bed with my clothes on and pulled the sheet up to my eyes. I held the revolver in my right hand under the cover and watched the window. The scent of the roses reminded me of funerals and weddings, but I felt more like a bridegroom than a corpse.

I lay all afternoon and watched the bright spot the sun made creep down the blind. My mind was keyed up tight. My nerves were taut and brittle, ready to snap. To relieve the tension that made me shiver slightly under the sheet, I thought of great things beyond my reach, the stars and planets, a million luminous balls kept in the air by a juggler nobody had ever seen. To make the sun move down my blind a foot in an hour, the earth's periphery whirled a thousand miles through space.

I thought of the inevitable past, Alec Judd crushed out with ten million others by the immense millstones of war, the millstones that were already powdering the bones of the men who had set them in motion. I thought of Herman Schneider, morally broken on a neat, cruel wheel devised by the son who had once been seed in his loins. I remembered the hunched despair of his well-fed shoulders when he walked away from the strange lovers in the fencing room, the lost and gone look in his eyes above the Lüger when he was going to shoot me, and the jagged hole that let the desperate conflict out of his head. I felt for him the kind of remote pity I felt for Agamemnon, a weak, well-meaning man betrayed and murdered in a forgotten language on a stage that time had crumbled into dust.

In the nightmare sequence of events that had seemed to grow out of each other, meaninglessly and malignantly, like cancer cells, I saw the push of giant uncontrollable forces on weak men, the waste of breakable wills and stout fragile bodies fractured in the clash of continents. But underneath the tired, cold impersonality of my vision I mourned for Alec Judd. I yearned steadily to plant the Schneider seed six feet deep.

When the sun's rays came straight through the opening at the bottom of the blind and lay horizontally across the room, a nurse brought me dinner. It was a good dinner, roast beef and Yorkshire pudding and mashed potatoes and gravy and a quarter of a lemon pie. I ate it with my left hand, watching the window. My right hand held the gun under the sheet.

The sun faded out of the room and darkness seeped

in slowly. I was glad that night was falling. I was more likely to have a visitor at night and I was lonely for someone to shoot.

The nurse came in and took away my tray. It was so dark I could barely see her face. The door opened and I could see a man's head and shoulders black against the light from the hall.

"Don't shoot," Sandiman said. "How's it going?"

"Fine. The dinner was excellent."

"I'll tell the dietitian. Well, see you later."

"No sign of Schneider?"

"No." He closed the door.

Now I could see only the dim outlines of the room, the walls which seemed more distant than before, the pale ridge my legs made under the sheet, the dark roses beside the window. I lay and watched the black mass of the roses, red in the sun and black at night like blood, rich and delicate to the touch like a loved woman, drowsy and dark like sleep and death. The rich, dark cloud of roses expanded and engulfed the room and the whole night.

I opened my eyes with a start and saw her standing in the room, a blurred figure glimmering faintly in the darkness by the window. No, it was a nurse. I could see her white uniform and cap. I must have been asleep. Thank God, he hadn't come when I was asleep.

I realized that he could have. The nurse was there by the window and I hadn't heard her enter. She seemed to be raising the shade.

"Leave it down," I said.

I could feel her start, but she said nothing for a moment. Then she said, "All right," and drew the shade.

Her low voice echoed in my mind. I closed my hand on the revolver under the sheet but there was no feeling in my fingers. I had been half-lying on my arm and it was asleep.

As I reached for the gun with my left hand, the

245

white blur slipped towards me and I saw the gleam of a face and the white shadow of an arm stretched out. In the split-second it took me to throw off the sheet I thought of several things: the evil whiteness of Melville's whale, the whiteness of sunless plants, the white bandaged head that had been on my pillow, the white look of death, and the bundle of caps and uniforms which the nurse had left in the room where Vlathek had been.

I caught the hand as it descended and tore the sand-bag out of it. It wrenched free and took my throat. I drew my right knee to my chin and kicked out against the silent thing above me. It staggered back across the room, jumped up before I could free my other leg from the sheet, and crashed through the blind out the window.

The gun was lost on the floor but I felt life in my right hand again. I dived out the open window through the wreckage of the blind and landed on all fours on the ground. There were shouts from somewhere and I saw the white shape streaking across the lawn towards the trees at the edge. I went after it.

Before he reached the trees, Nurse Schneider fell over his skirts and I jumped him with my knees in the small of his back. He twisted over and I caught a glimpse of his pale contorted face before his heel came into my stomach and sprawled me backwards on the grass.

I got up fighting for air and saw him crouched with his right hand under his starched skirt tugging at something. The hand came out with a black gun he had given birth to.

I heard men's voices and the sound of running feet somewhere behind me. He started to back away into the shadow of the trees and I walked towards him against my will faster than he retreated. The gun flashed and coughed.

I felt a freezing blow in the right thigh where the bullet struck but I got him by the wrist with my left hand and forced down the gun. His other hand tore my face but I kept hold of the twisting wrist. I circled his arm with my right arm and grasped my left wrist with my right hand and lifted.

The tendons in his shoulder tore softly like damp cardboard, and the gun dropped to the ground and lay impotent. He screamed on a high monotone and bit my arm. I let go of him with my right hand and hit him on the temple with all the will left in my body. He fell forward into the grass with his face turned sideways.

The ground shook under heavy feet and Sergeant Cummings came up beside me with a late gun in his hand. He turned a flashlight on the quiet face and said:

"It's him."

I said, "Yes," between gulps of air.

Above the dark-headed trees the stars began to waver and flare like torches at a celebration a long way off and I sat down in the grass because my right leg was made of rubber. My mind flew out like smoke in empty space and I rode a vertical wind through moving stars like fields of arcing fireflies. The earth was a small, forgotten thing, a withered apple for which black ants and red ants fought together. The diastole of exhaustion ended and the systole of unconsciousness closed on my head, narrowing the universe to a warm, dry tunnel where I ran lightly and easily in the friendly darkness. The terrible things had died in the dark behind. At the end of the tunnel Ruth was waiting with hair bright as sunlight and no sword in her hand.

ABOUT THE AUTHOR

ROSS MACDONALD was born near San Francisco in 1915. He was educated in Canadian schools, traveled widely in Europe, and acquired advanced degrees and a Phi Beta Kappa key at the University of Michigan. In 1938 he married a Canadian girl who is now well known as the novelist Margaret Millar. Mr. Macdonald (Kenneth Millar in private life) taught school and later college, and served as communications officer aboard an escort carrier in the Pacific. For over twenty years he has lived in Santa Barbara and written mystery novels about the fascinating and changing society of his native state. He is a past president of the Mystery Writers of America. In 1964 his novel *The Chill* was given a Silver Dagger award by the Crime Writers' Association of Great Britain. Mr. Macdonald's *The Far Side of the Dollar* was named the best crime novel of 1965 by the same organization. *The Moving Target* was made into the highly successful movie *Harper* (1966). *The Goodbye Look* was a national bestseller for more than three months, and *The Underground Man* (1971) even surpassed it in sales and critical acclaim.